In Richmond, Virginia, Deputy Mayor Dobson is brutally murdered. The FBI investigation reveals that this case isn't the only one in which an abusive husband died of unnatural causes. Special Agent Nicolas Hayes and his team begin the investigation but soon reach a dead end. There is no evidence and no suspect. When an old enemy appears on the scene, the investigation comes to a standstill, and Nicolas finds himself in mortal danger.

Cold Rage

ISBN: 978-1-4874-2941-6
Cover art by Martine Jardin

Published by eXtasy Books Inc or
Devine Destinies, an imprint of eXtasy Books Inc

Look for us online at:
www.eXtasybooks.com or www.devinedestinies.com

Cold Rage
Nicolas and Jacklyn Book 5

By

Ann Raina

Dedication

Muse, your love for new characters is unrivaled. I'm glad you complete their biographies and add your two cents – as always – to the humor of the story.

Prologue

The cover behind bushes and rock formations was excellent, the view on the country road unobstructed. The roadblock was a classic combat maneuver, one that Herb Sanders understood without a detailed explanation. During his three-hour wait, the weather conditions had improved from lashing rainfall to a slight drizzle that wasn't hampering his vision. Herb looked through the telescopic sight of his *HK MSG90 A1* to make any last adjustments. He liked the rifle more every day. It was reliable, dead on target, and lightweight to carry without tiring. Leroy Jennings, one of his two partners in crime, had joked that the weapons were more reliable than any woman he'd ever met. Of course, Leroy wouldn't know about such things, with his tragic track record of one-night stands.

Herb's headphone crackled.

"Transporter's on its way. ETA in two minutes."

Herb smiled. Leroy's voice sounded like he was making an announcement at a train station. Obviously, Herb's tension wasn't the same as that of Leroy in his elevated position.

"It's arriving exactly on time. Your redhead knows the moves. I still wonder—how did she get the information? Were nocturnal activities involved?"

"What does it matter now, Leroy?" Dwight Mueller asked, voice strained. "Shut up."

Leroy chuckled quietly. Herb imagined his friend's face splitting with suppressed laughter.

"We're here because she's paying us the big bucks,"

Dwight went on in his east coast drawl. "Shut your hatch and do your work."

Herb remembered the final mission briefing in their hideout. While Dwight, at forty-six and the oldest member of the team, had stuck to the facts like any good soldier, Leroy had fantasized aloud about the mysterious woman and her intentions, spiced with insinuations about sex in various positions. The more his descriptions turned specific, the more Dwight's composure dissipated. Eventually, Dwight shouted at Leroy, close to using his fists instead of reason. Herb had laughed at first, but as the scene progressed, he had seen no other choice but to interfere. He didn't want to lose Dwight's participation over such a stupid quarrel. Leroy had apologized later, but after a string of similar incidents, Herb had begun to doubt the young man's honesty.

"They're coming around the corner. Don't wet your pants, guys, it's showtime."

Herb hunkered down to look through the rifle sight once more. A police car rounded the elongated bend. The bus with the prisoners followed, displaying the logo of the Maryland Department of Corrections.

"There's a second black-and-white behind the bus," Leroy said, all humor gone from his voice. "Proceed or abort the attack?"

Herb curled his finger around the trigger. "Proceed. Everybody stays put."

"This wasn't the plan." Dwight sounded agitated even though he tried for a controlled voice. "There are at least two more guards than you calculated. We must abort and get away."

Herb knew his partner was an outstanding sniper as long as his nerves lasted. That was one of the reasons why the army had prematurely taken him out of service. It was also the reason why Dwight had chosen to supplement his income illegally. "Don't lose your cool, Dwight. We can do this. Stay where you are."

The police car was in range. The dark brown bus kept a steady distance from its fender. Dwight shot both the front and back tire of the police car and the front one of the bus in quick succession. Both vehicles swerved to the right, and Herb bet the drivers had a hard time keeping control until the brakes caught and the vehicles slowed to an inelegant stop. Herb moved the muzzle to the left, but Dwight shot at the same moment, as planned. Three bullets tore through the tires of the last car, one shattered the windshield. The black-and-white swiveled on its front axle, rammed the back end of the bus with its driver-side fender, and came to a skidding halt on the right shoulder. Smoke rose above the tires.

According to the plan, Herb and Dwight were to run toward the transport and free the quarry the client had paid for, but as Herb rose to get up, three uniformed men with pump shotguns emerged from the bus, took cover, and opened fire toward the hill. It was obvious they didn't see their enemies, but that didn't keep them from shooting. Herb took cover behind a large rock and aimed his rifle again. Further up the hill, Leroy shot at the uniforms, wounding one and forcing the others to retreat. Meanwhile, the police officers had exited their cars and hidden behind the vehicles' bulky front ends. As far as Herb could see, they were discussing their approach. One of them spoke into the microphone of his headset. Dwight sounded tense as a bowstring. "We can't make it. Sands, we must retreat, or we'll get killed."

"Not yet. Leroy?"

"Already on target." Leroy fired at the men huddled behind the first car. One of them fell backward with a cry. "Two down, five to go."

Herb was pleased to find that Leroy didn't lose his cool

even though things weren't going to plan. "We must keep them from calling assistance."

"They're in constant contact with HQ." Dwight fired at the officers hiding behind the second patrol car but didn't hit his mark. "We've got about ten minutes to pull this off or retreat. I'd prefer the latter."

"We can do this." Herb shot and knocked out another policeman. "Keep firing."

Dwight cursed. "Nine minutes and counting."

Herb watched a third officer collapse but suspected Dwight would lose the meager grip he had on his composure sooner than the nine minutes in his countdown. Dwight's breathing was audible through the headset, and Herb feared his associate was about to get up and make a run for it.

The side window of the bus shattered noisily, pulling Herb's awareness back to the action. Leroy had hit the bus driver. The officers were shouting to stay covered. The prison guards had stopped shooting. Herb swore he'd never again accept a job he hadn't evaluated himself. According to the lady's information, there should have been one patrol car with two uniforms and two guards on the bus, none of them heavily armed, for there were no important criminals on this trip to the court to warrant more manpower.

Two minutes passed.

Herb realized they wouldn't kill the remaining men in time to free the quarry and get away before reinforcements arrived. Police forces would be on their heels with trucks, fast cars, and a helicopter. Such an escape would be desperate, turning into a rat chase, and Herb had no intention of being a rat.

Leroy's next shot wounded one of the prison guards who had stood up to try to get a better view. Swearing loudly, a colleague pulled the man back to safety. Still, there were two men ready to defend the bus. Herb glanced at his watch. Once he left his cover, he risked being gunned down.

The police officers of the rear car were firing with pump shotguns, their bullets getting closer, now that they had calculated the sharpshooters' positions. Via headset, Herb heard Dwight's ongoing lament and a sudden cry of pain, followed by more cursing.

"Dwight, are you okay?" Leroy asked.

"Would I scream if I was okay, you sucker?" Dwight's voice was thick with pain. "Get us out of here, Sands. I don't want to end my life as cannon fodder and be the cause for some asshole's fucking promotion."

"Copy that." Herb lifted his rifle and loosened a staccato of bullets at the remaining police officers. "Dwight, get up and out of here. Leroy, wait for my mark."

"Roger." Leroy's shots riddled the rear police car, the cops ducked for cover, and that guaranteed Dwight's and Herb's retreat.

As Herb hurried uphill, he heard Dwight on his short legs wheezing behind him.

"Now, Leroy, move!"

Reaching the road, Herb opened the back door of the van, helped Dwight get in, dropped his gun on the floor, and slammed the door shut. Running to the driver's side, he slipped behind the wheel. Dwight groaned behind him, slumping in the seat and holding his left shoulder. Leroy followed half a minute later and eased into the shotgun seat. Two bullets hit the van, a warning that their enemies were following them and closing in.

"Go!" Leroy shouted.

Herb put the van in gear and headed south, glad that the roaring engine covered Dwight's complaints and accusations.

Chapter One

Jason Beckham reclined on his chair and watched his colleagues, Matthew Montagna and Nicolas Hayes, enter the large office. Both men were laughing and appeared to be in an amusing conversation about the previous weekend. Matthew quipped about the *unavoidable restrictions of a relationship,* and Nicolas replied that Matthew spent more time at the end of a leash than he did.

Without good reason, Jason felt anger bubble up. Nicolas, with his athletic Nordic complexion, was his partner at the FBI. Together, they dealt with dangerous criminals, pursued bank robbers and serial killers. They had an excellent detection rate. Jason had no intention of losing his best friend to an agent who had joined the team only recently. Matthew had been transferred from the bureau in Chicago eighteen months earlier and quickly made his mark while working with Nicolas on a case of brutal bank robberies in the Washington, DC, area. Jason envied Matthew's relaxed appearance and his courage when it came to combat situations. Matthew resembled Nicolas more than Jason liked to admit, and in the back of his mind, Jason was afraid his longtime partner preferred working with the agent from Chicago, who had nothing else to offer than his dedication to his job and a dog at home.

"Did you watch the news?" Jason asked, quashing his pessimism with a smile.

"No, what's up?" Nicolas, cup in hand, made his way to the coffee machine. "Matt? Coffee?"

"Sure." Matthew opened his jacket as he leaned against an

empty desk on the other side of the aisle. He crossed his ankles and put his hands on the desk. "Anything worth knowing?"

Jason held his tongue as Nicolas handed Matthew a cup of freshly brewed coffee. Instead of yelling at *Matthew the Intruder* that the coffee was made exclusively for Nicolas and himself, Jason sipped from his mug and nodded toward the screen.

"This morning, a prisoner transport on the way to the courthouse in DC was assaulted by three snipers. Thankfully, the officers and guards chased them off, but it took a heavy toll—one dead, four wounded."

"Did they catch them?"

"No, the three men got away. Reinforcements arrived too late, and the gangsters had already changed cars. CSU technicians are still at the crime scene."

"Do the police know about the target?"

Jason turned his attention to Nicolas, who sat down at his desk, blowing over his steaming coffee.

"Yes. Ricky Bianchi. He's—"

"He's the son of Alfredo Bianchi, one of the oldest mafia families on the east coast," Matthew said, snapping his fingers. "His escape would make Mother Maria Bianchi very happy." He laughed heartily. "She went ballistic when her son was arrested. I mean, she threw a hissy fit that quickly became an internet hit with more than one million clicks."

Jason had trouble keeping a blank face when he glanced at Matthew. His colleague's joy felt like a sting in his eye. "Right. I bet it was an interesting sight."

"Yep, it was. I didn't know the trial against him had already begun."

"It was moved up." Jason turned to Nicolas again. To his delight, his partner didn't share Matthew's jolliness. "There were two more prisoners on board we know—Theodor and

Benjamin Nelson, the evil twins."

Nicolas's eyes widened, and he put down his cup. "Really?"

"Yep. Nevertheless, the police assume Ricky was the target. The mob had announced his rescue a day after his incarceration. It was only a question of time until they'd strike." He glanced at Matthew. "That's why the judge agreed to proceed more quickly. They don't want daily threats against the court."

Matthew sipped his coffee, frowning. "Is there any evidence that Ricky's family's behind the assault? I mean, they'd need an insider to know about the transport."

"You think the Nelson sister did this?" Nicolas frowned deeply. "According to my research, she was seen at the airport in Charlotte on December fourth, leaving on a plane to Mexico City. She hasn't been spotted since."

"Yeah, I know. Tom Pinnock's drawing of Katherine was excellent, but is it possible she returned? Found a way to sneak back into the country?" Matthew held up his hand. "Before you say *no*, let's think about it. Two days before her oldest brother was shot and her younger brothers arrested, Katherine Nelson took a flight out of the country. We know she was the mastermind behind her brothers' bank robberies. Without her, it was only a matter of time until the rest of the gang was arrested. Tom didn't rat on her in the first place, and we suspect his allegiance helped her get away. I bet he was in love with her."

Nicolas grinned as he put down his cup. "Your idea of sending a bruiser to his cell block was great. Tom looked quite shaken when we interrogated him again."

"Oh, it was your idea, first of all. You knew about his cellmate, *Big Boy* Barrister, and his fondness for artists."

Nicolas burst out laughing. "Fondness! He would've eaten Tom raw for breakfast, brush and colors included."

Jason gritted his teeth so hard his jaw hurt. He didn't know a criminal named Barrister, had no idea about the decision to push Tom Pinnock to disclose Katherine Nelson's looks—not to mention draw a reliable picture of her—and he was angry he hadn't been involved in the manhunt for her. Though he'd been on sick leave because of an injury, he had expected his partner to keep him in the loop.

Nicolas's face sobered. "I don't think she'd risk coming back to the US, even if she had the means. We know now what she looks like. Every police station and border patrol got her picture. Like you said, she's smart. She took precautions to leave and avoid detection and arrest."

Matthew shrugged. "I think it depends on the strength of the family ties. The profiler assumed the siblings were close. We know the rest of the family died years ago. They've stuck together since they were little. They were careful, and Katherine obviously knew she had to remain almost invisible to develop a criminal career. I've never seen a woman with less interest in getting photographed. She's a kind of ghost of the modern times. No social media account, no email address, no permanent residence. Her name doesn't appear on any official document after she left school."

"That's what makes it so easy for her to disappear with a new ID," Jason said. He got up to refill his mug before Matthew, the good-for-nothing coffee thief, had a chance to empty the pot. "She's got a clean slate."

"For years, Katherine managed the robberies. We know that she's the brains of the family, maybe followed by Herman, who knew at least how to execute her plans. But the twins are a few cans short of a six-pack. About as sharp as an eraser. Without their sister, they walked around waving a flag and waiting to get caught." Matthew shook his head. "If she saw a chance to help the twins, I bet she'd do it." He emptied his mug and put it back next to the machine. "Thanks for the coffee, Jason. It was great, as always."

Matthew left, and Jason sat down at his desk, still angry without reason. "I bet the Bianchi family launched the attack. What do you think?"

Nicolas rubbed his neck, grimacing. "If the evil sister is back, I want to put her in handcuffs and drag her to prison."

Jason glimpsed fresh abrasions at his friend's wrists. "And who did that to you this weekend?"

"That, my friend, is not your concern." Nicolas pulled down his shirt sleeves, smiling secretively. "I'll tell you simply—it was an amazing weekend."

Jason's anger flared again, and he had trouble keeping his voice down. "Don't gimme that crap of an *amazing weekend* and then expect to talk work. I bet you told Matthew every juicy detail."

"No, I didn't. He made insinuations, and I didn't deny them. That's all." Nicolas looked back at the computer screen.

"But I want—" Jason stopped and shook his head. He realized he was going too far, and yet his uneasiness remained.

"What?"

"Are you thinking about changing partners?"

Nicolas's head shot up from the screen. "Pardon?"

"You heard me. You're getting more and more familiar with this pain in the neck from Illinois, and I—"

Nicolas nodded slowly. "He's a fellow agent, Jason. Sorry, but you're behaving irrationally. I'm not going to change partners, but maybe you could concentrate on our work now?"

Growling with bad temper about coffee being served randomly to everybody and a love life Nicolas didn't disclose, Jason checked his emails.

Herb's ears were ringing. Dwight's constant nagging about

the failed assault was unstoppable and very irritating. While Herb cleaned and dressed the superficial shoulder wound, his partner lamented that the team had never relied on a customer's plan without checking it themselves.

"Why did you believe her? Did she make eyes at you?"

Leroy laughed out loud. "A sexist question from you, Dwighty? Is it Christmas already?"

Dwight kept his questioning gaze. The gray stubble, as well as the faint pockmarks, added to the man's pale, unhealthy looks. "Tell me, why didn't you do reconnaissance? Why didn't you know that this Bianchi offspring would be on the bus? It was clear as mud that police and guards would show up in greater numbers with that bastard on board. You should—"

"You're right." Herb fastened the last strip tightly across the bandage, ignoring Dwight's pained gasp, then pulled up the shirt across the pudgy shoulder. "I should've doubted her, but she was very convincing."

Leroy stopped cleaning his rifle and turned around at the table. The look in his dark brown eyes was adamant. "Gimme a break, Sands. The news said it was the judge's decision to call for Bianchi *today*. No one—not even his lawyer—knew of the transport in advance. Miss Copper Head couldn't have known, and you couldn't have known, either." He shrugged. "Call her. Tell her what happened and ask if she's got another plan."

"You shouldn't even think about working for her a second time," Dwight groused as he moved his arm carefully. He shook his head, and the remaining few strands of blond hair moved as if the wind had touched them. His expression was that of a man looking into an abyss. "I won't shoot for at least a week."

Herb's smile came and went. He packed up the first aid kit and put it back on the shelf. "I doubt we'll get another chance so soon anyway." He reached for the phone, wiping the bridge of his nose fretfully. He was tired and worn-out. The shootout and getaway had taken its toll, and he wanted nothing more than to lie down and sleep. Usually, after a successful hit, he treated his aching forty-year-old body to a vacation to give it time to recover. But this had not been a successful hit. He hadn't suffered a failure in years, and it didn't merely disappoint him. It made him grumpy. Bracing for a difficult conversation, he dialed the client's number.

She took the call after the second ringing and didn't waste any time chatting.

"I thought you were the expert," she snapped. "I thought you'd be able to adapt your plan according to the ongoing situation. If you want to apologize, fine. But you owe me more than that. I want the job done quickly. Don't expect me to wait another month. It's far too risky."

"Fine." Herb broke eye contact with Dwight, ignoring the signal for him to end the conversation. "Did you have anything in mind?"

"Certainly. No one should ever leave the house without a plan B. Didn't you know that?"

Despite his grumpiness, Herb couldn't help but admire the lady's arrogance. From his first contact with her, he'd felt an attraction to her. She impressed him with her love for detail, with her clear and forthright expectations of him, not to mention her threat to ruin his life if he took her money and left her hanging out to dry. They had met once, and Herb had memorized her mass of red hair and fine features that no amount of make-up could cloak. He knew she'd dyed her hair to alter her appearance, but the style suited her and matched her personality – she was wild and determined, like a cruel but beautiful witch in a fantasy movie.

"What do you want me to do?"

At the table, Leroy made distinctive and obscene gestures

with his hips and hands. Dwight grunted with disgust, and Herb looked away to quash a smile.

"Another assault would be useless. You'll go directly to the prison and get them out."

"We will? How?"

"I'll meet you at the Irish Inn at Glen Echo in three hours."

"And the timing for this proposed break-in?"

"In three days."

She hung up, and Herb rubbed his itching head. "Dwight, you have to mend a tad faster. The next job is in three days."

Dwight bemoaned his position loudly once more. This time his lament focused on his unbearable pain and the hardship he had to suffer from working with Herb and Leroy, those half-wits who didn't deserve his support.

Victor Morrison despised the term *bodyguard,* preferring *security adviser* instead. While the bodyguard took care of his client's survival, the security adviser had a much wider range of influence and responsibility. Victor considered himself a personal assistant rather than a man who would jump into the line of fire. The description was reflected in his appearance. He dressed in a tailored suit and tie, matched with a white dress shirts, and wore leather shoes as immaculately shiny as his frequently shaved bald head. He wanted to impress with a classy outfit. So far, his strategy worked—the list of clients was growing, and he had recently hired two more men with the same work attitude to enlarge his security company. The income sufficed to maintain a small but exclusive office in downtown Richmond and to buy a new luxury car.

Right now, he was driving the impressive limousine of Deputy Mayor Bryan *Buck* Dobson, a man dedicated to his job, cigarettes, and women, not necessarily in that order. Dobson was reclining in the back seat, smoking and reading. The first appointment of the day was with a real estate agent in Windsor Farms. Some friends in the Richmond government had told Dobson that real estate was the most rewarding economy branch, and he shouldn't wait too long to buy a summer residence as a secret resort. Afraid that prices would go through the roof the following month, Dobson had spent more time than was decent to inspect suitable houses close to Richmond.

It wasn't an adviser's job to criticize his employer's behavior, but Morrison wouldn't vote for his boss at the upcoming election for mayor of Richmond. The security advisor glanced in the rearview mirror, through the thick smoke, to see Dobson mumbling to himself, turning pages, and reaching for the next cigarette while the one between his fingers was still smoldering. Dobson was oblivious to the scrutiny. He was interested in the voters' decision, in polls, and in his opponent's failures. A politician through and through, Dobson possessed an uncanny ability to find the correct words to impress voters and stress how important his work was for the community. Because of gang rivalries and shootouts, Dobson had taken up the cause of fighting against gangs and drug dealers in the greater Richmond area. He vowed that once he was elected, he would increase police personnel, buy new service cars, and more and better weapons. He claimed that no police officer should fight a hardcore criminal with weapons of less penetration power than the gangster's. He hadn't revealed where the money would come from to underwrite his plans, and Morrison doubted that his boss even knew how to read a budget, but his announcements on the subject sounded convincing enough to the people for him to be a real contender.

During the last five months, Dobson had constantly been rallying, speaking to the masses, and presenting his family to show his voters that he was an ordinary man with the same fears and hopes as them. In his role as head of security, Morrison had combed the audience for possible killers, for suspicious persons with bulky bags. He'd been hired to keep Dobson from being shot or stabbed by angry criminals who were taking their crimes up another level. But it had to be said that, so far, Dobson appeared as threatening to a violent gang as a ballet dancer to a group of Navy SEALS.

Morrison stopped the car in the driveway to get out and check the surroundings before he opened the back passenger door, ignoring the noxious stench of stale nicotine that hung over the politician like a rain cloud.

Dobson grunted and exited the car in a plume of smoke, reaching for his lighter before the door closed. He smoothed his tie and adjusted the sleeves of his dress shirt. Due to his nicotine addiction, he was slim, but his skin had a touch of gray, and the index and middle finger of his right hand were saffron yellow. If he wanted to appear healthy, his make-up assistant had to work on his face for more than thirty minutes.

"Well, now look at this nice piece of ass," he mumbled.

Morrison followed Dobson's gaze toward today's curvy real estate agent, then turned his attention back to the garden and possible threats. Seemingly unaware that he might become a shooter's victim, Dobson strutted toward the lady, who waited on the last step of the wide porch. Morrison had no choice but to hurry after him. He knew from past experience that there was no point in trying to hold back his client.

The real estate agent had the voluptuous figure of an hourglass, a Gina Lollobrigida of the present age, and her appearance in a modest but classy two-piece suit appealed to the deputy mayor's lust in the most blatant of ways. When his boss's first saccharine compliments rained down on her, Morrison stared at the floor, clasping his hands and hoping this appointment would turn out to be professional, at least from her side.

Dobson held the lady's gloved hand for a quick kiss on its back. "Oh, what a wonderful sight, and that doesn't include the crafted banister and the color of the doors, if you get my meaning."

Morrison knew he was in no position to reprimand his employer, but he felt like apologizing for Dobson's gibberish. However, the real estate agent appeared flattered and her smile genuine.

"Thank you, sir. I'm Teresa Olbridge and very pleased to meet you."

"Oh, the pleasure is all mine, believe me."

"I hope that this house will increase your pleasure and give you the feeling of being on a lasting vacation."

"With you at my side, that wouldn't be too hard." Dobson laughed and patted her hand again. "But, please, show me more before I decide on how the day will continue. Maybe we should start with the bedroom."

"There are three bedrooms in this house, sir." Her smile was warm, her tone convincing. "I think you'll like the one with the view of the pool best."

Morrison admired the lady's composure faced with Dobson's sleazy attempts at flattery. He followed his boss and Miss Olbridge into the wide lobby, looked left and right, but didn't see any suspicious movement or anything that might pose a threat. Once again, Morrison felt like a puppet that had only been taken along to make the deputy mayor appear more important than he actually was. Morrison pondered whether the rest of the appointments on this day would be equally irrelevant.

The house interior was chic, with cream-colored walls and gold-framed paintings, the floor made of expensive wood, polished to shine. The few pieces of furniture, meant as a sample of how the room might look, were designed to match the exquisite taste of the future owner. Morrison hoped one day he'd make enough money to move into such an exclusive estate.

In a well-tempered voice and without any discernable accent, Miss Olbridge reported about when the house was built, its size and advantages, its outstanding view, and the guaranteed increase in the value of such property. Without appearing distant or impolite, she kept Dobson from touching her backside while they walked through the door toward the living room. Morrison's admiration climbed another level when the real estate agent stepped to the side the moment Dobson made another approach at her derrière. Still, she smiled like an untouchable goddess and continued her sales talk without interruption. Morrison grinned and almost missed the soft hiss above him. He looked up to find a short spray can attached to the door frame, dispersing a white fog into his face. He coughed and retreated at once, yet his eyes teared and he had trouble breathing. He wanted to call out to Dobson, but the words stuck in his throat. His knees buckled, and he went down hard on the parquet flooring. Before losing consciousness, he heard Dobson yell, "What's goin' on here?"

CHAPTER TWO

Jason met Nicolas on the way to the garage at FBI headquarters. It was early in the morning, and Jason handed his partner a travel mug with coffee from his machine at the office. In contrast to Nicolas, Jason arrived at the office wide awake and prepared for the day.

"Thanks." Nicolas sipped the coffee while Jason got the keys to their car. "What's so important that you called me in the middle of the night?"

"Deputy Mayor Dobson of Richmond was murdered yesterday morning. Richmond PD was at the crime scene first, but then their chief decided they'd better drop the file onto our desk. I can't tell if someone put pressure on him, but now it's our case."

"Okay." Nicolas slipped behind the wheel and put the mug into a holder. "What took them so long? Internal quarrels we should know of?"

"No. Dobson's bodyguard called the police yesterday in the afternoon and—"

"In the afternoon? Didn't you just say the mayor was murdered in the morning?"

Jason grunted in his beard. "If you'd let me finish, it'll become clear." He held his breath and the door handle as Nicolas gunned the engine and the sedan roared up the slope toward the street. No matter what level of urgency, his partner was addicted to speed like a race car driver. "Dobson's bodyguard, Victor Morrison, reported the crime when he woke up. He stated he'd been knocked out by some kind of gas from a spray can. He found his employer beaten to death in the living room of the house the deputy mayor was being shown around by a real estate agent. The woman's description has already been sent to police stations in the districts. They're searching for her."

"Knocked out by some kind of gas?"

"Morrison stated he was about to follow Dobson and the lady when he was hit by the gas. Dobson wasn't affected, and Morrison went down so quickly he can't tell what happened next."

"Shouldn't he have entered the next room first?"

"That might be so, usually, but it didn't happen in this case."

Nicolas whistled through his teeth. He stopped the car at a red light and turned to look at his partner. "CSU was also at the crime scene?"

"Our team will arrive with us, but the main evidence was photographed and sifted already. It's a mess."

Nicolas drove on. "The evidence?"

"The mayor was clubbed to death, Nick. He was tied to a chair, and then someone used a baseball club to smash his body. Messy."

"And what happened to the real estate agent?"

"Goes by the name of Teresa Olbridge and hasn't been found yet. We don't know if she was kidnapped or if she got away before the murder was committed."

"Let's hope for the latter." Nicolas drove onto the highway leading out of Washington.

"If she got away—why didn't she call the police? Why didn't she help the bodyguard?" Jason shook his head. "I'm sorry, but I think we're dealing with a murder and a kidnapping or two murders with one body missing."

"But think about it. The killer knocks out the bodyguard and takes control of Olbridge and Dobson. The killing of the mayor took time. Did he make her watch the murder?"

"Maybe he knocked her out and carried her away later. Or he killed her, too, and we'll find her in a dumpster."

Nicolas mumbled about scenarios and illogical behavior while Jason imagined the poor woman being forced to witness a brutal killing and then dragged away to an unknown destiny, fearing for her life.

He cringed, thinking of his beloved Elaine trapped in such a situation. Since he'd begun the relationship with the lovely FBI secretary, Jason felt like a man reborn from sadness. Elaine loved him even though he was a miserable poker player, lost to her at every virtual game, and never won at air hockey. She pampered him like a mother hen, and he was grateful he'd gathered his courage to ask her out.

"We're on the safe side calling her a victim and hoping she'll be found alive."

Nicolas made a face. For a moment, Jason couldn't tell whether he was angered by a slow driver in front of him or irritated by the case and its circumstances.

"The murderer sounds driven by an overbearing and excessive aggressiveness. Surely, he wouldn't kill the mayor and then take her like some kind of trophy. If he acted in a frenzy, he'd have killed her and the bodyguard, too."

"The vicinity was searched. No other body." Jason skipped through the thin file he'd received from the police department in Richmond. "There's still hope he's got her someplace. Maybe taking her with him was a spontaneous decision."

"No. Something doesn't fit."

"Tell me, what did you do with Jacklyn or the other way around? I mean, you had two days off. There must be something—"

Nicolas let go of his breath loudly. "Jason, please, stick to the case. I don't ask you for bedtime stories."

"If you would, I'd tell you."

Jason's sly grin was met by Nicolas's open frustration.

"Ah, buddy, come on, you owe me some good stories. No other couple I know has a dungeon in the house."

"It's our bedroom, okay? It's a . . . part-time dungeon."

Jason laughed out loud. "That's a pretty strange description. Just because you sleep there from time to time, hmm? If she lets you sleep at all."

Nicolas pursed his lips as if weighing up the hours of sleep compared to those of entertainment. "We slept together."

Nicolas's mock seriousness caused Jason to laugh again. "You're playing the modest lover here." He shook his head. "Man, you've got a life! Chasing murderers during the day and playing submissive lover at night."

"You don't envy me," Nicolas said quietly. He steered the car down the ramp and turned right at the next corner. "There's no way I can imagine you tied up in a stressful position."

Jason sighed. "No. Maybe it's not the part of being tied up, just the part of reaching levels of satisfaction I'll never reach." When Nicolas didn't reply, Jason went on. "I pulled some information about this bondage lifestyle. It said that the amount of hormones distributing to the feelings of lust are five times higher than during normal sex."

"There are statistics about that?"

"Yep. Many couples state they live a very fulfilling and also relaxed life because the roles in their partnership are clearly defined. Once the roles are established—this must be heaven on earth. No discussions, no arguments." Jason beamed at Nicolas. "That's the part I envy you for."

Nicolas frowned, and much to Jason's chagrin, didn't go into details about the weekend.

"What do we know about the bodyguard? Could this be a hoax?" Nicolas asked after a while.

"Morrison has run his own business for five years without

complaints. Many happy clients. He's been expanding due to his growing income and increasing demands from the persons he protects. Ex-US Army, last rank master sergeant. No negative entries here, either. The army wanted to keep him, but he preferred to be independent, maybe preferring not to follow orders anymore but to give them instead. I say it's highly unlikely he framed his employer and clubbed him to death."

"Never jump to conclusions." Nicolas pulled into the street at Windsor Farms, where a row of police cars was parked. A line of officers kept pedestrians and a number of reporters from entering the area.

Nicolas and Jason showed their IDs, passed under the yellow police tape, and went toward the living room.

Jason braced for the sight of the dead deputy mayor, but it was worse than the photos in the file. The politician's face wasn't recognizable anymore. Blood had splattered his suit, shirt, and even his shoes. The parquet was soiled with bloody smeared stains where the killer had stood.

"Footprints on both sides of the chair." Jason pulled plastic covers over his shoes. "Either the killer wanted to work his wrath from both sides, or there were two attackers involved."

"Two men. The sizes are different." Nicolas stepped toward the body carefully. CSU technicians told them in harsh voices to keep a distance. "The prints are smeared, so it's hard to tell the size. It looks like they wore plastic covers over their shoes."

"Yes, I agree with that. And they are of average height or smaller. Why? Because that fits with the height of impact," Miller, CSU technician with the FBI, said, butting into the conversation.

As far as Jason could tell, the man's voice was tinged by enthusiasm rather than horror.

"The killers swung the clubs at waist level and hit the victim's chest." He demonstrated the swinging. "Then, with more effort, they smashed his face."

Nicolas made a step to the left. "No gag. The killers weren't afraid of anyone overhearing the murder."

"He must've screamed in sheer agony." Jason avoided taking a deep breath. The stench of blood and excrement was threatening to overwhelm his sense of smell. "Looks like they broke his hands, too."

Miller nodded, causing a strand of hair to fall across his forehead. "I can't tell exactly, but I assume the killers started with his hands and arms, then beat his chest and finally killed him by the blows to his head."

"The violence was out of control."

Jason turned away from the body. "At least one of them must've known the mayor personally and bore a grudge against him. This isn't a crime committed by chance."

Nicolas straightened to his full height and rubbed his neck. When the homicide detective arrived, they introduced each other, and Nicolas asked, "Still no news about Miss Olbridge?"

"Nope." Detective Callahan made a face that deepened the wrinkles around his eyes and mouth.

Jason thought of a Shar-Pei, which fit the officer's rheumy eyes and the permanent sad expression. "My men canvassed the vicinity, checked gardens, the neighborhood, asked residents, and they are now sifting through traffic camera footage."

"What about Miss Olbridge's car?" Jason asked. "Did anyone see her leave? Is her car still there?"

"No. No car here. Either she drove it away, or someone else did. We're searching for that, too, of course." The detective's expression changed from sad to hopeless. "My men also checked the data of known criminals who are of less than average height. No matches." He scratched his head and pointed across his shoulder. "Did you see the houses along the street? If the owners are home, they stay to themselves. Other houses are empty because the owners spend weeks overseas. There are more gardeners and housekeepers around than owners, at least at this time of the year. The employees do their work and leave again. We tracked down most of them, but they didn't see anything. The residences are secluded, too. High fences or hedges. The neighbors aren't interested in a garden chat." He shrugged, and his loose suit swished around his body.

Jason suspected the man had been overweight until the last year and hadn't had time yet to buy new clothes. "Of course, we'll keep looking, if you want us to." Callahan looked from Nicolas to Jason. "If you send your people, I'd appreciate that. We've got enough cases on our desks. We don't need this one."

"Is there a reason . . ."

Callahan snorted and lowered his head and his voice. "My captain thinks that a hate group perpetrated this crime. He didn't name a gang, but that's what he means. The deputy mayor suffered some trouble with gangs during the last few weeks—destroyed advertisements, Molotov cocktails against the election office, and other kinds of vandalism. I call it luck that no one was hurt. The election is in less than a month. No one at the department wants to be responsible for the investigation and what it might turn up. Don't get me wrong—I'd investigate this case like any other, but that's not what is expected from me. My captain wants this case solved ASAP, and I despise the . . . political implication."

"I get it." Jason felt sympathy for the tired-looking detective. Judging by his looks and moves, he was close to retirement. "We'll take it from here and let you know what we find out."

"Great." Callahan's face lit up for a moment. "So, I can really start my vacation as planned. That's a first. I'll send you my report and the results from the tech lab as soon as I get them."

"Thanks." Jason watched Callahan leave and thought the old detective had a jauntier swing in his steps than before. "Okay, local police are out of the race. What's our next step?"

Nicolas put his hands on his hips, and his focus was back on the body. "I'm thinking about Miss Olbridge's role in this. Could she be an accomplice?"

"An accomplice? Why?"

"Her car's gone, there's no trace of her. She didn't make contact, either."

"But you consider her a criminal rather than a victim. Okay, what makes you think so?"

"First, the size of the footprints. Small for a man, right?" He smiled when Jason made a face and looked down at his own small feet. "The killers knew where the deputy mayor would be at the time and set the trap. They were clever enough to knock out the bodyguard and take their time to kill Dobson. Somebody must've tipped them off. That would explain why she wasn't found and didn't call the police."

Jason whistled softly through his teeth and directed Nicolas out of the house. "You're saying, she didn't witness the crime but worked with the killers? That's strong stuff, and I don't want to think that way. I mean, she's a real estate agent. Those people may be pulling your leg, but they won't murder anybody."

"Another possibility would be that she told the killers where to find Dobson and then left before the killing started." Nicolas shrugged. "It's also possible she only played the role, and the lady from the company is dead, too. We'll have to check the company's employees later. Let's talk with the bodyguard."

"Security adviser," a man beside them said. He reached out for a handshake. The left side of his light brown face was bruised from temple to chin. "Victor Morrison. I was Mr. Dobson's security adviser and drove him yesterday morning." He pointed across his shoulder. "A police officer sent me here, telling me the FBI wanted to see me."

"That's right." Jason schooled his expression. Apparently, Callahan was in a hurry to turn the case over to the FBI. "Tell us what happened after you arrived."

Morrison summed up the events, then pursed his lips and directed his gaze to the tips of his shoes. "I kept telling Mr. Dobson to let me secure the area before he entered a building. He said I obstructed his view." Morrison looked up. "If I'd been given time to search the house, I would've seen the attackers, but he rushed in as if he had nothing to fear."

"We understand your concern for Mr. Dobson," Nicolas said soothingly. "Did you do a background check on Miss Olbridge?"

"No. I checked the homepage of the real estate agent, *Lindberg Global Estate*. Mr. Lindberg is an elderly man, has been in the business for more than thirty years. The homepage didn't include pictures of all employees, but I found her name." He frowned. "Do you think she wasn't the person who she claimed to be?"

"It's possible. We have to check that." Jason looked Morrison in the eyes. "Why didn't you pass through the door into the living room first?"

"I already told the police that I wanted to do that, but Mr. Dobson didn't take me seriously. He hired me because of some threats by haters, some fanatics who said they wanted to see him dead. Local police had their eyes on a gang in town. If you ask me, I'd say Mr. Dobson took me to be an addition to his campaign, like announcing to his followers that he was willing to take risks to push his political agenda, no matter his physical safety." Morrison shook his head. "My pleas to let me do my job were answered by disrespect."

"You were hit by the gas and went down. Do you know what sort of gas? What about the spray can?" Nicolas turned around. "Did you secure it? And there were no remnants of adhesive tape or anything else."

"It was gone when I came to. And I can't tell you why I was out cold for hours." Morrison shook his head. "I don't know of any gas that causes such a long-lasting effect. It couldn't be identified at the hospital, either. There were no traces on my face or in my blood. The only thing the doc found was the remnants of baby oil, like what's used in those small baby wipes." He shrugged. "I don't have the faintest idea what the killer used, but he wanted to leave no traces, obviously."

Nicolas lowered his chin. "A good explanation. Almost too good."

Morrison's eyes narrowed, and his voice was tinted with anger. "Are you accusing me of lying?"

"Who knew about Mr. Dobson's appointment?" Jason asked and scanned through his notes. "I understand it was a private one?"

"Yes, it was private." Morrison frowned, then huffed. "I don't think he placed the call himself, so his secretary, Miss Simmons, made the arrangement. Then there's his wife. I assume he let her know that he was looking for a house. And then there's Miss Olbridge. She might've boasted about her famous client."

"We'll talk to her as soon as we find her." Nicolas put his hands on his hips.

Jason read the distrust on his face clearly.

"You were unconscious for six hours straight. In that time,

your client was beaten to death, and a real estate agent is missing. What did you see when you arrived? On the street? In the garden? In the foyer?"

Morrison didn't flinch. "I didn't see anything out of the ordinary in the garden or at the house. Otherwise, I'd have stopped Mr. Dobson and pushed him back into the car. I didn't see another person or car besides a red *Chrysler* sedan, in which Miss Olbridge might've come to the house." When Nicolas's gaze didn't waver, Morrison said, "No, I didn't check the Chrysler for weapons. If you think the lady has anything to do with the murder, you're mistaken. She's . . . harmless. A sweet and very professional woman who tried to sell a house and make a living. In spite of Dobson's sleazy advances, she gave him the impression that she liked his flattery." He made a face. "Could she be this good and fool us both?"

"Do you know of any threats to kill the deputy mayor?"

"No, not the people. The hate letters he received were the trigger for hiring me, but there were no tangible threats from individuals that I could identify. The police couldn't name any suspects at all."

"We'll get back to you later." Jason maintained eye contact. "If you remember anything else that might be useful—"

"There was one thing—a large gray plastic bag in one corner of the living room. It was gone when I came to."

"Any idea about the contents?"

"No. I considered it odd because the rest of the house was clean as a surgery room."

"All right. We'll check that."

"I want to catch that bastard as much as you do," Morrison stated. "If you need help or information, feel free to contact me anytime."

Katherine, now known as Jolina Bertoni, was still in mourning. Her beloved brother Herman, the gentle giant, who had been positive, optimistic, a real charmer, was dead, buried in an anonymous grave. The news after the shootout in the shopping center had revealed the shocking truth—Herman would never again embrace her, hold her, and give her solace. She wouldn't hear his smooth voice anymore, laugh at his feeble jokes or scold him for his recklessness. She wouldn't fight with him anymore about how to treat the twins.

Katherine was choking on her anger. More than anything, she needed to avenge Herman's murder.

Without her as a mental guardian, and in less than a week, the twins had degenerated into numbskull idiots completely without a sense for danger. Consequently, they had been spotted, reported to the police, and pursued. Their miserable attempt at escaping the FBI had failed and left Herman to die wastefully in a parking lot. Katherine had watched the news broadcasts and also the videos made by pedestrians on their cell phones. The media had had a field day with Herman's killing, along with the arrest of Theo and Ben. Katherine didn't know what made her more furious—her brothers' dumb behavior or the FBI's shoot-to-kill attitude.

Though she was angry, her grief nagged her even more. She couldn't let her brothers rot behind bars with the possibility they might be killed during their first year in prison. She knew their recklessness would lead them into arguments, fights, and ultimately to a dark place where gangs ruled the corridors and their leaders would decide the brothers were a nuisance they didn't tolerate.

As she strolled along the path to the meeting point, Katherine pondered her strategy and evaluated her decisions, as she had done many times before. She loathed working with strangers but had learned that money was a universal language soldiers of fortune understood. Herb Sanders was no different. According to the news reports, he and his two partners had tried to raid the prisoner transport and aborted the mission at the last moment to get away. Though their failure was regrettable, she had another plan that she couldn't wait to see put into action.

Herb Sanders turned the corner at the park entrance, looking left and right as if expecting an FBI ambush. Katherine smiled. If Herb failed her, there would be no need for a federal agent to pull the trigger and end the sniper's life.

Despite himself, Herb was impressed that Miss Copper Head had not one but two elaborate plans to offer. It was as if her brain ran on overtime, creating escape plans faster than an expert could assemble a Russian rifle without looking. He listened intently, added his two cents, and promised to work according to her timetable once he was convinced her details had been correctly researched. The lady had no illusion that she was ordering people harmed, maybe even killed. Her ruthlessness matched his own, and he felt drawn to her as if she was the female partner he missed. He didn't say a word about his feelings, of course, for the lady was focused on her brothers' freedom. She wouldn't know his emotions even if he painted his thoughts on the wall. They parted quietly and without a handshake. Herb had the money, and Miss Copper Head had the conviction that plans B or C—preferably both—would work.

Herb made two phone calls before he informed Leroy and Dwight about their imminent tasks. They departed from their hideout, and Herb moved into his observation post at dusk.

It was important to know about the gangs and their bosses once you decided to stay for more than a few days in the city. For a criminal who wanted to maintain a hideout in the city, it was wise to get acquainted with the locals, treat them with necessary politeness and make clear you weren't easy prey they could chase away. Having worked in the DC area for three years, Herb knew some hired muscle he could call for easy jobs he wouldn't lower himself to do. The five men he'd recruited for tonight's assignment belonging to a gang from Washington's south, loved to fight, and were easily convinced to do the dirty work if the payment was good enough.

Herb stood with his binoculars in the shadow behind a large tree and watched the bar entrance. Still dressed for work in a suit and tie, Nicolas Hayes had met with a friend two hours ago. It was a regular weekly meeting, as Miss Copper Head had told him. The guys were chatting and drinking whiskey on ice, obviously at ease with each other. Judging by the second man's looks and bearing, he might work for the police or the military. When Hayes got up, he signaled the barkeeper for the check, and after a short exchange of words, the barkeeper took the phone. Herb expected him to call a cab, the right decision after the amount of alcohol the two men had consumed. Hayes went to the restroom while the other guy paid for the drinks. When Hayes returned, they left the bar and walked toward the parking lot. Their cars were parked close to each other. Both men pulled out their keys from their pockets, but neither went to get behind the wheel. Instead, they headed for the trunks and set about gathering their belongings. Hayes fetched his backpack and slammed the trunk shut.

That same moment, a gray van with patchy bodywork rolled along the street. Tires and engine squealed and rattled, adding to the impression the van wouldn't drive another mile.

From his lookout, Herb watched with a smile on his haggard face. The van stopped, and the passenger got out, leaving the door open. He had a street map in one hand and a puzzled slant on his boyish face and approached Hayes gesturing toward the next corner. Herb didn't hear words, but Hayes reacted as anticipated—he moved toward the stranger on the sidewalk, shouldering the backpack and smiling like a boy scout with an overwhelming eagerness to be of service.

Herb had instructed the gang members to patiently wait until Hayes was close to the van, distracted by his duty to help the young men find their way. Herb counted to ten, and then as if the men had heard him, the sliding door opened, and three more gangsters jumped out to grab Hayes.

Herb nodded his approval. Though they weren't the brightest lights in a chandelier, the gangsters had listened to his instructions. Hayes recoiled, arms raised in defense. He dropped his backpack to gain an advantage. Two gangsters attacked him, but Hayes delivered a series of hard punches that kept them at bay. The young guy let go of the map and joined the fight. Hayes evaded his attack and kicked the man's stomach so hard the attacker crumpled and fell on his knees close to the van's front tire. From the parking lot, Hayes's friend came running at top speed.

Herb cursed. If the job couldn't be committed in thirty seconds, the assault would attract the attention of pedestrians, car drivers, and maybe even guests inside the bar. In less than a minute, the police would be informed and on their way. Irritated by the turn of events, Herb glanced at his watch. Either the fight was over in fifteen seconds, or the gangsters must retreat and leave their prey behind. Herb counted the seconds as he watched the fight. Hayes's friend wasn't just an excellent runner. He had such a hard punch that Herb heard the gangster's cry of pain across the street. The fight had turned, and the driver yelled at his battered comrades to get into the van. The men scrambled into the back, the sliding door closed, and the van lurched away with squealing tires, leaving only the caustic smell of burning hanging on the air.

Hayes lay on the sidewalk, stretched out on his back, motionless. His friend was holding his right side, breathing raggedly and calling out to Hayes. With considerable effort, he made it to his feet and stumbled to check Hayes's vitals. Blood trickled from his nose, and he wiped it away before he reached for his cell phone.

Herb pondered the idea of crossing the street and offering help but decided it would trigger too much attention once he tried to finish off the action by knocking out the friend and pulling the unconscious Hayes toward his car. Dragging a dead weight of one-hundred-eighty pounds would take time—not to mention it would be laborious—and he couldn't risk anyone seeing his face. Cursing viciously, Herb stepped back into shadows as two guests left the bar, saw Hayes and his friend, and pulled their phones to call for assistance.

Without being spotted, Herb left the crime scene and walked back to his car.

Chapter Three

Jason missed the time he'd been the first one on Nicolas's emergency call list. When he entered the hospital, Jacklyn was already waiting for him, glancing at a doctor and a nurse as they passed by.

"Tell me what's going on," Jason demanded without any formalities.

Jacklyn's lips twitched, and belatedly Jason saw the remnants of tears on her powdered cheeks. He apologized with a look, and he thought she understood.

"The police called me an hour ago. Nicolas and Thomas were attacked when they left the bar. They fought off the bad guys, but—" She glanced at the emergency room. "Nicolas has several bad bruises and probably a concussion. The doc's testing him as we speak. Tom's nose was broken. He looks as if he's won a prize fight—all smiles and no sign of pain. The police don't know who did this. The witness statements contradict each other—the street was so dark. Tom said four men attacked Nicolas on the sidewalk, must have been with the intention of kidnapping him." She fought back tears and paused to control her voice. "Without Tom's help, they might—" Jacklyn shook her head. "I don't understand why this happened. Is it your new case? Does anyone want Nicolas out of the way?"

Jason scratched his nose, cleared his throat, and thought about quoting flowery phrases the FBI used to soothe nervous witnesses.

"Honestly, I don't know. We haven't started investigating

our new case yet. It's much too early to claim that we've found incriminating evidence that would trigger the killer to act against us." He shrugged. "Even if the attack's connected to the ongoing murder investigation—who'd involve a gang? They're unreliable and work for their own agenda. So the attack would only make sense if the gang was behind the murder. So far, I don't have a clue. Sorry." He stared at his shoes, at the floor, and turned his head when a nurse appeared from behind the curtain.

"Can I see him now?" Jacklyn asked.

"Sure." She left, rushing toward the next booth.

Jason followed Jacklyn, deep in thought. The current case was either much more complicated than the FBI had assumed so far, or was related to another crime. An idea leaped into his mind demanding attention, but Jason pushed it back as he entered the bay and the extent of his partner's injuries became apparent.

The cut above Nicolas's left eye had been treated, and he was lucky it was only puffed half-shut. His lips were split and swollen, and a purple bruise showed on his chin. His right hand was bandaged, but the left one was scabbed, too, evidence of a serious knuckle fight. By the stiff way Nicolas was moving, Jason knew there were more bruises on his body. Nicolas tried to smile when Jacklyn bent to kiss him gently, but obviously, the pain was too strong to ignore.

"Hi, nice of you guys to drop by." His speech was slurred, and Jason had the impression that Nicolas couldn't focus on him.

"How're you feeling, pal?"

"Dizzy." Nicolas turned his attention to Jacklyn. "The doc said he'll keep me here for the night, just to be sure . . ."

Jacklyn caressed his face, then rested her hand on his shoulder. "Yes, it's better you stay here, maybe two days. Don't try to play hero, okay?"

"I'll be fine. If it's a concussion at all, it's a mild one. I don't feel so bad."

"Yeah, right." Her smile was a shadow of its usual exuberant brilliance. "Do you remember what happened?"

"Sure do. The gangsters thought I was a sitting duck, but I taught them better than that. What about Tom? Is he okay?"

"He considers himself the winner of the night's major prizefight. He's still in treatment. He's got a broken nose and looks pretty shaken up, though. Charlene's with him."

"Oh." Nicolas frowned with sympathy. "What about her?"

"She looks worse than he does." Jacklyn made a sound of frustration. "That woman's a mess, if you ask me. She's crying her eyes out and behaves as if he's on the brink of death. If she doesn't get a grip, she'll have a nervous breakdown."

"She's a troubled soul."

"Do you want me to talk with her?" Jacklyn asked.

Nicolas looked up to her full of love and gratefulness. "No, you can't help her. You're so much stronger, and she doesn't want anyone telling her that she's overreacting." He lifted his chin, and Jacklyn bent down for a kiss. "I love you for your strength."

"Yes, and not telling you to take it slow. So I'll keep the trembling to myself and keep my head high." She sighed. "If you're up for it, I bet, Jason's got some questions only you can answer."

Jason's brows twitched. He found her words and her look more than condescending. He didn't like to be treated like a supplicant. But he schooled his features to be neutral as Jacklyn left the room, knowing Nicolas wouldn't approve of any word against his lover. At the moment, Jason was more concerned about Nicolas's concussion and tried to blank out the fact that Nicolas's sick leave would mean he would have to work with Matthew once more.

"Jacklyn already summed up what happened. Anything

you'd like to add? Did you know the attackers, recognize any of them?"

"No, but I can describe them." By the way he moved, Jason assumed Nicolas's torso had taken some hard punches and kicks. "Their intention was obvious—they wanted to overwhelm and drag me into the van." He closed his eyes and sighed. "I've thought about a possible reason—I mean, who'd hire hoodlums to kidnap me? We have nothing to do with gang crime, so their motivation must have been money."

"My thought exactly." Jason rested his arms on the foot rail. "I already ruled out that it's a crime connected to the deputy mayor's murder. It doesn't make sense. That leaves former crimes for evaluation."

"Maybe my investigation in Florence Town—"

"Exactly. Tyrone's still on the run."

Nicolas opened his eyes, and his look was angry. "Tyrone wouldn't find his ass in the dark. He wouldn't be able to hire a gang in a foreign town. That's ridiculous."

"Okay, don't yell at me." Jason preferred not to mention that despite considerable police efforts, Tyrone was still at large. "Are there others on the loose who could support him?"

"Maybe. I don't know."

Jason took a mental step back. Nicolas was irritated and tired. "Then, there's the bank robber case."

Nicolas frowned. "You think—"

"Yes, I do that sometimes." Jason lifted his hands to emphasize his argument. "The assault on the prison bus failed and—"

"The assault was directed at Bianchi."

"That's what the police assume, yes, but let's take into consideration that the Bianchi family had no means to know about Ricky being on that prison bus."

Nicolas wet his lips, then turned his head to the small table at the bedside. Jason was faster and handed him the glass of water.

"Thanks."

"You're welcome. The judge made the decision the same morning, no announcement to anyone. It was known, though, that the Nelson twins would be on that bus. From this, it follows that the twins were the target of the assault. However, the twins are still in prison and—"

"You think Katherine wanted me kidnapped to blackmail the state?" He stopped shaking his head, grimacing. "That's farfetched."

"No. It's bold, and it's doable. It's the same way she worked on all the robberies—the hits were planned with a love of detail. Think of tonight—you meet with Tom every week, if time allows. If she followed you, she knew about your meetings. A piece of cake."

"But then—" Nicolas's frown deepened, and Jason waited, giving him time to transfer his thought into words. "That would mean Katherine remained in the country the whole time. She didn't leave at all."

"That's a possibility. She told the gangsters where to find you, and she sent enough muscle to overwhelm a trained agent. She miscalculated Tom's involvement, though."

"Yeah, he saved my ass."

"That's the only piece of the plan that was a flop. You're both excellent fighters." He waited for Nicolas to appreciate the compliment with a nod. "So, back to her plans. Katherine had already worked out a contingency—to kidnap you and blackmail the state into releasing the twins?"

"That wouldn't work." Nicolas closed his eyes. His face was paling noticeably and his words were quieter than a breath. "We don't deal with terrorists."

Jason smiled, though his friend didn't see it. "Yeah, we're tough FBI agents. We kick ass." Quietly, he left the room. He knew what he had to do.

"Hey, Jason, it's you and me again, hmm?" Matthew boxed Jason's shoulder playfully. His cheerfulness this morning was in stark contrast to Jason's reluctance to work with him. "What do you say? The widow first? I've got her address and called. She's home."

"That was my plan exactly."

"Fine."

Jason evaded another hearty slap, took his jacket off the chair, and put it on. "Spare me your cheeriness, okay? I'm not in the mood."

"Oh, okay." Matthew swept his hand dramatically to usher Jason out the door first. "You interrogate her and the family. I'll trail along."

Jason detected mockery in Matthew's look in spite of the other man's attempt at hiding his attitude. There was no way to avoid the partnership, and Jason needed to take some action, to do something. He hated the gang members even more for roughing up Nicolas.

"I bet you can't keep your mouth shut for five minutes," he snorted ruefully.

"That certainly depends on the quality of your interrogation."

Jason clenched his teeth with frustration, walked into the garage biting back a list of caustic replies, but then realized he had the unique opportunity of driving the service car to the widow's home. The day was looking up.

The Dobson estate was under siege by the press. Two police cars blocked the entrance and kept reporters at bay. Two more black-and-whites secured the street. Jason and Matthew had to show their IDs to pass and were immediately surrounded by reporters who pushed microphones in their faces, clamoring questions at the top of their voices.

Matthew gave the standard answer—the FBI couldn't comment on an ongoing investigation and asked the press to respect the widow and her family at this time of mourning. More questions flooded like a wave against them, and Jason was relieved when a police officer told three of the most impertinent TV reporters to move away from the driveway.

Jason smoothed his tie before ringing the bell. Matthew stood half a step behind him, hands clasped behind his back. Jason had been surprised that, against his nature, his temporary partner kept his word and stayed quiet for the ride, a fact that irritated Jason more than his colleague's usual yakking and singing along to the songs on the radio.

A servant opened the door, and Jason introduced Matthew and himself to Mrs. Dobson in the hallway. She was a woman of about forty-five years, neither slender nor overweight, with an oval face and large green eyes. She might've been a beauty, but her face was puffy, the dyed blonde hair stringy, and there were abrasions along her chin the make-up didn't cover. She pulled down the sleeve of her blouse, and Jason noticed the bandage beneath it. Contrary to his assumption, however, the widow was not dissolving in tears but was very calm. She kept a stiff posture as she invited the agents to sit down in the living room and told the butler to serve coffee and biscuits.

Mrs. Dobson smoothed her green skirt toward her knees. Through the pantyhose, Jason saw swollen bruises along her shins. "I know you've come to ask me about my husband's enemies, if there were any. I told the police that I don't know much about his work, no details that would mean anything for the investigation." She looked up when a woman entered with an inquisitive glance at Jason and Matthew. "May I introduce—my sister Annie. She's here to keep me company and help with the preparations . . . for the funeral."

"I understand. We'll keep this as brief as we can." Jason pulled out his notebook and a pen. "You were present during his rallies, I assume?"

"On some of them." She lowered her gaze. "I'm not . . . well. I had other obligations so I couldn't be with him every time. But as far as I know, the rallies went smoothly. When my husband announced that he planned to take action against organized crime, there were threats from gangs, probably the usual things that happen once a politician decides to do more than just talk. But if anything had happened, you'd probably have heard about it in the news." The butler delivered a silver tray with coffee, cups, and a silver platter with apple pastries. The bitter aroma of the crushed beans was mouth-wateringly delicious. Mrs. Dobson insisted on pouring herself and handed Matthew and Jason a cup each.

"Thank you, ma'am."

"You're welcome. At that time—when the first threats came in—Buck hired a bodyguard." While she tried to smile, Annie, who had taken a seat beside her sister, scoffed. "I know, you think it was for show, but—" Mrs. Dobson lowered her chin and closed her eyes for a moment. "You see, not even Victor could prevent . . ." Her voice trailed off, and she groped for a tissue.

"We all know he wanted to make the world a better place," Annie said and handed her sister a tissue from the table dispenser. "He had a very unique way of implementing his . . . *ideals*." Annie had the same green eyes as her sister, but instead of sorrow, Jason read suppressed anger in her look. When she took her sister's hand, Annie's mouth twitched as if she wanted to say more and didn't dare.

"Would you mind explaining that?" Matthew asked. His baritone was smooth as honey, and Annie's attention turned to him. Her lips curled in an almost smile, and her eyes widened as if she had seen an object of interest.

"He was a man who strictly followed his goals. He had a clear vision of his life and how it should evolve, how it would evolve, no matter the obstacles people threw in his way."

"You're referring to his political career?" Matthew put down his coffee cup and took a pastry. "Or did he treat his family the same way as his political opponents?"

Jason held his breath. He had noticed Mrs. Dobson's purple jawbone and her stiff walk, too, but decided to wait for any delicate questions. The widow's lips twitched as she tried to keep her face blank. However, the pain remained visible, and it had nothing to do with her mourning. Mrs. Dobson held her sister's hand tighter and, with a glance, invited Annie to take over the conversation.

"You have it right." Annie's interested gaze was fixed on Matthew. "Buck wasn't the loving and caring husband he should've been. During the last three years . . ." She hesitated, searching for her words carefully. "Living conditions in this household worsened."

"That sounds like a euphemism." Matthew lifted his brows as he looked at Mrs. Dobson. "You were hurt recently?"

With a trembling hand, Mrs. Dobson pushed a strand of hair behind her ear. Her voice quivered. "Buck was under immense stress—"

"Don't do it again," Annie growled. "He's dead. For once in your life, be honest. You and your son deserve that the world learns of the truth."

Tears trickled down Mrs. Dobson's face, and she sobbed. Then, as if driven by an organizer demon, she frantically rearranged magazines and flyers on the glass table. In her haste, she almost toppled the vase in the table center. With incredible presence of mind, Annie saved the glass and put it out of range. "Stop it!" she hissed.

Sighing, Mrs. Dobson drew up her arms around her breasts and hugged herself, her gaze still fixed on the now neat table.

"He wasn't a bad man. That's not fair to say. He always wanted the best . . . for all of us."

Jason put down the coffee cup and looked around the tastefully decorated room. There were family pictures on the mantel, memories from past times when the Dobsons appeared to have been happy with their newborn son. Other pictures showed Mr. Dobson shaking hands with various famous politicians from town and county. There were no recent family photographs.

"Clare, don't lie to yourself, that's worse than lying to the FBI."

Annie gave Matthew another quick glance that Jason caught and tried to decipher. Was Annie giving his partner the eye? He dropped the thought. It was far too disconcerting.

"I know this must be very hard for you, Mrs. Dobson, but did Mr. Dobson mistreat you and—you can correct me on this—your son, too?"

Jason cleared his throat. Mrs. Dobson bit her lip but remained as motionless as a marble sculpture.

Matthew pushed, "Did you do anything about the situation? Did you contact the authorities?"

Mrs. Dobson's face flushed, and her eyes widened. "By God, no! Do you see the avalanche of the media outside our house? These greedy bastards would sell their mothers for a story about the deputy mayor's private issues! How dare you think I would've done this to my husband?"

Matthew replied quietly, "He violated you. You had every right to go to the police."

Annie embraced her crying sister as she looked at Jason and Matthew. "You don't understand. They've been married for twenty years. Buck had always wanted to become a leading politician in this country. His goals meant the world to him, and a family was part of reaching that goal. My sister knew that and would never have ruined his career. That was unthinkable."

Jason had to break eye contact to conceal his frustration

and growing anger. He disliked politicians at large, but Mr. Dobson's behavior was intolerable. He tried to console himself with the fact that the violator had found his just punishment, but he had to hide his attitude in front of the sisters.

"Thank you for your concern," Annie said with yet another small smile that seemed out of place in a house of mourning. "There's no doubt about his stance, and the benevolent people in this house would say Buck was a complicated man. During the last three years, his ambitions got the best of him because he'd lost the election and had to deal with being second best. As a result, nothing was good enough for him, and he criticized everyone for nothing and then some. If you ask me, he made one enemy too many, and this person took revenge."

"Do you have someone in mind? Maybe a political opponent, or members of organized crime?" Jason asked and watched her reaction intently.

Annie's sarcastic smile deepened, and she looked him straight in the eyes. "If so, it's all right by me. I don't agree with vigilante justice, but—" She shrugged and left the sentence unfinished. Instead, she hugged her sister tighter and whispered in her ear, "We'll get through this and begin to look forward."

Matthew pulled out the artist's impression of Miss Olbridge, according to Mr. Morrison's description. "Do you know this woman?"

Mrs. Dobson and her sister shook their heads. "Should we?"

"She might've seen what happened." Matthew put away the picture.

"Sorry, but, no, we don't know her."

Jason lifted his gaze when a lanky teenager of about fifteen years appeared on the threshold. His features left no doubt he was Mr. Dobson's son. It was impossible not to notice the boy's black eye and the cast encasing his left arm. As if hiding behind a curtain of his brown hair, the young man scowled, realizing he was interrupting a conversation.

Mrs. Dobson freed herself from Annie's embrace and looked up. She wiped her eyes. "I'll be with you shortly, Clark. Please, wait in your room."

"But you wanted me to—"

"Yes, hon, I know. I'll come to you as soon as I can."

"Okay, Mom." Clark turned around and went back upstairs, the sound of his steps slowly receding.

Jason glanced at Matthew. The longer Jason stayed in this house, the more he wanted to kill Mr. Dobson if he hadn't been dead already.

"You understand that your husband's ongoing aggressive behavior toward you could be a motive for murder?" Matthew looked from Mrs. Dobson to Annie and back. "Where were you yesterday morning?"

"Do you really think I killed my husband?" Mrs. Dobson gaped at Matthew. "Are you out of your mind?"

Annie shook her head, vigorously. "You aren't accusing Clare of murder, are you? That's total nonsense! She just told you she wouldn't have accused him of domestic violence, and now you ask whether she murdered him? What's that? FBI-twisted logic?"

"It's a standard question." Matthew was unmoved by the women's outburst. "I could give you statistics, but it boils down to this—"

"No need to argue," Annie replied, lifting her hand. "Clare was at Clark's school yesterday morning and gave the children a lecture on how to avoid ending up in a gang. And I—" She looked smug. "I was at the county office to pay for my parking tickets. I guess that vouches for both of us."

"It does. Still, we'll have to check your bank accounts for unusual movements of money."

"You do that," Annie said defensively. "But you won't find anything. We had nothing to do with this!"

Matthew looked at Mrs. Dobson. "Who else lives in the house?"

"My son, the butler and his wife, the gardener. He has a small house at the rear wall. Sometimes friends come to visit and stay for a few days. We've got three guest rooms, so—" She finished the sentence with an apologetic shrug.

"What about the bodyguard?"

"Victor doesn't live here. He or his partner, Jeff O'Connor, come here for their shifts."

"Do you have other relatives, Mrs. Dobson?"

"Yes, two brothers, but they don't live here. Michael has a company in Minnesota, and Greg is a geologist. I've got no idea where he is at the moment."

"Did your husband attack your employees, too?"

"No! Never!"

Jason made another mental note that the politician had been an asshole in the true sense of the meaning. "Did they witness any of his actions?"

Mrs. Dobson lowered her gaze and shook her head. Her voice was quiet again. "No. Buck was . . . concerned about . . ."

"About being the perfect politician. He was very discreet." Annie huffed. Her anger showed in her words and look. "You're right. He was a bad husband and a successful politician. As weird as it sounds, but to the public, he was an angel of righteousness, not least because Mr. Fitch took care of his image."

"Mr. Fitch is—"

"Buck's greatest and most devoted admirer. He managed his campaign."

"I understand." Jason stood and put back his pen and notebook. "Thank you for your patience. There might be more questions, so we have to ask that you stay in the city."

"We're preparing for a funeral, agent." Annie's gaze hardened. "Find the killer and give us closure so we can mourn."

Jason had the impression Annie chose words to meet a social obligation, and he didn't buy her attitude of indignation. "The FBI will keep you informed on the progress."

Back in their car, Jason leaned against the headrest and closed his eyes. "How's it possible she endured that for all those years?"

"She loved him more than he deserved. I bet she loved the living standard, too, not to mention the public acceptance. Maybe she hoped he'd change after the election. If he had won." Matthew buckled up, then stopped. "Shall I drive? You look kinda shaken."

Jason turned the key in the ignition. "I'm fine, just angry."

"When it comes to that—welcome to the club. I bet there were a lot of the wife's friends and relatives who wanted to see Dobson dead as a doornail."

"That only applies if she shared such intimate details of her marriage with anyone besides Annie."

Matthew settled comfortably in his seat while Jason steered the car back onto the street, where the throng of reporters was still looking for answers. Jason loathed that their visit would be part of the prime-time news.

Matthew frowned. "Annie looked like someone who'd pay a killer to get rid of Mr. Dobson."

"Did she truly try to flirt with you?"

"Yeah. Anyway," Matthew said, ignoring Jason's nonplussed expression, "I wouldn't put it past her, she couldn't watch her sister's misery any longer and took action to avoid more harm. I'll look into her finances, check her whereabouts in the last two weeks, and confirm her alibi. That shouldn't be too difficult."

"They both delivered the perfect alibis." Jason stopped the car at a stop sign. "As if they knew it would be needed."

"Hmm. A hired killer would take a pistol and shoot the deputy mayor in the head or twice in his chest. He wouldn't make an effort to tie him to a chair and club him to death. Much too risky and time-consuming. No, that crime shows very personal preferences—a lot of hate."

"Maybe the need for information. Remember, the man's hands were broken, too. The killers tortured him for an hour, maybe longer. He might've known something important a gangster wanted."

"From what I read about Dobson, he wasn't a man with secrets or a hidden agenda." Matthew took a deep breath. "This looks like someone wanted to give back the violence Mr. Dobson had used against his family—all at once. Though I understand the killers' motivation, it gives me the creeps that they might belong to the family."

"We have to check them all." Jason sighed. "That will take time."

CHAPTER FOUR

More than her elder brother's quips and words of comfort, Katherine missed Herman's presence and the strength he had presented. With him, she felt safe. After his much too early death, Katherine felt as if she'd lost much more than a brother—a soulmate, an anchor to the real world. She wondered if she'd ever be able to love again, for she was filled with rage and yearned for revenge on the FBI agents responsible for Herman's murder. She knew which ones to blame. In her mind, she'd played various scenarios of their slow and painful deaths, and with every new brutal idea, a shudder of delight flashed through her, especially when she considered the blond agent. He even looked a little like Herman, and she knew destroying his face and body would finally grant her peace.

She'd watched the news about the shootout at the mall that resulted in Herman's death and the arrest of Theo and Ben more than twenty times. She'd memorized every detail—from the first arrival of the TV crews at the crime scene to the last interview the FBI senior agent had granted the waiting press in front of the FBI building in Washington, DC. The agent had announced that the Nelson brothers could expect the highest sentence a court could impose.

Forced to flee the city, Katherine had hibernated in a secluded resort where no one knew her name or face. Altering appearance and behavior, she'd played the touchy and slightly egocentric wife of a mysterious and unnamed rich guy from Italy. After two days of escaping her hissy fits, the staff had left her alone, and after another day and a growling argument with a lady on the patio, she didn't see any of the other guests, either.

Brooding in the solitary loneliness she had chosen, she collected newspaper clips and recorded reports from several TV stations. She hungered for information about the leading agents of the investigation, hoping for an epiphany that would unveil a plan of how to deal with them and let them bleed the way Herman had bled his life out on the concrete.

Planning her younger brothers' escape from prison was hard work because security was tight, and the authorities knew about Theo's and Ben's abilities. It would be a great victory if she could help her brothers escape the country, like flipping the middle finger to the FBI. However, that would not be enough to drain the cup of her rage. She needed more than an example showing the FBI's ineptitude in finding her and keeping her brothers in prison. She wanted it broadcast on all the prime-time news channels—horrifying images of their bodies shattered by bullets in a parking lot or beaten beyond recognition on every front page.

Then she would sit with Theo and Ben and laugh until their bellies hurt.

That ambition kept her senses sharp. She'd never before been so effective and inventive. After having found Herbert Sandemann—or Herb Sanders, as he now called himself—she'd decided to hire him and his crew to execute her plans.

Sandemann's biography was impressive—a former German soldier, Special Forces trainee, but then dismissed dishonorably because of his liking for illicit drugs. Sandemann had fought to stay in the army but was dismissed, nevertheless. Because of a girlfriend who had studied in Germany and returned to Georgia, Sandemann had turned his back on his home country and accepted a job as a security guard at an international company for spices in Atlanta until he received his green card and the US citizenship four years later. He changed his name and his occupation. Together with Leroy Jennings and Dwight Mueller, Herb founded an assassination trio, which built up a reputation and thus demanded high fees for their work. Three sharpshooters without remorse were hard to find, and Katherine had called in many favors just to get hold of Herb's contact number.

But it hadn't quite gone as she had envisaged. She hadn't expected his crew to be sloppy. She hadn't expected Herb to delegate the important job of kidnapping Nicolas Hayes to a bunch of drug-addicted youngsters with fewer brain cells than an amoeba. To avoid changing the crew on the final road to victory, she had allowed Leroy and Dwight to execute plan C, but with the distinct hint that she couldn't tolerate another failure.

"What's the news from the lab?" Matthew asked upon arrival. He placed his butt on the empty table opposite to Jason's desk after greeting him with a conciliatory cup of coffee he had bought on the way.

Jason ignored the kindness, instead bracing himself for another hour with his pesky colleague. "Miller sent the report via email—"

"Because Nicolas isn't here to take it." Matthew nodded like a psychiatrist who just discovered an interesting behavior oddity.

"There were no signs of foreign DNA on Dobson's body or in the room."

"That's impossible, even if the suit was fresh from the cleaners."

"It implies the murderers wore body-wraps from head to toe, right." Jason couldn't help himself and smiled when Matthew burst out laughing. Colleagues were turning their heads, but Matthew held his belly and still chortled as Jason went on. "Let's say, the murderers were extremely careful." He frowned. "Well, if you look at it—the bag Morrison mentioned could've been filled with plastic wrapping such as CSU technicians wear at crime scenes."

"That's a good point." Matthew nodded in appreciation. "But that means that Miss Olbridge knew about the assault or she was participating. Otherwise, she would've taken the bag out of sight, wouldn't she?"

"That's right. Miller says the murder weapon was a baseball bat, but it didn't leave traceable marks or chips of wood to help identify the origin or the brand. He assumes it was made of metal. The coroner writes the bone fractures were so numerous he couldn't determine the one causing Dobson's death. The blood on the floor is Dobson's, and there was nothing in the footprints. They wore special shoes for the occasion, the same as the forensic team. The rest of the report is equally disheartening."

"But it tells us a lot." Matthew sipped his coffee. "First, the murderers were very careful—no murder in a rush. This was planned to the last detail, which means they're organized killers, probably committed other crimes the same way. We should check this in a query, nationwide, if possible. Second, the murderers are very ruthless and in perfect harmony with each other. They knew Dobson would come with a bodyguard and planned to take him out first, but not to kill him. The dose of tranquilizer was so high, Morrison was out for more than six hours, enough time for the murderers to take their time on Dobson's death. Third, they're sadistic bastards."

"A very familiar FBI phrase."

"As I read in the coroner's report, they broke Dobson's fingers and hands, virtually every bone in his body that finally led to the mayor's death. Fourth, they were so clear-headed they refrained from any assault on the bodyguard. This leaves me the hope that the real estate agent is still alive—if she is innocent."

"That's your conclusion? I fear that we are gonna find her any minute with a broken skull. The killers wouldn't want her to testify."

Matthew shrugged. "Like I said—she could be an accomplice."

"That means the killers have a female associate we're searching for. Morrison's description was excellent. We've given it to all police stations and the media."

"Didn't Morrison state the woman's hair might've been a wig? What if the rest of her appearance was . . . say, not the real thing? There are several possibilities to alter a woman's looks, not just make-up."

"This is getting weirder by the minute." Jason frowned. "But when I think of it—Morrison claims the woman had very eye-catching hips—"

Matthew nodded. "*She had a figure like an hourglass,* he said."

Jason warmed up to the subject. "If we assume the lady is an accomplice, she lured Dobson into the house to leave the killers with him after Morrison was out for the count. She must be as ruthless as they are."

"Maybe. She could've been blackmailed to help them. That takes us back to the main suspects—local gangs and other hardcore criminals in Richmond, who'd lose big time once Dobson took action against them. The women in these gangs aren't really angels. I'll contact the local homicide and the gang crime division and see what I'll find out." He pushed off the table. "Do you know when Nicolas will be back on deck?"

"No, but I'll let you know."

"I bet you will."

After five hours of intensive research and a late lunch break, Matthew entered the office and was about to open his mouth when Jason held up a hand to stop him as his cell phone bleeped. "I've got to take this." He pulled out the phone. "Yes, Nicolas, what's up?"

"I've had a lot of time to mull over the attack yesterday."

"How're you feeling?"

"Better. You do remember the disaster at the Federal Triangle, don't you?"

"How could I forget?" Jason leaned back and, with a gesture of his hand, motioned for Matthew to take a seat at Nicolas's desk.

"Katherine had told the brothers to leave the car behind and change clothes, then to blend in with the passengers and escape."

"So?"

"She was extremely clever to prepare the brothers for an escape on the train. So, in this case, when the assault on the prison bus failed, she already had another plan up her sleeve."

"All right. First, the assault on the bus, second, the attempt at kidnapping you. Both failed."

Nicolas sounded weary. "She won't give up."

"Agreed. I'll tell the prison warden he'd better tighten security around the twins before they slip through his fingers."

"You do that."

"Will the doc let you go today?"

"Later this afternoon. But I don't think I'll be back at work tomorrow."

"That's okay." Jason stared at the floor. "Take your time."

"Keep me posted, please."

"Will do." Jason finished the phone call and searched for the number of the Baltimore Penitentiary.

"Your ring tone for Nicolas is the theme from *The*

Avengers?" Matthew failed to keep a blank face. "I don't believe it."

Jason ignored the banter, dialed, and asked for the warden. When James Colton took the call, Jason outlined the situation briefly and instructed the warden to increase security around the twins.

"So, you already know."

"What do I know?" Jason sat up straight and reached for pen and notepad.

"About the blackmailing."

Jason's heart skipped a beat, and in his mind, he saw the Nelson brothers already board a ship bound for Africa, waving and smiling at the FBI agents who came too late. "Did they escape and you forgot to report about it?"

"Don't even think I'd dare not report this!" Colton bristled, but his voice was strained. "The twins are still behind bars, but . . . the family of a guard was kidnapped, and the kidnappers instructed Barton Cooper—he's the father and has worked here for seven years—to smuggle the twins out in a garbage truck. If we don't fulfill their demands, his wife and kid will die." He huffed. "Now, what do you want me to do, Agent Beckham? I already told your colleague, but he ordered me to stay put and do nothing until they've evaluated the seriousness of the threat."

"I haven't received—" Jason stopped, realizing he hadn't been part of the investigation and arrest. He wrote *check your emails* on a piece of paper and pushed it to Matthew. "We'll handle this," Jason said to the warden. "What's the time frame?"

"The garbage truck comes the day after tomorrow, in the morning."

"I see. Give me a few minutes, then I'll call you back."

"Whatever you say. But I'll tell you this—if the FBI doesn't come up with a plan, we have to let the twins go. I won't accept the death of a woman and her eight-year-old child because of this scum. It's your task to catch the kidnappers!"

The warden slammed the phone down before Jason had a chance to tell him that the FBI couldn't provide security for every staff member of every prison in the country. He turned to Matthew. "Anything from the department?"

"The email's only a few minutes old," Matthew replied. "Addleton took the call. Yes, the warden reported the blackmailing after Cooper confided in him and asked for support, but he certainly doesn't want the hostages endangered." He looked around the monitor. "Any proposals on how to proceed?"

Jason pursed his lips. "We can't move against the twins as long as we don't know about the hostages' whereabouts."

"Hmm." Matthew looked up to Senior Agent Sullivan's office. "I think I know what our boss will say about this."

Jacklyn unlocked the door, pretending she didn't notice Nicolas's obvious weariness as he slumped against the door frame. She knew it had been too early for his release from the hospital, but she had learned one thing in their relationship—an FBI agent didn't whine but gathered himself to continue his work. She dropped the keys on the small desk in the hall and waited as discreetly as possible for Nicolas to take off his shoes.

"Hungry?"

"No." He ran a hand across his short-cropped hair and went for the bathroom. He was pale and sounded weary. "I'll take a shower and grab a bite later."

"Sure." Jacklyn didn't mention she had prepared dinner before leaving for the hospital, and she didn't intend to let her lover go to bed without a meal. No one would call her a mother hen and live, but she knew which measures to take to get him back on his feet.

She smiled while she set the table. Lesley, her best friend and a fierce mistress who owned a highly frequented dungeon in Washington, would scold her for pampering Nicolas. She wouldn't understand that a loving relationship was built on more than sex and domination games. She would urge her to put Nicolas under her heel and not let him out anymore.

Nicolas emerged from the bathroom in shorts and shirt, and Jacklyn persuaded him to eat and drink before he lay down on the bed.

"I offer my skills to massage your sore body," Jacklyn cooed and sat down beside him.

"You do? You're too kind."

"Sometimes. Close your eyes." She undressed him and poured a cool, soothing lotion onto her hands. "Stop frowning. Just don't think of anything right now. Relax."

He opened his eyes to a slit. "How can I think of nothing while you sit beside me, wearing *nothing*?"

"Oh . . ." Jacklyn looked down at her body as if she hadn't noticed she was in the buff. "Then let your hands be your eyes." She smoothed the lotion over his shoulders and arms and went on to his chest. "Yeah, that's much better." When he winced, she eased the pressure on his muscles and proceeded more carefully.

Massaging his hips and thighs, she let her thoughts go fondly back to the first night she had spent with him in her apartment. She had known of his interest in her, but because he was a gentleman, he hadn't pushed her toward the bedroom. In the end, Jacklyn had seduced him and left him no way out but to satisfy her. She couldn't recall why her heart had chosen a young man, inexperienced and insecure, not to mention a rookie at the sex games she loved. Even after more than two years, she couldn't determine the day or the moment she had fallen in love with him, but she told everyone that he'd been too good a catch to let him slip away. On the one hand, Nicolas had made it easy for her. Even though his love life had been conservative before, he was neither shy nor reluctant to follow her lead. On the other hand, Jacklyn had taken her time to explain her motivation and how much she got aroused seeing him tied up.

This night wasn't about arousal and sexual satisfaction. Jacklyn hoped the massage would loosen Nicolas's sore muscles and help him relax. She massaged his back, paying particular attention to a large bruise over his lowest rib, and when she was done, Nicolas was asleep.

Gently touching the curve of his ear, Jacklyn got off the bed, put on her night clothes, and curled up beside him. Without waking him, she pulled the cover over both of them, happy and satisfied in a way only a true lover could be.

"I know you won't like it," Matthew said on the way to their car, "but we've got a lead that takes us to a gang named *The Ultimados*. Richmond PD told me they're known for armed robbery, assault, and blackmailing. Murder might be on their list, but the police couldn't put together enough evidence to connect their leader, Radek Cuch, or Gizmo for short, to the death of a young local politician in Richmond two years ago. Officers told me they're clever, fast, and know how to avoid detection, which makes the gang first on our suspect list." He fastened his seat belt and smiled. "Be honest—you enjoy driving. Why don't you do it when Nicolas is here?"

Jason maneuvered the sedan out of Washington with his usual caution. "He's the better driver."

"Which doesn't make a difference when you're not on a high-speed chase, right?"

"Matthew, is there anything else you want to add that's relevant for the case?"

"All right, don't bite me. I asked Morrison to join us at the gang's hangout, a bar named *Bullet on Top*. He might identify the real estate agent, aka accomplice. The realtor Morrison mentioned—Mr. Lindberg—describes Teresa Olbridge as an *elderly, portly woman*. He was close to a heart attack learning that criminals had used his *extraordinarily beautiful* estate for a murder. But don't be mistaken—he wasn't grieving the loss of the deputy mayor, but the loss of money because no one would want to buy the house now. He asked me if we cleaned up the house after leaving. Imagine that!" Matthew rolled his eyes. "The world's full of money makers with no moral standards. At least he was worried about the real Miss Olbridge. Two uniforms checked her apartment to find out whether she's all right. They had to break open her door but found her alive. She said she'd eaten her favorite pastry, but after two bites, she was so sick she couldn't leave the bathroom, not even to make a call for help. She's been hospitalized with food poisoning and dehydration, but will recover." Matthew lifted his brows. "Sounds like a vicious plan to me."

"Now we know the woman's involved in the crime." Jason frowned. He didn't deny the possibility of a female suspect and had seen enough female criminals, and yet, he wished that women were kind and loving like his fiancé, Elaine. Jason didn't want to believe that the false Miss Olbridge had tolerated or even participated in the crime. "What else?"

"This leads to the conclusion she knew of Dobson's appointment in advance, knocked out Mr. Lindberg's coworker, and took her place. But—and here it comes—the plan must've been done quickly because, according to Morrison's testimony, Dobson had told him of the appointment only two days in advance."

"We're searching for someone with access to the mayor's

calendar." Jason smacked his lips. "Back to relatives and friends."

"And to Mr. Lindberg and his associates."

Jason gave him a look of pure incredulity. "You don't think the real estate agent bore a grudge against the deputy mayor?"

"No, but someone in his company might. I won't rule anything out because we've got too few clues right now. Are you with me?"

Jason growled into his beard but didn't say a word.

"I thought so." After a while, Matthew asked, "What about the Nelson twins? What's your plan?"

"Addleton and Spring delivered the surveillance gear, and another FBI agent Katherine doesn't know will drive the garbage truck. We'll let the twins take the truck only to catch them the moment we know of the whereabouts of Mrs. Cooper and her daughter."

"What does Sullivan say?"

"He said he'll cut off my head if the twins escape, but he agreed on three patrol cars that'll monitor the truck. We can ask for the support of the local police, too."

"Okay. So you either lock up the twins again or come to work a few inches shorter. Fair enough."

Jason snarled. "You're such a cheerful and supportive colleague! But what should I expect from you?"

"Hmm, I was thinking about stopping Sullivan reaching for a weapon, but if that's what you think of me, I might just hand him a battle ax and watch gleefully."

"As if—"

"That's Morrison's car. I hope he hasn't made a move yet. He was pretty pissed that his client was murdered on his shift.

That's bad for the business, especially one that's trying to expand." Matthew got out of the car. "A failure like this will cost him clients."

Jason locked the car and stood for a moment rooted to the spot. As in any bad movie, it wasn't a policeman's best idea to walk into a filthy bar, but Jason had no choice.

Morrison greeted them with a grimace behind his smile. "You think the killers are here, in a bar?"

"We think this gang might bear the future mayor a grudge. After all, Dobson carried the flag of righteousness, and these guys have criminal records longer than your arms."

Morrison made a face that Jason interpreted as disbelief.

"Do you think Dobson would have really changed anything?" Jason asked while they walked toward the entrance.

Morrison pursed his lips. "I think that Dobson was like any other politician—he said what his potential voters wanted to hear and would've made excuses the moment he won the election. When dealing with the mob or violent gangs, you need more policemen on the streets, more officers to work on organized crime, and a whole lot of new equipment, and that all costs money." He shrugged. "Maybe he would've wanted to make changes, but the budget wouldn't let him."

Matthew showed his badge, and none of the hard-looking men with beards and tattoos up to their ears standing in front of the entrance hindered their entrance into the semi-darkness. The room smelled of smoke, alcohol, and a repelling mix of sweat, perfume, and unwashed gear. It was filled with twenty men and several women, all sporting figure-hugging leather outfits. Three men played poker, and a group of four men stood around a pool table. They all looked up and stopped playing, bristling as if awaiting trouble at any moment.

"We're here to investigate the murder of Deputy Mayor Dobson," Matthew announced, trying to pitch his voice loud enough so he could be heard over the howling music. He held up his badge. "Please, turn down the volume so that we can talk."

A feisty man with a reddish beard signaled to the barkeeper, and a moment later, the room was so quiet you could hear the humming of the beer fridge on the other side of the counter. Jason felt that the quietness was louder and more threatening than the aggressive music. Every man and woman was now turned in the agents' direction. The tension was palpable.

Matthew smiled and stowed his badge. "Thank you."

"What do you want from us?" Mr. Red Beard asked, stepping closer. Though he didn't raise his voice, the threat was louder than a shout. "We've got nothing to do with any murder here."

"We need an alibi from all those present in the room from ten o'clock the day before yesterday morning until late afternoon."

"Are you kidding me, G-man? I couldn't tell you where I've been this morning," a young man to Jason's left blurted out. "I've got trouble remembering how I got here." The men at the pool table laughed out loud and rapped their cues on the floor.

"You didn't leave yesterday!" another man shouted across the table, and once more laughter bubbled up.

The young man flipped the bird at his friends. "What's so fucking important about the time?"

"It's the time Mr. Dobson was murdered," Jason explained. He glanced at Morrison, who strolled through the crowd looking for a woman suiting the description of the fake Teresa Olbridge. "So, sir, can you tell me where you've been?"

"We can all vouch for each other." Mr. Red Beard crossed his massive arms in front of his massive body. "We were here, drinking beer, having fun, listening to music." He shrugged and bent forward like any virtuous man would do at his office desk. "The usual things, you know."

"Is any member of your club missing?" Matthew asked, looking around the room.

"No. That's the entire club. We were about to go play golf with the governor as we do every week. If there're no more questions—"

"Yes, there are." Jason passed him to meet Morrison. He had an eye on two men waiting close to the rear exit. They spoke quietly to each other, and Jason expected them to bolt through the door at any moment. "What's up?"

"The woman over there—she's got a resemblance to Miss Olbridge," Morrison murmured.

"Fine. Let's ask her some questions." Matthew ignored Mr. Red Beard's angry yelling and went straight for the woman at the end of the bar. "Ma'am, I'm Agent Montagna, and this is Agent Beckham. We're here to investigate the murder of Deputy Mayor Dobson. Can you tell me where you were the day before yesterday, in the morning?"

"This is a joke, right?" the woman snarled. Her voice was rough and deep. "You don't think I'd ever get close to some fucking politician, right? Not in this life." She frowned and made a face of disgust. She was missing a piece of one of her front teeth. "Get out of here before my boys re-arrange your faces with some broken bottles."

Jason exchanged glances with Morrison, who shook his head.

"What about the other women in the room?"

Morrison lifted and dropped his hands, profound skepticism on his handsome face. "No, none of them gets even close to the looks."

"This was about looks, you morons?" the woman asked. She propped her hands on her very female hips and raised her voice. "You're telling me I've got no looks, or what? Is that it?" She cocked her head and lifted her brows. "You're searching for some brat with some looks?"

"Very special looks," Matthew corrected but refrained from any further explanation when the woman couldn't be soothed.

"You say I'm not good enough?" She pointed at the agents as if she were to stab them. "Not good enough to—what? Fuck the mayor?"

"What?" Mr. Red Beard yelled across the room. "Is he saying you screwed some damn lying bastard?"

He parted the crowd with his arms, and Jason had the impression of a drum rolling in his direction to flatten him. His first idea was to turn tail and leave the confrontation to Matthew. His second idea consisted of shame, regret, and that he'd be the butt of jokes for more than a day because Matthew would use his cowardice against him.

Mr. Red Beard stopped in front of Jason, even more impressive than at a distance. His breath smelled of beer, his body stank of sweat, and his words were spiced with spittle. His words, though, were directed at Matthew, who stood his ground, unflinchingly. "She can suck your brain out through your cock, okay? But she wouldn't boff no mayor! You got that?" He reached out to poke Matthew's chest but refrained from pulling his lapels.

"Thank you for the clarification, sir. We got it." Matthew looked Mr. Red Beard in the eyes. "She's not the one we're looking for."

"Better for you. She's a straight woman with morals, not some whore. Better show respect, right?" Mr. Red Beard made eye contact with the woman at the bar. "You okay?"

"I'll live." The woman looked smug when she smoothed her black top to emphasize her cleavage. "Y'know, Gizmo, I wouldn't want anyone but you. I need impressive junk."

"Yeah, and that's what you get." He used his right hand to

caress the named body part. "Anytime, anywhere, baby."

"Though . . . sucking out such a small brain would be fun, a real challenge."

Matthew looked from Red Beard to the smiling woman. "Yeah, but we're talking about real brain mass, not cotton candy. You'd choke, lady."

Jason held his breath, but then the audience burst out laughing, and the agents decided to leave while they were winning.

Jason breathed a sigh of relief when they were on their way back to their company car. Sweat trickled down his spine and along his sides, and he thanked whatever god held his hand over FBI agents. If he had smoked, he'd have pulled a pack of cigarettes to light two at a time. Matthew took over that action and shared his cigarettes with Morrison while they walked toward their cars. Both blew out smoke, obviously pondering the minutes inside the bar.

"Not what you expected," Matthew stated in his lowest possible voice.

"We were lucky they weren't out for a brawl." Jason hated how breathless he sounded. The stench of his own sweat crept into his nose, and he wanted to drive home, take a long shower, and forget about the encounter completely.

"With FBI agents? Get real, Jason, most of them are show-offs. They don't want to spend time in the pen for clubbing us. They might be criminals, but they're not that stupid."

For a second, Jason had expected Matthew to call him *son* and was—once again—angry with his colleague. Growling into his beard, Jason wiped his brow and opened the car door. He knew it was a wild-goose chase to lecture Matthew about unnecessary risks. "There's still a chance the woman we're searching for wasn't there tonight."

"I don't think so." Morrison pulled the keys to his sedan.

"Miss Olbridge was a sophisticated lady with good manners, intelligent, witty. Her nails were polished, her pantyhose had no snag, and even the heels of her shoes were flawless. She was a woman who looked after herself. I didn't doubt for a second that she was a real estate agent with a good reputation."

"You're saying?"

"I'm saying the fake Miss Olbridge, and the women inside this bar have as much in common as a toad and a flamingo. I should've known. So, sorry for the lost hour. A girl from the street won't pull off such an act—switch behavior, moves, looks. When I listened to their conversations—"

"What you can call a conversation," Matthew quipped.

"They were talking slang, never finished a sentence. None of the women could act like a realtor, you see? We're searching for a woman with a higher education who speaks English flawlessly."

"And again, back to family and friends, someone we've overlooked so far. Any idea, Mr. Morrison, who that could be?"

"No. If I had an idea, I'd have told you. No one in Dobson's close circle resembles the imposter."

"Maybe Clare or Annie hired someone." Jason sighed. "Or maybe the neighbors voted against Dobson and his political agenda. Who knows? Thank you for your time, Mr. Morrison."

"You're welcome."

Morrison left, and Jason dropped onto the driver's seat. "We've got to check the schedule for the day after tomorrow."

"Addleton reported the preparations were almost done. We'll take care to make sure the twins won't get away, so you can keep your head on."

Jason growled into his beard as Matthew started whistling the old Joe Cocker song.

CHAPTER FIVE

The chief of the Richmond PD provided the FBI agents with two desks in their homicide division's open-plan office. It spared them the hassle of carrying their files around and driving back to Washington, DC, after every interrogation. Jason was grateful but also uneasy among twenty homicide detectives, who he suspected where looking over his shoulder. Once more, Jason felt inferior to Matthew's easy-going manner and how the older agent handled the officers' gruff behavior. There wasn't a minute Matthew appeared to be unsettled or offended. He was like a smooth skier gliding around poles without ever touching one or losing speed. He had a joke for everyone and befriended most men and women within a few hours.

Grumpy and hoping for a quick solution to the case, Jason remained at the desk and studied the leads they had found. He refrained from setting up a whiteboard, even though it would have helped him think. As an alternative, he spread the sheets of paper on his desk, listing the important events and results of interrogations on a separate piece of paper. He used another large sheet of paper for the timeline and to record who they had interrogated so far.

Mrs. Dobson's two brothers had clean slates. They worked hard, spent their money on family and business, and had no exceptional expenses. Political opponents such as the sitting mayor of Richmond were aghast to learn of Dobson's death and the circumstances. Jason and Matthew were convinced that none of the men and women they talked to had either the guts to kill Dobson or a reason to hire two brutal killers to make it look like a personal murder. The search for known criminals with an agenda to murder for money hadn't revealed any suspect, either.

"So far, it's a dead end."

"No, it's not."

Matthew looked much too cheerful for Jason's brooding mood.

Jason took a deep breath as he steered the car through Richmond's traffic. "Okay, fire away."

"Gladly. I ran a query on murders with the same MO. There were two, one of them from way back in the seventies. A man by the name of Leon Hill murdered four men. His partner was never found. Some assume Hill killed him last, but there's no proof for that theory. Fact is, Hill and his partner took their victims to lonely houses, clubbed them to death, and departed without leaving any traces to follow. Yes, forensics wasn't as sophisticated as it is today, but still—the MO was the same."

"The men left the victims to be found by the police?"

"Yes, but since the houses were empty because of renovations or because owners had moved long before, the victims weren't found for a while. Hill was caught when he took the fifth victim to another building. He hadn't checked, and the house had a new owner, who happened to be inspecting the rooms that night. The owner made it out of the house without being spotted and called the police." Matthew grinned. "Maybe the partner found himself a new mate and continues the . . . work."

"The victims were men who abused their wives?"

"The victims were brutes of many kinds. They bullied their neighbors or colleagues, harassed their girlfriends, or were generally just a pain in the ass. So, yes, they were abusive bastards, and very few people mourned their passing."

"What was the connection between the victims?"

"Hill lived in the neighborhood of a large car repair shop and worked as a gardener, a helping hand for daily repairs. He heard and saw a lot of what was going on."

Jason pondered for a while. He rounded the corner to the city hall and parked on the other side of the street. "How old would his partner be by now?"

"Since he was never identified, no one can tell." Matthew got out of the car and buttoned his jacket. "Hill was forty-two and assumed to be the leader. His partner could've been younger." Matthew fell in beside Jason as they crossed the street. "It's a shot in the dark. The killers could be copycats who simply adopted his flawless style."

"Don't say that as if it was . . . an art or an achievement. They're brutal killers." Jason wiped his face. "And clever ones, too. That's still not an art. And the other one?"

"A man was murdered with a baseball bat. As it turns out, his fiancé had been beaten almost to death before. There were no leads, no DNA of the killer, nothing. The case is still open."

"Where did the murder take place?"

"Eighteen months ago, in an empty house in Lakeside."

"We should have a look at the file."

They took the elevator to the second floor and entered the office of the deputy mayor. His secretary, Beth Simmons, looked up from behind a large desk that was overflowing with files. She was in her fifties, a short, portly lady with soft brown eyes, little make-up, and a haircut that framed her oval face. She put back a strand of her light brown hair, smiling a business-like smile.

"How can I help you?"

Jason and Matthew showed their IDs. "I know that the police already spoke with you, but we've got some more questions about the murder of Mr. Dobson."

"Oh." Miss Simmons's expression darkened instantly. Her

gaze dropped to the files. "It was a shock, as you can imagine. He was aspiring to be mayor of Richmond, but you know that. Now there's a mountain of work to be done until his successor arrives and I—" She cleared her throat, then paused for a moment. "You didn't come here to chat about my work. So, how can I be of help?"

Jason read no grief in her look, no hasty moves that would confirm she was in shock. Her eyes were clear, focused, and without the stains of weeping. She sat straight and met his gaze like any woman who had nothing to hide. Her classic white blouse, closed to the last button, added to her aura of inscrutability.

"You made his appointments? Managed his obligations?"

"Yes, I did. Either he told me what he wanted, or I proposed appointments that might be interesting or important for him. Though he had a campaign manager, he left a good deal of this branch of work to me in addition to managing his private appointments."

Matthew nodded with a friendly smile as if he'd known Miss Simmons for a long time. "You worked for him many years, I assume."

"I handled him . . . I mean, I handled his daily obligations and handed him a schedule for every single day. He was busy, even more so since the rallies began. He wanted to attend the major events but also get in contact with the people. You know, meetings with mothers and their children at the kindergarten and talking to the elderly at their favorite coffee shops." Her smile was forced. "The more attention the media granted him, the more he was convinced he'd win the election. His rallies were always large and planned to the last detail. He didn't leave anything to chance."

"Did you have contact with his family, too?"

Jason envied Matthew the smooth baritone that worked especially well with women.

"Partly." Miss Simmons lowered her gaze. "I organized the office work—emails, meetings, press relations if not managed by Mr. Fitch. I talked to Mrs. Dobson from time to time, though. Because her husband wanted it, she had an office on the same floor as him. It was . . . unavoidable that our paths crossed from time to time."

Jason watched Miss Simmons blush. Matthew tilted his head to make eye contact again, and Jason realized it was advantageous to keep his mouth shut and let his partner continue the interrogation.

"Is it correct, then, to assume you knew about the cause of Mrs. Dobson's injuries?"

Once more, Miss Simmons took her time to answer. "Yes, I noticed. At first, it was an occasional bruise on her arm or chin, and she claimed she was clumsy. But then there was—" She looked unblinking at Matthew, and her words had a fierce edge. "You just know when a woman is maltreated. Well, *I* know." She glanced at the monitor in front of her when the ping announced an incoming email. "Clare is not a woman to openly complain about her husband. She loved him. She adored him, even though he didn't deserve it."

Jason followed a hunch. "If you knew of Mr. Dobson's actions—did you offer help?"

"Oh, I did! I told her about ways to inform the cops without risking public attention. She didn't want to hear me out. I told her about support groups. I know of one connected to the St. Mary's Medical Center, so it would've been easy to arrange a meeting. I urged her to make contact, but I don't know if she did." Miss Simmons huffed, then reached for a handkerchief. "She said she was thinking about it. The last thing I know is that Mr. Dobson claimed that Clark had broken his arm during some kind of sports practice." She blew her nose. "If you know Clark—he's more into playing chess and computer games than football or basketball. He's not the outdoor kind of boy who'd climb trees. I asked Clare, and she started crying." Miss Simmons looked from Jason back to Matthew. She plucked the tissue into small pieces, then scrunched the pieces together and dropped them into the bin under her desk with a sniff. "That was when I urged her once more to ask for help from a support group, at least. She couldn't bear this alone. She shouldn't have to."

"Her sister appeared to help her."

"Her sister considered Mr. Dobson to be a zit on the ass of society." A small smile came and went. "Her words, not mine. She would've taken her sister and nephew out of that marriage a long time ago." Miss Simmons reached for her cup of tea but stopped in mid-motion. "Don't even think either Clare or Annie would be able to kill Mr. Dobson. That is impossible."

"Did Mrs. Dobson know of her husband's appointment with the real estate agent in Windsor Farms?"

"Yes, she did, and she was excited about it. She'd longed for a smaller house and hoped he'd make the right choice. I showed her the model homes. So, yes, she knew where he'd be."

"Mrs. Dobson never considered leaving her husband?"

"Even if she'd thought about it in private, she wouldn't have told me. I'm not her best friend, and I don't know whether she has someone she really trusts. I consider her a close-mouthed type of woman. Anyway, it's a fact she supported her husband. She wouldn't have left him during the campaign, even if she wanted to. She would've stayed at least until after the election." Miss Simmons put down the cup, frowning. "I admit that Clark's injury shattered her faith in her husband." She narrowed her eyes, and her voice dropped a notch. "You know, being hurt by the man you love can be . . . disheartening, and such an assault makes you think about your value as a woman or if you did something wrong.

If your kid's hurt—that's the end of the line, because the kid's innocent. No matter what happens between the couple, the kids have to be left untouched." She rubbed her right wrist. "Do you have any more questions?"

Jason showed her the drawing of the false Miss Olbridge, but Miss Simmons didn't recognize her. "Did you tell anyone else about the appointment with the realtor?"

"Mr. Dobson's schedule was no secret, so I can't tell who else might've been informed. I didn't tell anyone in particular about it, but his campaign manager would've known."

"Mr. Fitch."

"That's right. You'll find him down the hall, grieving like the survivor of a plane crash."

Jason had trouble remaining serious. "You're saying?"

Miss Simmons sat up straight behind her desk, looking smug. "Find out for yourself."

"Very well. Thank you for your time and information."

Jason left the office while Matthew told Miss Simmons they might be back for further questions.

Mr. Fitch's face was as cheerful as the inside of a garbage can. He was a slim man with graying hair, a large mustache, and silver-framed glasses. Jason estimated his age at forty years, though he looked older because of his bent posture, stressed by the loose-fitting jacket. He stood at his desk, gesticulating wildly while having an argument on the phone about schedules and dates and the costs for terminating a caterer. Without further ado, he threw the phone on the table and looked at Jason and Matthew, obviously determined to take out his bad temper on the agents.

"Who are you, and what do you want?" He reached for the cigarette in the ashtray, knocked off the ashes, and inhaled deeply. "I don't have time for any chitchat."

Matthew flipped his badge. "Agents Beckham and Montagna, FBI."

Fitch squinted to decipher the name on the ID. "So, what, Agent *Mon-tag-na*? Are there any charges against me?"

"Should there be charges against you, sir? For killing Deputy Mayor Dobson?" Jason watched Fitch. The campaign manager choked on the smoke, coughing violently as if his lungs would fly out at any moment. After he had recovered, he shook his head. "Or for hiring a killer?"

"Man, are you sickos?" Fitch coughed again, put out the cigarette, and fetched a small water bottle from the fridge. "I worked for him for years! Without me, none of his campaigns would've worked! I was the brain of every campaign, every rally, every speech! Damn you. I've got no time for your accusations. Get the hell out of here and let me pick up the pieces. Find the killer or have a donut at a shop. But leave me alone, will ya?"

"Why don't we sit down and you answer our questions?" Jason pointed toward Fitch's broad armchair. "We might stay for a while."

"You've got no idea, agents, what I've got to do." He sat down, gulped water, and played with the bottle cap. His words tumbled out like staccato bullets from a machine gun. "Buck's death ripped me apart. We were so close to winning the election, and now he's gone! I don't understand how some fucking bastard could kill him! He was . . . a gift to the citizens. He was a man true to his word. If he'd been elected, he'd have changed a lot. I know that. I developed the campaign's main topics."

"So, without you, he wouldn't have got the job done," Matthew suggested as he chose the leather armchair in front of the desk.

"Damn right! Buck was great going out to the people. He was great at presenting his ideas. I was the man in the back where the stitches kept running together."

"He was the face and you were the brain?"

Fitch stopped playing with the bottle cap as if hit by a club. He stared at Matthew, nostrils wide, anger flaring. "You're insinuating he was dumb? Is that it?"

"You said that, sir." Jason warmed up to the interrogation. "Without you, he wouldn't have been as successful as he was."

"Yes . . . well, that may be true." Fitch drank again and continued playing with the bottle cap. The deep frown remained.

"Did you know about his family situation?"

Fitch threw the cap on the table and bent forward. His gray eyes were wild, his jaw muscles tight. "Does his wife say I had anything to do with his murder? Does she?"

"Do you think she has reason to do so?"

"Fuck! No!" Fitch made a dismissive gesture, drank, and slammed the bottle on the table. He wiped away the drops from a sheet of paper, mumbling curses. "Maybe he wasn't the nicest person at home, but that wasn't my concern." Fitch coughed again roughly and wiped his mouth. "I didn't care what he did in private."

Jason detected a defensive tone. "So you knew he abused his wife and son. Did you talk with him about the subject?"

"He assured me his wife wouldn't go public, and that was enough for me. She accompanied him on the rallies, waved and smiled, and did what she was asked to do." Another gesture followed, and Fitch let go of his breath as if tired of the conversation. "I didn't care about anything that took place behind closed doors. I was in charge of his public appearance, his speeches, his appointments. *The face he showed to the nation,* you know? Not how he dealt with his family in his home."

"If the abuse had become public, it would've damaged his image, wouldn't it?"

"What a dumb question! Of course, every tiny bit of negative publicity would've ruined his chances of being elected. Every child knows that. Did you see the press sharks? They would've ripped him to pieces. I told him that I wasn't interested in his behavior or if his wife deserved the treatment. I told him to make sure nobody knew about it." Fitch lifted his chin. His look was challenging, and the words tumbled out of his mouth even more quickly. "You think I should've told him to stop? To educate him? Get real, agents. No one climbs up the ladder of political success without a certain kind of ruthlessness. You're gonna have to be a tough guy if you want to make a difference in life. That's what he was—a tough guy. He had an attitude. He had a goal. He would've been good for the people."

"You had a profound knowledge of the abuse and chose to remain silent in order for him to win the election." Matthew's voice dripped with irony. "Because you considered Mr. Dobson a gift for society. Is that it? A man hits his wife and child, and you think he would've been a great mayor? Who are you to—"

Jason cleared his throat, and Matthew fell silent, not without shaking his head and glaring at Fitch. "Back to the day of the murder, Mr. Fitch. You knew about Mr. Dobson's appointment with the realtor?"

"Yes, of course. I urged him to make it quick because we had to go through the speech he was supposed to give at four PM." Fitch reclaimed the bottle cap and rolled it between his fingers. "It was a great speech. I had worked on it all night." The cell phone hummed, and he quickly checked the name of the caller. "He'd spent several hours over the last weeks with this irrational search for a summer residence, hours he should've spent on preparing presentations or meeting with supporters. I don't know what had happened or who had urged him to buy a house, but that's how he was—determined to get what he wanted." Fitch put down the phone. His look told of growing annoyance. "Gentlemen, as much as I enjoy talking to you—I've got a lot of work to do to clean up the mess."

"A mess?" Matthew frowned. "We're talking about a murder case, Mr. Fitch, and you're concerned about the *mess* it makes?"

Fitch squirmed on his chair, obviously embarrassed about the choice of words. "Listen, agents, I work for a living, and I do my job very well. Buck wouldn't have come this far without my support. That's a fact. Now he's dead, his campaign is over, and I'll be employed until the end of the month. Do you understand that? I've got three weeks, including weekends, to pay the checks, close the files, and reorganize some of the material for his successor." He snorted. "And that will be the sitting mayor, I tell you that. You should search for the killer among the mayor's followers and helpers. His manager—Raymond Gallow—he really is an aggressive guy. I wouldn't put it beyond him to take any road that leads to success for the man he works for." He shook his head, suppressing another coughing fit. "Though murder seems a tad too violent, even for him."

"Does anyone else come to mind who might be interested in killing Mr. Dobson?"

"Agent Beckham, in this line of work—a politician with a mission to root out crime—you make a lot of enemies." His tone was patronizing. "The list would be too long to write it down in a day."

"We are talking about personal adversaries," Matthew continued tenaciously. "People with a motive to kill the deputy mayor."

"Buck knew he had enemies—a lot of them. That's why he hired a bodyguard team. But it didn't help him, did it?" Fitch seemed to lose the verve he had shown thus far. "He was killed at a private appointment, not shot while giving a speech. What does that tell you?"

Matthew showed him the drawing of the false Miss Olbridge. "Do you know this woman?"

"She killed him?"

"Do you know her?"

"No." He smacked his lips and twitched his brows. His look said he would know what to do with her between sheets. "But she looks good, really."

Matthew stood. "Thank you for your time, Mr. Fitch. We may be back with more questions."

"Sure. Waste my time anytime you want." He waved goodbye to them and reached for another cigarette. "I'll be here for three fucking weeks."

Outside the building, Jason inhaled the fresh air as if he'd been close to suffocating from the stale smoke in Fitch's office. "He'd have danced the happy dance if Dobson had been killed like Kennedy."

"Yep." Matthew lit a cigarette. "I know. I should quit. Don't look at me as if I was smoking crack, okay?"

"I don't think Fitch has got anything to do with the murder."

"He's an asshole, but no killer." Matthew picked up Jason's pace toward the parking lot. "Thanks for stopping me. I almost went for his throat."

"I thought you had a better grip on your emotion."

"Usually. My lenience ended the moment he considered Dobson's behavior nothing more than a nuisance. Imagine if Dobson had been elected." He waved his cigarette. "What kind of example is a mayor who abuses his wife and kid? And I promise it wouldn't have remained a secret for long."

"We need to pursue his hint about the sitting mayor and

his men—I'll have Spring check the election team." Jason hit the button to open the car. "What about Miss Simmons?"

Matthew stubbed out his cigarette, slipped onto the passenger seat, and fastened his seat belt. "A former abuse victim. I bet she tried very hard to convince Clare Dobson to take action against her husband or at least leave him. Did you see the scar on her right arm? Looked like a burn wound to me. Barbeque tongs, if I had to guess."

"Ugly, yes. She mentioned a support group at the hospital. Let's check it out."

Nicolas turned on his back and squinted into the bright sunlight flowing through the large windows. One of them stood open, and the warm June air swept the whiff of freshly mowed lawn into the room. He wiped his face and was about to turn to the nightstand to check the time when Jacklyn entered the bedroom.

"You're still here?" he asked in a raspy voice. "Shouldn't you be at the clinic?"

Jacklyn sat on the bed and bent forward to kiss Nicolas's lips. "I rescheduled four of my patients, so here I am. How are you feeling?"

"Much better. Rested. I hadn't thought I'd sleep this long. What time is it?"

"Past eleven. I was wondering—what was it like to be attacked?" She lifted a hand when he flinched. "Listen before you turn me down. I understand that you can't tell me much about your job, but this was private. I want to know—"

"What I felt?" Nicolas caressed her cheek while he dropped into the memory. "Fear. I knew they were out to get me alive. Otherwise, they'd have shot me from the van. The attack was fast, but they didn't anticipate my defense. I saw the surprise in their eyes and knew I had a chance. I dealt out blows as hard as I could and ignored the pain when they hit me." Her compassionate expression made him look away. "I might not have been able to ward them off alone, but Tom was there suddenly, and the thugs turned tail when they realized they couldn't win." He lifted his gaze again when she kissed his palm. "I know how to defend my hide, but I was outnumbered, and they would've beaten me and dragged me away without Tom's help. So, I'm no superhero, *ma chérie*, just an average guy with some martial arts training."

Jacklyn bent to kiss his lips sensuously. "You're my hero, and I've got no words to tell you how grateful I am that they didn't get you. Do you know who they were?"

"Some gang members hired to kidnap me."

Jacklyn frowned.

She looked lovely without a trace of make-up, and he pulled her down for another kiss, ignoring the dangerous fact that some thugs were still out there planning to take him away. His hands explored her bare back, and she lay on his chest, long hair flowing across her shoulders. The kiss made up for all the worries they had shared. He felt loved and safe, as if her presence chased away any peril.

"They didn't act on their own, did they?" she asked when they had broken the kiss and were able to breathe again.

"No, most certainly not. They did this for money."

"Who hired them?"

"I don't know. I handed the information I had to the cops. They'll deal with the gang. It's not my turf."

"You don't want to know?" The frown was back, and he read a hint of distrust in her eyes. "Isn't it important to get to know your enemy? He could hire someone else and try again."

"He might." Nicolas couldn't stand her inquisition and turned to get out of the bed.

She held him back. "Okay, drop the thought. I didn't take

the morning off to see you up and around. I stayed to take care of you."

He lay back again and looked up to her as innocently as he could. "You did?"

"Oh, I read your very manly thoughts, and you're right." Laughing, she kissed his forehead. "I'll grant you a few minutes to freshen up and—"

"No need to." He embraced her gently. "Just love me like you want me."

"You sure?"

"I'm sure."

Every time he entered a hospital, Jason got the impression he had fallen into a beehive. There were busy people around him, passing him by, pushing him, excusing themselves for being in a hurry. Doctors and nurses appeared ever alert, ready to jump into action once the news came in of a major incident. Though he admired professionalism, Jason wished one of them wasn't running to treat a patient and had time to point him in the right direction. He asked the friendly woman at the counter about the support group, and she handed him a flyer, telling him the group met twice a week in a room down the corridor to his right.

Frowning, Jason turned the flyer in his hand.

"I've seen this before," Matthew said, looking over Jason's shoulder.

Jason had a faint ringing, a tinnitus of the mind, distant but present. He had a hard time catching a clear thought in the chaos within the beehive. "Yes, I thought the same. Do you know where?"

Matthew directed Jason to the side of the corridor, narrowly missing being run over by two male nurses pushing a stretcher at breakneck speed down the hall. "At Dobson's house. Remember Mrs. Dobson arranging the papers on the table?"

"Yes, that's right. She hid the flyer under some magazines." Jason's mood lifted instantly. "Let's talk to the person in charge and see if anyone knows Mrs. Dobson."

Within two minutes of conversation, Jason realized that officials of the law—whether in uniform or plain clothes—were not welcome to ask questions, no matter the seriousness of the subject. Lara Billingham, in charge of the support-group, treated the agents with the greatest possible distaste and tried to get rid of them as if they were a contagious disease she intended not to catch. She crossed her arms in front of her remarkable bosom and stared at Jason through thick, black-framed glasses, choosing her words as carefully as the change for the bus ticket.

"I told you, every woman—or man, you would be surprised how many men are mistreated—who comes into the meeting is treated with the greatest respect for privacy. Do you hear my words? Privacy. The women don't want their husbands or partners to know that they're searching for a way out of a relationship that's very bad for them. They want to leave their partners, but fear pursuit and even more backlash. We promise every woman or man that we'll never hand their names to anyone, not even the police. So, no matter how you put your question, I won't tell you the names of our participants."

"I understand that," Matthew said obligingly. "We respect your work more than you can imagine. It's good that those in need find a safe haven and receive help to settle their difficult situation. I wish there were more helping hands like yours. The world would be a better place."

Mrs. Billingham was obviously flattered. She smiled briefly before remembering that she had chosen to be hard as nails.

"I'm not the one who initiated this support-group. Mrs. Nyeburn—Jill Nyeburn—did this. She's a lawyer and an angel in one person." Her smile stressed her admiration. "You should talk to her."

"What kind of help do you offer to those coming to you?"

"First, in a one-on-one interview, we try to find out what kind of family problem the woman or the man has. After that, Mrs. Nyeburn offers legal advice and the chance to participate in group therapy. For many women, it's the first time they're able to talk about their abuse or learn about other women's similar predicaments. Knowing that you're not the only one is a great help." Mrs. Billingham's glare softened. "Many of them go home with a better idea of how to handle their husbands. We give them strategies of how to avoid quarrels or at least take the edge off them. If possible, we try to improve life conditions—be it with therapy, assistance with talking to the police, or with advice on how to file for divorce. Many don't want a divorce from their husbands because of the kids."

A woman of average height entered the room through a side door. Her wavy dark blonde hair was cut to a fashionable bob, her wardrobe had a heavy touch of class, and her winning expression told Jason, without further ado, he was about to meet the actual person in charge.

"Jill Nyeburn." Her voice was warm but had a defining undertone. She shook hands with Jason and Matthew, then smiled at Mrs. Billingham. "I assume you already introduced our support group to the agents?"

"Without giving away any names," Mrs. Billingham stressed and fell back to her glaring. "They've come to talk about the murdered deputy mayor and thought they could drain me of information." She lifted her chin. "Of course, they couldn't."

Mrs. Nyeburn's smile didn't waver, and maybe it was Jason's impression that there was a sparkle of amusement in her green eyes. It was hard to tell behind the professional façade. She folded her hands in front of her body, lifted and dropped her shoulders, and asked, "Can I be of any more help to you?"

Jason was close to blurting out that he expected her to help him solve a murder case and didn't want any more chitchat, but he kept himself in check. He expected that as a lawyer, she would understand an FBI investigation better than Mrs. Billingham. Matthew summed up the facts and asked if Mrs. Dobson had searched for help within the support-group.

"I'd be forced to disclose the participants of this group only if you showed me a court order." She strolled toward a couch, sat down, and offered the agents the opposite seats. Elegantly, she crossed her legs and corrected her glasses. "Groups like these have to respect our clients' wish for anonymity or would fail their purpose."

"It's possible there's a connection between the domestic violence Mr. Dobson perpetrated and his murder. That's why we need to know if she came here, maybe with her son, Clark. Did she talk about her problems?"

"I can't tell you, agents." Her smile showed very white teeth. She could've been the model of the month of a lawyer's magazine cover. "If you want this information, please, ask Mrs. Dobson."

"Do you have safe houses for women who can't return home?" Matthew asked.

Mrs. Nyeburn's smile lost its shine as she turned wary of Matthew's intention. "There are possibilities to accommodate women who'd be in danger of being molested at home. It depends on the severity of the case and, of course, on our resources. As you know, the city maintains a shelter for battered women."

"I'm sure you agree with me that a woman like Mrs. Dobson wouldn't take refuge in a public shelter and risk being seen by the press."

Mrs. Nyeburn pursed her lips but didn't confirm Matthew's statement.

"Once more, Mrs. Nyeburn, it is of immense importance to learn if Mr. Dobson's wife sought help within your group and to learn if anyone close to this group might've taken action in order to protect her. For example, we need to know if she befriended anyone who might feel obliged to help her in this very difficult situation, may it be with a new home or with action against her husband. Some political opponents could've seen this as a chance to harm Mr. Dobson, if not in person, then his political career."

Mrs. Nyeburn's voice was businesslike, her demeanor indicating she would not budge. "Agents, this group is open for every man or woman who is maltreated at home, suffers from a brutal husband, wife or abusive parents. Some women and men are strong enough to make the difficult decision to part with their miserable lives and start over again. I can't imagine how much courage that would take or that anyone who would want to start such a new life—make the change—would commit murder, no matter whether the abusive partner deserves it. The people in this group support each other with words and with hugs, sometimes. They have no intention to make their lives even worse by committing a crime. That's ridiculous."

She lifted her brows. "You don't understand how despair disables people. Coming here, taking part in a group session is a great step forward. Statistics show that eighty-five percent of cases of domestic violence are left unsolved." Though she tried to keep the anger out of her voice, Jason could hear the passion behind her words. "The partner suffers, resigns themselves to it, and then suffers again. The few women and men who break this vicious circle summon all their courage to search for help because they want the suffering to end. They don't want to see their partner dead, just to leave him or her behind."

Jason understood he wouldn't get any more by pressing her for more information. He stood and thanked her for her cooperation.

Matthew let go of his breath loudly, clearly frustrated. "You know that you're obstructing an official investigation?"

"You can come back with a court order, Agent Montagna," Mrs. Nyeburn replied, still friendly and still with a professional smile. She stood and smoothed her business pants. "Until then, my priorities lie with the women and men, whatever their status in life. I can tell you this much—I'd treat the president's wife with the same respect to her case."

"I might decide to do things with you that you don't have on your wish list." Jacklyn placed kisses all over Nicolas's face. "What do you say about that?"

"I'll flow with your imagination. I always do."

"Hmm." Jacklyn caressed his stubbly cheek, then got up. "Don't go away."

Nicolas carefully stretched to examine whether any movement still hurt. He knew he'd been lucky after the confrontation with the four thugs. For the period of Jacklyn's absence, he mulled over possible adversaries, old cases, and whether either Katherine Nelson or any member of the Turner family had plotted against him in order to . . . what? Gain an advantage? Blackmail the FBI to drop the charges against the Tuners or release the Nelson twins from prison? Or was this attack connected to an earlier case? He couldn't believe anyone was stupid or daring enough to kidnap an FBI agent hoping to gain an advantage.

He was relieved when Jacklyn returned but frowned upon seeing the equipment. "Towels and a razor? I admit—"

"You *sub*mit, my wonderful beast, you don't decide, not in

here." Jacklyn smiled a very sweet but also wicked smile. "Please, rest your exquisite butt on the towel and spread your arms and legs. You know the drill."

"Aww . . ." Nicolas obliged, and his pulse quickened when she closed broad leather cuffs around his wrists and pushed his legs further apart to chain them, too. The bondage bed had more metal rings than a punk had piercings, so Jacklyn had no difficulty securing him to the frame. Nicolas trusted her completely, so he wouldn't need their safe word, nor did he think about the possibility that he couldn't free himself from the shackles. While this had been difficult for him to accept a year ago, it was now a part of the game. He wanted her to take the game seriously. He wanted her to tie him up so that he had no way out. The stimulation of being helpless made him horny in two minutes flat.

Jacklyn ran her nails up his legs and through his growing pubic hair. "It's time to make you look like a real sub again. It's been too long since your last grooming."

He strained to look along his body. Jacklyn playfully licked his belly button. "It's been a week, *ma Belle*, not a year."

She pinched his sides. "Shut your eyes and your mouth, beast, or I'll change into a really nasty mistress."

"Ouch." He grinned, seeing that sting of nastiness in her eyes. "I like your dress, by the way."

Jacklyn waggled her butt, insufficiently covered by some small pieces of lace. The black bra consisted of hardly any more fabric but was classy and—as he knew—expensive.

"Always there to impress you." Jacklyn lathered his chest, abdomen, and the area around his genitals.

Nicolas moaned when she put the razor to work. Jacklyn made an art out of grooming him, so he enjoyed every minute, especially her effort to arouse him before taking away his pubic hair. It was a prelude to sex, minutes of pure sensation that made him pull at the restraints and bend his back. The bruises along his torso hurt, but the stimulation outmatched the pain, and he flowed with the rhythm until Jacklyn decided he had enough. The razor did its work, and a warm wet towel cleaned up the foam.

"Turn onto your belly."

"I thought—"

"Once more, you don't think, you don't talk, you don't look. Do as ordered!"

Nicolas understood why the chains were longer than usual when he turned. He had to cross his arms to accomplish the task. He mumbled to himself that shaving his butt was no fun.

Jacklyn laughed and slapped him playfully. "This isn't about fun, this is about serving me. Don't give me an attitude, beast, because I won't tolerate it. On all fours!"

Jacklyn placed a large pillow under his belly so that she could still access his genitals. Nicolas had hoped she'd forego her plan and play with him, but the shaving stayed on her priority list, and he endured his butt losing every single hair. Nicolas was grateful she didn't extend the shaving to the inside of his thighs and down to his knees as he had heard from Lesley, who didn't tolerate any hair in areas where she'd go with her tongue. In fact, Lesley's comments about how to deal with a submissive had made the rest of his hair stand on end, and he wondered how many of Lesley's habits influenced Jacklyn's actions in their private dungeon. He didn't need his FBI training to decide that he'd never walk into Lesley's professional dungeon freely.

Nicolas heard the towel drop at the side of the bed. Jacklyn's hands kneaded his smooth buttocks and the back of his thighs. For some time, her breathing was the only sound in the room, and Nicolas imagined her touching herself to get into the right mood. She had trained him to be aroused while bound, even without the prospect of fulfillment. Nicolas didn't demand satisfaction. In fact, he accepted that he sacrificed any demand for how the game would evolve. Jacklyn commanded their roleplay, and he was the lover who had chosen to become her sub.

She parted his buttocks and lubed his hole to insert a prostate massager she had used on him before. It was a double-edged sword—she could use it for stimulation as part of their game or make him ejaculate without reaching a climax. He never knew which way Jacklyn would choose and was eager to please her so he wouldn't be left hanging out to dry. As much as he wanted to urge her, he kept his mouth shut, didn't even moan. Hands clenched to fists, he breathed shallowly, feeling the pulsing of his cock throughout his abdomen. While her right hand moved the massager, her left hand played leisurely with his balls, never touching his member in a way that would increase his arousal.

"Stay calm, beast, or I'll do this for an hour," Jacklyn warned when Nicolas dared to lift his ass and get closer to her hand. "Don't move a muscle."

He tried to relax, but it was impossible. Trained to feel desire the moment the handcuffs closed around his wrists and announced the day's playtime, Nicolas was literally unable to calm down. No matter how intensely he thought about icy storms, cold, and pain, he reacted to Jacklyn's touch, his imagination adding to what he didn't see. Fulfillment could be close or an hour away, he could never tell. But he knew that Jacklyn loved him and would never intentionally hurt him.

Her fingertips glided across his glans. He was so sensitive he jerked and gave her a reason to continue the teasing game. He leaked pre-cum, prayed for the prostate massager to leave him alone, but knew from experience that Jacklyn never threatened him without consequence.

"The bad misbehaving beast gets nothing more than this. I'll milk you dry, and that's it for the day. You hear me?"

It was a rhetorical question, and he knew his answer was not required. The massager was still in play, forcing semen through his penis without getting close to a climax. Nicolas had anticipated she wouldn't whip him while he was recovering from the fight, but her treatment was worse than being lashed. He wanted her to arouse him, to fulfill his growing desire and yet she made him wait, hold still, and beg without words.

"Yes, that's better, my beast. Finally, you're behaving in an acceptable way."

Nicolas forced his lower body to remain motionless while the massager was pulled out. He admitted that obedience was part of the game—he'd never before considered it the hardest part. He was close to jumping with relief when Jacklyn closed her fingers around his member and started rubbing him.

"Don't be too eager, beast." She stopped the stimulation.

Nicolas panted, trapped in a world of his own desire. His heart hammered against his ribs. He felt no pain. He focused on Jacklyn's hand around his pulsing meat, wishing she would continue, and when she did, he was close to spurting without permission.

"You're a beast, not a little puppy. You can hold that a while longer."

Nicolas grunted sounds well beyond the confines of the English language. His leg muscles quivered as she took her time to massage his balls, pulling them down and letting them go again. She continued teasing his junk until he was ready to throw caution in the wind and beg her to make him come. Under her command, he had no problem getting hard by serving her demands. He couldn't remember the time when making love was a gentle act, dominated by him. He'd been careful with women, never harmed his lovers, but had also never before experienced the peaks of fulfillment Jacklyn provided.

If she let him come at all.

Nicolas pulled at the restraints, fists still clenched—the only way he dared to show his impatience. Jacklyn pulled back his testicles while rubbing his member harder now. The combination of pain and anticipation of the climax was too much.

"Let me come! Please!"

"Not yet!"

She slapped his balls as a punishment, but instead of stopping him, it was the straw that broke the camel's back. His semen burst from him forcefully as if he hadn't had an orgasm for weeks. Groaning as much with relief as fear of her punishment, Nicolas felt all tension leave his body as he lifted upward from the thick pillow, only held in place by the chains.

Her face wasn't as dreamlike and satisfied as he had anticipated. Instead, she appeared ready to spit fire at any moment.

"You had no permission to come, beast! Not at all!"

"Did you know that you've got this wonderful . . . amazing . . . body?"

Jacklyn glared at him but broke eye contact when her amusement showed. "That's your outburst of eloquence today, huh? Let me tell you this—I'll use the hands of this amazing body to punish you for your misbehavior. You hear me? I won't let you go. Not today."

Nicolas smiled at her. "Just love me like you want me."

Close to the hospital exit doors, Jason stopped. His frustration grew with every step, and he was unwilling to leave without sufficient answers. He turned on his heels and walked back toward the counter. The elderly African American nurse behind it smiled at him warmly as if he were the only person around. He read her nametag.

"Tell me, Nurse Asha, every new patient comes here for information and direction, right?"

Her smile broadened, and its white-toothed shine seemed to bring light to her workplace. "Yes, that's right."

"I'm here to investigate a murder case, and I really need your help. Did you see Mrs. Dobson, the wife of Deputy Mayor Brian Dobson, enter the hospital in need of medical attention? If so, when did she come here?"

Nurse Asha glanced over her shoulder as if she expected a reprimand for talking with an FBI agent, but ignored the rules as she confessed in a whisper, "Yes. The last time she came here, she had her son with her and a small suitcase."

"When was that?"

"A few days ago." She looked at a large wall calendar, pursing her lips. "May twenty-ninth." She shook her head, and her face and voice were filled with honest compassion. "The boy looked awful. She was . . . completely upset about his condition though—judging by the way she looked—she hadn't fared any better."

"Do you know who treated her?"

The nurse's features creased into a frown. "Sir, I want to help you, but that's confidential information, and I don't want to get into trouble."

"I respect that, of course. Did you see her speak with members of the support group?"

"No, but . . . I saw her walk down the corridor." She shrugged. "Maybe she talked with someone, but I can't see that from here, you know."

"Do you know why she had a suitcase? Did she look like she was about to leave town?"

"I don't know. If so, she didn't make it. Her husband arrived with another man—a tall one who looked like a tough guard—and they escorted Mrs. Dobson and her son out after they'd been treated."

Jason put his palm on the counter and smiled his warmest smile. "Thank you so much, Nurse Asha, you've helped me more than I can tell."

The bright smile was back on her round face. "You're very welcome."

Jason turned away and walked with lighter steps through the doors.

Matthew waited outside, nonchalantly smoking a cigarette in front of the *No Smoking In This Area* sign. "Did she tell you something useful?"

Jason slapped Matthew's chest with the back of his hand. "The coffee's on me today."

Chapter Six

Agent Spring delivered a tedious monologue about the mayor's campaign team. He had checked their backgrounds as thoroughly as available data permitted and found nothing of any interest. He finished with a disheartened shrug.

"Nothing. Some debts from betting, some debts from unpaid child support, trouble with neighbors about a carport. There's no one without flaws, but also no one with enough to be a legitimate suspect. And none of the workers love their mayor so deeply or fanatically he or she would murder the nearest competitor."

"A dead end." Jason finger-combed his hair, sighing. "What about known gangs? Any information from that department?"

"None. I circulated our profile, and the officers who interrogated the gang members didn't find any woman fitting the description. Given the details, the officers doubted that such a woman would be part of a gang, and I bet he's right."

Jason thanked Spring for his work. "Okay, here's what I got about Mrs. Jill Nyeburn."

"I hope it's more interesting than Spring's report." Matthew yawned, lifted his empty mug, and went to refill it at Jason's coffee pot. "Sorry, Jason, but without coffee, I'll be asleep in two minutes. No offense, Spring."

"None taken." Spring grinned like a teenager. "I was bored collecting this stuff, believe me."

"Fine. Help yourself." Jason lifted his gaze to look at Agent

Addleton, who joined the meeting. As usual, his black hair was sleeked back, and he used his reflection in a nearby monitor to straighten his tie. "Do you have anything to add to the case?"

"No, not this case. I called the prison warden. He says the twins are being prepared for tomorrow. They'll be scheduled to help with the garbage and then get added to the pile. I hope in a plastic sack, tightly knotted." He cleared his throat. "Agent Cardena will drive the truck. He knows what he's getting into." He looked left and right. "He claimed to be an experienced truck driver. Did it in his youth."

"Then that's settled." Jason tried to sound confident, even though he couldn't shake the haunting ghost of failure. He didn't want to be responsible for the twins' escape. He was also afraid of what Sullivan would do to him if he failed. Although the plan for the coming day was carefully worked out, Jason decided to go over all the details again at the end of his shift. He glanced at his notes. "Back to the lawyer at the support-group. Jill Nyeburn was born Jill Hampton of the Boston tycoon family *Hampton and Sons, fine furniture*." He looked up. Matthew returned to his chair, the only one who nodded. "Old English leather chairs and sofas, if that means anything to you. She attended law school, met Donald Nyeburn at a family reception, and married him. According to the rainbow press articles and statements of friends, it was her family's decision because he came from a known and well-off family. Nyeburn was about to become CEO of his father's cement business and planned to expand it big time. The marriage had no children. Three years ago, Donald Nyeburn was stabbed in front of his wife—"

Spring drew in a sharp intake of breath.

"He died in the bedroom. The homicide report sums up the scene as a *brutal, unprovoked act of violence without any distinct clues to the motive*. Mrs. Nyeburn was ruled out as the killer, and her description of the intruder was vague because she was under the influence of valium and two different pain killers. The tox screen confirmed she had taken the drugs ahead of the murder. She told the officers the man had been hooded, dressed in black, and was very fast. She said she had sat for about an hour on the bed until she was able to dial nine-one-one." He looked from Spring to Matthew. "Though the house and the area were searched, the murderer has never been found. He's like a ghost that appeared only once and vanished to never return."

"What did the neighbors say about the marriage? Was it happy?"

Jason flipped through the pages. "The neighbors described the couple as friendly but reclusive. The estates are large, the people rich and eccentric, and if they listened to any quarrel, they didn't say." He studied the photographs of the crime scene. "Three stab wounds in the back, below the third rib. Nyeburn didn't see the attacker coming. He collapsed face-down on the sheet and died within seconds. And only his wife could've seen anything."

"She was too far gone to understand the danger." Matthew frowned as he blew over his coffee. "The killer came in to murder Nyeburn but left her alone even though she was a witness. Did the police investigate her involvement in the crime? Did she have reasons to hire a killer, maybe?"

"The detectives didn't find anything out of the ordinary, no money transfer, nothing. Aside from his parents' regret about the still missing grandchildren, they didn't complain about their daughter-in-law's behavior. Her parents' testimony was a eulogy about their daughter. They claimed she'd tried everything to make her husband happy even though he wanted her to stay at home. Friends and neighbors stated that the marriage appeared to be happy, at least content. If there was any trouble, they carried it privately."

"For how long had they been married?"

"Two years."

"Was anything stolen?"

Jason went over the report and nodded. "Jewelry and cash, about eight-hundred dollars. Mrs. Nyeburn stated that she didn't know how long the killer stayed in the house. Maybe he searched the house, but she couldn't remember. She never expanded on the list of stolen items. Of course, she didn't have to—the inheritance was huge. The detective in charge took down that Mrs. Nyeburn became hysterical when questioned about the murder and its circumstances. She claimed she was unable to testify, too traumatized by the murder. She kept the house but remodeled it completely, especially the bedroom."

"That's perfectly understandable." Matthew shifted on his seat and looked down at the pictures Jason handed him. He pondered a minute, then said, "Try to imagine the scene. The couple's already in their nightclothes. The murderer enters the bedroom, stabs the husband in the back so that he collapses. He never touches the wife, but—as if he wanted to do that the whole time—turns to look for money and jewelry. Does that appear odd to you?"

"Were there other crimes in the vicinity that month or year?" Spring asked.

"None of that kind." Jason lifted his hands. "The question of how the killer entered the house wasn't sufficiently answered, either. An open patio door seems strange to me, but the police accepted it as plausible. It was a hot night. And it's usually a safe neighborhood." He shrugged. "The couple didn't worry about burglars, and the neighbors stated they did the same—leave the doors open for the night."

"Is it possible Mrs. Nyeburn was in league with the killer, and the robbery was a cover-up?" Matthew leaned back and swung on his chair, frowning deeply. "I would've pestered her with more questions concerning her marriage. Call it a hunch, but now she's a lawyer for victims of domestic violence. Is it possible that she chose the line of work because of her experience? Is she in a relationship now?"

Jason shook his head. "She's been single since then. I don't doubt the police work. The detective investigated the case thoroughly but couldn't find any clues that led to Mrs. Nyeburn being an accomplice of the crime. If anything had been odd or suspicious—like typical injuries on her arms or face—he would've added it to his report."

"There are different forms of abuse," Spring said quietly in his dark and smooth voice. He pushed his hands into his pants pockets. "He might've forced her to do things, or punished her with mockery or taken away her money. Who knows? Anyway, it's possible the wife had something to do with the murder but was clever enough to cover her tracks."

Jason shook his head. "Even if it sounds tempting, we have no evidence to support it."

"Back to the recent case." Matthew stood, put down the photographs, and stretched his arms, groaning like an old man. "I'd like to talk to the bodyguard once more. I'm convinced he knew of his employer's actions but didn't tell us right away. I wonder why he kept back the information and why he didn't take action."

Jason looked at the chaos of his cluttered desk. He silently wished he had his whiteboard.

Jason offered Victor Morrison a chair at the desk. "My colleague and I would like to talk with you about the relationship you had with your employer."

Morrison frowned as he sat down and smoothed his tie. "I had a professional relationship, if you want to call it a relationship at all. Mr. Dobson hired me for protection, and I accompanied him on his appointments, looking for possible threats."

Matthew looked through the window of the interrogation room into the large room where officers of the Richmond PD went about their businesses. Their supposedly inconspicuous looks made it clear how much they were interested in the work of FBI colleagues and yet did not dare to ask direct questions. He pursed his lips. "What about the threat that Dobson posed to his family?" He looked Morrison in the eyes. "Did you know how he treated his wife and son?"

The bodyguard rested his hands on his thighs, exhaling as if he knew the question was unavoidable. "I knew. I never witnessed him hitting his wife, but I saw the injuries." His look was full of regret. "I wanted to report him to the police, but Clare urged me not to, even after Clark had been at the ER with his broken arm. She wanted to keep this private and yelled at me when I tried to convince her. She was very concerned about her husband's reputation and his chances of winning the election."

"Why didn't you tell us this before?"

"I promised her not to tell this to anybody. I keep my promises."

"But your employer was dead when we spoke to you for the first time. The family circumstances are quite interesting to us, and you would have known that."

"You think it's a motive for murder." Morrison's tone turned defiant. "But then, if you think Clare would have her husband killed, you're wrong. She's a caring woman. She loved her husband in spite of his awful behavior. She had the strength to stand beside him on stage and waved to the crowd as if she still loved him."

"Never mind your personal appraisal," Jason snapped. "It is a motive. Since you didn't tell us of your observation, let me be blunt with you—your statement of the events on the morning of Dobson's murder occurred is vague. You claimed you were knocked out, but the gas bottle wasn't found. There were no traces of any narcotic agents on your skin or in your blood."

"But why—"

"Your alibi is your unconsciousness because the only witness cannot be found. Considering your training and strength, you were perfectly able to commit the crime. Not to mention that you were the one who found Dobson's body."

"That's nonsense!" Morrison bent forward. "I worked for Mr. Dobson and would never have acted against him. I was hired to keep him from harm, to protect him against criminals. Why would I kill him?"

"Talking to you just now, I have developed the impression that you and Clare Dobson get along very well."

"You're insinuating—"

"It's a fact that the murder carries a very personal signature. This crime was committed out of hate and revenge. You watched his wife being abused, then Dobson hurt his son, too. You just admitted that you knew of Dobson's actions all along. Nevertheless, it was your job to protect the man, even though you would've preferred to smash his face. Isn't that the real truth?"

Morrison shook his head, lifting and dropping his hands. "You're right. I found it hard to watch her suffering, but you can't help anyone if the person doesn't want to be helped. Should I have insisted? Should I have gone to the police in spite of her pleas? I didn't do it. So, yes, I'm guilty of respecting her wish. You can ask her. She'll confirm it."

"That may be the case." Matthew made a gesture that Morrison was free to go. "But it doesn't rule out your participation. Please, stay in the city."

Jason watched Morrison take the elevator before he left to call Nicolas at home from the quiet solitude of the corridor. The constant hum of noise in the large office was giving him an intense headache, and he wanted to return to his desk at the FBI building in DC more than ever. He felt like an alien in Richmond. Nicolas took the call with a distinct groan.

"Did I wake you up?" Jason asked and checked his watch. It was about dinner time, and his stomach growled. "Are you all right?"

Nicolas's voice was hoarse and hardly discernible. "I'm all right. What's up?"

"I wouldn't bother you, but I really need you to come to work tomorrow." Jason lifted his gaze as two officers pushed past, heading for the staircase. They were talking to each other and didn't look at Jason at all. He sensed, though, that every move of the FBI agents was closely watched and judged. Jason loosened his tie and opened his jacket buttons.

"So, you already killed Matthew and need me to cover it up?" Nicolas joked, his voice becoming stronger with each word.

"We need all hands on deck for the surveillance mission concerning the Nelson twins. I'll tell you the details once we meet. And, no, I didn't kill Matthew, but I'm getting close. I can't bear him to be in my car all day."

"Your car?"

Jason flinched. "Never mind. Are you fit enough to come?"

After another groan, Nicolas said, "Sure. Anything else?"

Jason knew his partner and read his voice like other people read their favorite books. "Are you sure everything's okay? You sound as if you're still in pain. More than before."

"In a way."

Jason bit his lips. He didn't want to hear about an extended sick leave, which would lead to more days with *Matthew the Charmer*. He would chuck up his dinner if he learned he had to serve another week with Matthew on the case.

"The beating was harder than expected, hmm?"

To his surprise, Nicolas chuckled. "I'll survive. Where do you want me to be tomorrow?"

"I'll be at your home at six AM. We're going to Dillwyn."

Chapter Seven

"Any good news?" Nicolas asked when he settled on the passenger seat, hissing through his teeth. He adjusted his butt and sighed with relief.

Jason was astonished his colleague didn't insist on driving and blamed it on his friend's injuries. He steered the car away from the curb. "Yes. Richmond PD caught the gangsters who tried to kidnap you. They gave a description of the man who hired them, and the drawing has been sent to every police station. You don't come cheap! For two thousand dollars, the gang was to take you to a hideout and deliver you to another bunch of thugs. That's all they knew, and the police are searching for those gangsters, too." Jason glanced at Nicolas. "I thought it would brighten your day."

"It does," Nicolas assured him, but then his face became serious. "You're wearing a new suit."

"Yes. Elaine bought it for me. It's great, isn't it?"

"Classy. Okay, back to the case. The twins. Bring me up to date, please."

"Sullivan agreed to let the Nelson twins leave the prison in a garbage truck as long as we catch them the moment the Cooper family is free." He nodded toward the small monitor between their seats. "The truck and the twins' clothes are bugged so we can watch their escape and arrest them as soon as we know about the hostages' whereabouts."

"Who's in the team?"

"Spring, Addleton, Montagna. We've got air surveillance, too. The HRT sent us Agent Fowler. She's our contact."

"I thought the team would be larger."

"I thought you knew Sullivan." Jason's gaze told him what he didn't want to say out loud.

Nicolas complied. "We know Katherine's MO. She'll have the snipers placed along the route."

"Yes, I thought about that. Free sight on the roads—a place from where a shooter could cause maximum damage. I ordered the State Police to keep all fuel trucks and those with chemicals on board away from the highways our truck takes."

"Okay. And Dobson? Any new leads I need to know of?"

"None. The fake realtor hasn't been found, and there were no useful fingerprints outside the house Dobson visited. Even if there were any—the house has been on the market for three months. A lot of people walked in and out during that time."

"Sullivan's pissed, I suppose?"

"When is he not? We know for sure that Clare Dobson and her son were at the hospital on May twenty-ninth. She might've talked with someone from the support group, but then her husband showed up and escorted both his wife and son back home." He looked at Nicolas. "She had a suitcase with her. It looks like she wanted to leave him, in spite of her allegiance."

"Dobson might've known her decision and made a last, desperate attempt to hold her back."

"An attempt that cost him his life? Brutal but not impossible." Jason let his breath out slowly. He'd been mulling over the possibilities for a long time. "Anyway, Matthew found out there had been a killer duo back in the seventies with a similar MO. They dragged their victims—abusive men, threats to society—to lonely houses and killed them with baseball bats. One of the murderers was arrested, the other one might still be on the loose. He was never identified."

"You think he started over, and this time killed an abusive politician?" Nicolas frowned. "Farfetched, if you ask me."

"Copycats, more likely. That's my assumption, too." He was grateful Nicolas shared his evaluation. Even if it was mean, he felt like flipping the bird at Matthew. "But we have no lead on the killer. Gangs can be ruled out, and the widow's family and employees have clean slates. The bodyguard, Morrison, is still on my list. He had the time and the means."

"But his shoe size doesn't fit the ones we detected around the body. They appeared to be smaller. And Miller says the point of impact was low."

"That may be." Jason stopped the car at a red light. "Could it have been faked, a ruse?"

"I'm not sure, since the footprints couldn't be matched to a single shoe size. But I assume Morrison would have walked on his tiptoes to leave such prints. Doable, but not likely." Nicolas frowned. "The men were smaller than the bodyguard."

"Still, I don't rule out Morrison as an accomplice to the crime and told him to stay in the city." After a pause, he said, "Matthew found another *Murder by Baseball Bat*. The abused woman had been hospitalized at the Richmond Health Clinic and was close to dying when her husband was murdered. The killer's still on the loose."

"Interesting. What's our position today?"

Jason drove up the intersection and maneuvered into traffic. "We'll stay close to the truck but out of sight. It goes without saying the kidnappers demanded everyone to stay away from the truck. Sullivan ordered that we shouldn't provoke the kidnappers to kill the hostages. He wants them to be protected as much as possible."

"So, we keep a distance and rely on the bugs?"

Jason shrugged. "Sullivan's expression told me he doesn't give a damn about the hostages really, but he'll cut off my head if I lose two hardcore criminals." Jason glanced at his partner. "So, don't let me down, okay? I can't afford failure. Elaine and I signed a contract for a small house out of town.

We plan to get married." Try as he might, he couldn't stop his mouth sliding into an inane grin.

"Wow! And you're telling me this like it's as important as a new pair of socks? Congratulations, buddy!" Nicolas slapped Jason's shoulder heartily. "That's great news! Do you already have a date?"

"No, not yet, but this year. Elaine wants to move into the house, marry me, and, well . . . if everything goes as planned, we'll start a family."

"I don't believe this!" Nicolas pointed at him. "Or . . . are you trying to tell me she's already pregnant?"

"No, she's not." Jason grinned, pleased as punch about Nicolas's reaction. "Not as far as I know. And I bet she would've told me."

"First round tonight's on me. We've got to celebrate this. And make sure you keep your head, we don't want a headless groom!"

"Let's save the hostages, put the twins behind bars, and then it's off to a fancy bar. I'd like to take advantage of you being so generous. It doesn't happen very often."

During the ride, Jason chatted about Elaine's and his plans about the house and his future family. Nicolas nodded, smiled, and asked questions when questions seemed appropriate until Jason looked at him knowingly.

"Okay, you heard my story. Now, tell me yours. I know you're happy for me, but your love life seems to be suffering a glitch."

"There's no time for it. We're almost at our rendezvous point."

"Thirty miles." Jason lifted his brows and shook his head. "We're ahead of schedule."

"Jason, I—"

"Overruled. I've been with you on this relationship journey from the beginning. I took the card out of the wastepaper and told you to call her. Remember? What did Jacklyn do with you that makes you shudder with doubt?"

Nicolas smiled helplessly. "You know me well."

"Yep."

"I don't know how to put it. Sometimes I feel like I'm a pawn she uses for her desire."

"That's the submissive's role. If you don't speak up, she'll do as she pleases. And so far, that was all right by you."

Nicolas inhaled before replying as he admitted to himself that Jason's reasoning was correct. In the beginning, Jacklyn had told him what she was about to do with him, and she had asked him for permission. After more than two years, she lived out her fantasies in their dungeon, and he enjoyed the thrill ride without fear.

"Did she go too far, and you didn't dare resist?" Jason asked quietly.

"I'm still trying to figure out what she did that I found odd. I want to please her, follow her train of thought, but last night—"

"You were on sick leave and had sex?" Jason blurted out.

Nicolas made a face and shrugged. "Guilty."

"Now, come on, that's rich. But, please, go on."

"I missed the love she'd shown so far."

"Love?" Jason cleared his throat. "If I have it right, this roleplay is about the idea of slipping out of your normal positions and becoming someone else. Jacklyn's the mistress, and you're her servant. It's a game, and she's playing it tougher every time." He whistled through his teeth as he steered the car toward a parking lot, killed the engine, and took out his binoculars. "Jacklyn acts out what she loves most." He made eye contact, and Nicolas thought his friend looked directly into his soul. "Finally, you're frightened of what she's capable of. I think it's time for a conversation before you're gagged the next time."

Nicolas wanted to reply, but Jason signaled him *no* as he opened the channel to listen to the agents' reports of their position and status. The four surveillance cars were positioned along the route the truck would take toward the dump, and the FBI agent driving the truck was ordered to follow the route exactly the way the routine driver would've taken. Jason stressed that he wanted to maintain the illusion of following the gangsters' plan as long as possible. Nicolas agreed that they should free the hostages first and catch the twins later.

"Do you think Katherine hired more men?"

Jason looked back at the highway. "Assuming that Katherine hired the snipers through an intermediary to attack the prison bus and to kidnap you, then it's a safe bet she's got herself help now. Maybe more men than before. She can't wait in a car to intercept the truck's route and force the driver to deliver her brothers." He lowered the binoculars. "She always stayed in the background to pull the strings. I bet she hired a team of four to five men to do the dirty work. The gang members could be a part of it."

Nicolas frowned when the truck passed by their position. The signal from the surveillance was strong, and Jason nodded, satisfied.

"What if the gangsters kill the driver to take over?" Nicolas asked.

"Agent Cardena's got a bullet-proof vest. That's all he can do. He volunteered for the job."

"He's the new guy," Nicolas said regretfully. "He's trying to earn his stripes. Was that a wise choice?"

"He's not reckless, and we all started this way. I know it might've been better to let Matthew take the wheel, but this solution appeared to be better."

Nicolas switched off the intercom. "How bad is your relationship with Matthew?"

"Don't frown at me like that. He doesn't do anything aside from—" He stopped when Agent Spring reported the new position of the truck. "Confirmed. We're on our way." Jason put the car in gear and steered into traffic to keep the truck in view.

Nicolas opened the channel again and listened to the incoming reports. The truck was heading toward the dump on a straight route, keeping to the speed limit. It took US 60 east and changed to the Old Courthouse Road, heading for Lynchburg.

Nicolas looked around with growing nervousness. The unwelcome knot in his guts tightened. He waited for a sign, for something that told him the place for the attack, a place for a roadblock, a staged accident that would leave enough room for the truck to pass but not for its pursuers. He studied the map and looked up again. The landscape on both sides alternated between farm buildings and woodland.

"The sharpshooters can attack from any position, five hundred or more yards away."

"That doesn't—"

The truck braked, slowing down crazily and swerving to the right, narrowly missing the barrier and then veering back into the road.

"A shot . . . gas . . . can't see!" Cardena's strained voice cackled as he coughed severely. His words were hardly understandable. "Gotta stop . . . dizzy . . . don't—" His voice broke off. The garbage truck came to a squealing stop at the curb while the engine ran idle. White smoke rose through the passenger window and dissipated in the wind.

"I didn't see a bullet hit the window!" Agent Spring shouted. "Damn it!"

On the right lane, two cars slowed down, then sped up

again and drove to the left. Honking followed while four more cars braked hard to avoid a collision.

Jason drove on slowly while Nicolas took the binoculars.

"One man's coming up from the trees. He's wearing a ski mask, is about five-feet-eight, dressed in dark greens and army boots. Considering the bulge in his overalls, he's wearing a bullet-proof vest under it. He's armed with a *MAC-ten* slung over his shoulder." Nicolas swallowed hard. "Nine-millimeter, no suppressor, prolonged magazine. He's got quite a range and firepower with that gun."

"Don't shoot," Jason ordered.

Nicolas admired his colleague for staying calm under pressure.

"Spring, take a position somewhere behind the truck so he can't see you."

"Roger."

"Report," Nicolas demanded when the ensuing traffic blocked the truck and the surroundings.

Spring's voice was strained. "The man's running around the front, now he's opening the driver's door. Cardena's either unconscious or dead. The gangster's pulling him out. Fuck this!"

Nicolas watched more white smoke escape from the cab. "Did he—"

"He's pulling him around the front of the truck onto the sidewalk. I can't see him anymore!"

Into the shocked silence, Matthew yelled, "Go on, damn it! Tell us what you see!"

"Cardena's on the other side of the truck. It's blocking my view."

"The gangster will kill him, you moron! We must move in!"

"No!" Jason hollered. "No one moves until we know about the hostages. I repeat, stay where you are!"

"Are you out of your mind?" Matthew barked. "He can

shoot him at any moment!"

"If he wanted him dead, he would have already killed him," Nicolas interjected firmly.

He heard Spring's hard breathing. "Okay, the shooter has climbed up into the cab, and he's driving on. He'll be at your position shortly."

"Damn it!" Jason watched the rearview mirror and stayed in the center lane until the truck gained speed. "Spring, what about Cardena? Is he all right?"

"I'm with him. He's not responding, but I can't see a bullet wound. Slow pulse but steady. I'll call a medic."

"Roger. Anything about the position of the hostages?"

"No."

Jason swore as the garbage truck changed to the center lane, bumped into an SUV, and drove on with increasing speed. The driver of the SUV lost control, steered the car to the left, and collided with a yellow transporter that stopped immediately. Jason braked hard and tried to swerve around the right side, but was blocked by a large black tour bus that didn't give way.

"Fuck this!" Jason hit the horn but didn't go any faster. "Get out of the way!"

Nicolas realized they'd lose visual contact with the truck within seconds. "Matthew, where are you?"

"I'm waiting at the exit leading to the dump. What's going on?"

"We got stuck in traffic. The truck caused an accident to block the road. It's heading west on the Campbell Highway. It'll take us a few minutes to get through here."

"I have them on the monitor. They won't go anywhere without us knowing."

"Twenty miles until the truck reaches Lynchburg." Jason's hand clenched the steering wheel. "Spring, what about Cardena?"

"He's coming to."

"Ask him—"

"He says the gangster put something in his pocket. I'm searching—it's a piece of paper, handwritten numbers."

"What kind of numbers?" Jason honked again, then steered the car toward the sidewalk between the tour bus and a compact to overtake the stopping vehicles. They were lucky there had been no pedestrians around.

"Coordinates. I just checked the navigation. It's a factory building in Gainesville, no longer in use. A large area. Shall I send the helicopter?"

"Get on to the local PD and give me confirmation ASAP! Use infrared imaging, if possible." Jason steered the car back onto the highway and hit the gas. The truck was already out of sight.

"Will do."

Jason wiped his brow with the back of his hand. "Signal still strong?"

Nicolas knew it was only a question of time until Jason lost his composure. There was no use trying to talk him down. "Still strong. We won't lose them, buddy."

Jason's expression was grim. "You said Katherine's an excellent strategist. I'm still waiting for this genius to show."

Nicolas didn't answer. During the bank robberies, her flawless planning had helped her brothers escape the police every time. Katherine had always found a clever way to slip through the lines. It was obvious she'd studied the MO of the local police and the FBI to be one step ahead. The gut feeling of having missed a crucial point in the operation increased with every mile. Nicolas expected a shootout, a bomb attack, even an assault with drones—there was no limit to his imagination because he knew there was no limit to hers.

"Addleton, where are you?" Jason asked.

"Stuck in traffic. We're way behind you, but Agent Cardena has regained consciousness and is on his way to the hospital. He seemed to be okay."

"Good news, at least. Try to catch up!"

Fifteen miles later, the truck was still on its route to Lynchburg. The traffic was getting heavier, and Nicolas saw a truck loaded with wood continuing below speed level in the center lane. In a moment of clear understanding of the situation, he experienced an epiphany of what was about to happen. The truck's large cab swerved to the left and the overlong trailer crossed over the lanes. The clamps holding the tree trunks gave way. As if filmed in slow motion, the trunks dropped onto the roadway one by one. They hit the sides and fenders of cars, skittered across the lanes, and forced all vehicles to try to evade them. Cars and transporters behind the trailer came to a squealing stop. Other cars had no luck and bashed into the ones in front of them. Ahead of the mayhem, the garbage truck gained speed and crossed the bridge at the junction of US 460 and Campbell Avenue.

"We lost the signal!" Matthew shouted. "I can't see the truck. It didn't take the exit."

"Follow back to Campbell Avenue," Nicolas ordered, looking at the map. "It must be in the area. Maybe the driver took a straight route and left at Mayflower Drive."

"Roger. I'll check that."

"I can't believe this!" Jason maneuvered along two cars whose drivers sat stunned as they watched the results of the accident unfold in front of them. The tree trunks blocked the lanes, there was a small explosion, and a fire developed directly behind the cab. The driver opened the door, and two passengers from other cars were quick-witted to help him down and lead him away. In a panic over the growing fire, the cars behind the trailer tried to back up and couldn't. Drivers and passengers left their vehicles to get to a safe distance.

Within thirty seconds, the lanes were filled with escaping people abandoning their vehicles while dense wood smoke rose into the warm air to envelop the scene.

"It'll blow up." Nicolas couldn't believe it had fallen apart so quickly. "The sniper's close by. Damn it! And we're blind."

"They're using a jammer," Matthew said. "I'm at the crossroads, but I can't see the truck."

Jason finished easing his way between the empty cars as he picked out an escape route through the car jungle and slammed his foot hard on the accelerator. "We'll be with you shortly. Keep looking!"

"What do you think I'm doing, wisenheimer?" There was a short crackling, then Matthew could be heard again. " . . . close by, interfering with our radio, too. I'll check the traffic cameras."

"We're gaining on them."

Nicolas couldn't tell whether this was true or if Jason just wished it to be so. With a thunderous roar, the gas tank of the truck exploded behind them, and a large column of fire and black smoke rose to the sky.

With no warning, a bullet ruptured Jason's right front tire. It was just a small explosion, unheard in the noisy confusion surrounding them. The vehicle turned to the right and collided with the rear of the vehicle in the neighboring lane. Both airbags were triggered, and the last thing Nicolas heard was the deafening crash of metal folding in on itself.

Chapter Eight

Herb Sanders waited with bated breath. As the radio silence continued, he tried to imagine Leroy's position and how much time he needed to reach the rendezvous point at an underpass. Like any good plan, it was simple and easy to execute. The lady had impressed him with her strategy—there were two alternatives at every junction in case the police tried to stop the brothers' escape. He wondered how many henchmen Katherine employed to put her plan into action, but she'd guarded her intentions and not given him more information than he needed. Her smile had been seductive as well as regretful. He knew he would never gain her trust, no matter how hard he worked.

A quad waited beside the four-wheel-drive truck, key in the ignition. On the other side of the road, an unknown man sat in a garbage truck, similar to the one Leroy was driving. The engine ran idly, and the man behind the wheel was chewing on a toothpick. He didn't glance at Herb but looked through the windshield while he listened to music on the radio. The driver appeared at ease, as if nothing in the world could dampen his bright mood. From time to time, he glanced lazily in the side mirror.

Herb shook his head. He wished he could see into the woman's mind, understand her feelings, and give her what she needed. He envied the brothers for their devoted sister. He was convinced that some terrible event in the siblings' past had forced them to become criminals and choose a road they wouldn't have taken if the circumstances had been better.

That was a link they shared. Herb considered himself a pawn slaughtered on the block of righteousness. The German Army had had no right to deny him a career, and yet, without much ado, his superior had recommended his dismissal. Fuming with rage, Herb had turned his back on his country and sworn he would live a great life, making more money than any soldier ever dreamed of. In a way, he'd reached this goal. Miss Copper Head had paid him enough money to make anything possible. Once the job was completed, he would leave West Virginia and spend time chilling on a beach in Florida.

Herb was pulled from his introspection by a throaty diesel-fumed roar as the garbage truck rounded the corner and coasted to a stop. Leroy killed the engine and jumped out of the cab, grinning like a fool and opening his arms wide. With his black hood and black gloves, he looked like the unbelievable villain from a comic book. His exuberance showed in his voice. He was close to singing with joy.

"Now, how did I do?"

The second driver put the large engine into gear and rolled toward the main street, where he accelerated, rounded the corner, and was out of sight within five seconds.

Herb snorted as he walked past Leroy toward the side of the truck. "Let's get them out quickly. It's no fun sitting among the garbage in this kind of weather."

"Yeah, and congratulations, Leroy, for mastering the FBI and their dumbass agents." Leroy patted his shoulder. "I think I heard them swearing behind me. Man, they knew some colorful words!"

"You left the message?"

"I did. I assume they understood the numbers." He laughed, shaking his head. "Fools. They'll be searching until dusk."

Herb opened the side door of the truck, where the prison warden and Cooper had managed to place a wooden box so that the twins had some room to breathe. Still, they had been in the closed compartment for one and a half hours and looked half-baked. They were sweating and shivering at the same time—two muscular men with stringy hair and unkempt blond beards. They could have jumped out of an end-of-time movie, in which the last living protagonists fought for survival, disregarding the basics of cleanness.

Herb schooled his features. The twins were dirty, smelled terrible, and were in the grumpiest mood anyone could imagine. Squinting, spluttering, and swearing, they stumbled onto the concrete. One of them fell down to his knees, coughing and spitting, while the other one stood, grimacing as if he were about to attack his rescuer. He pointed at Leroy.

"You can't drive, you cocksucker!"

Leroy rolled his eyes. "Such gratitude. You're very welcome, you morons. Didn't your mother teach you to say *thank you* when someone helps you escape from thirty years of prison?"

"Where's our sister?" the other brother demanded to know as he pulled himself back to his feet with help from his brother. His voice was hoarse, and he stumbled more than he walked. His eyes, though, were filled with feverish urgency.

"You'll meet her shortly." Herb handed him a small water bottle and pointed toward the cargo bed of the red pickup truck. "There are clothes, food, and more water under the cover. Hurry! We don't have time to chat."

"You brought some booze, I hope." The first one washed his mouth with water and spat, then handed the bottle to his brother.

"Yeah, and two whores to fuck you," Leroy said as he went toward the quad. "It was a pleasure to be your driver." He took the helmet from the seat and put it on. "See you soon." He tipped the helmet in a salute and drove off.

"I hope so," Herb mumbled. He helped the men settle under the cover and handed them headsets. "Stay put, okay? No more movement than necessary. Do what I say."

"Yeah, fine, whatever."

Herb, repelled by the man's stench, kept his distance and breathed shallowly. "Change your clothes and stuff yours into the plastic sacks. Do it now!"

"Okay, okay, don't freak out." The first brother slipped under the cover. He lost his canvas shoe, but Herb didn't try to retrieve it. "Oh, fucking great! From one box to another! I hope for your sake that this doesn't take all day!"

"Do as I say and you'll be out of this in an hour." Herb pulled the cover over and closed it, relieved to be rid of the men's stench as well as their obnoxious behavior.

He slipped behind the wheel, listening to the sounds. He knew Dwight's distraction had worked. Otherwise, he would have been surrounded by FBI agents already pointing heavy guns at his head. Above him on the intersection, the sirens announced incoming fire trucks and ambulances. He switched on the radio—a major accident hampered Lynchburg traffic on the Richmond Highway.

"You don't say." Herb smiled, turned the pickup around, and drove back onto Martin Street.

Jacklyn stirred the tomato soup, her cell phone wedged between her ear and her shoulder. She reached for the box with oregano but stopped in mid-motion. "Yes, Mom, I know you expect us both to attend your Fourth of July dinner, but I can't promise that Nicolas will join us. His work comes first."

"He should be honored to receive an invitation and do everything in his power to join us."

Jacklyn rolled her eyes and counted to five to skip the petulant answers that came to her mind. "Mom, in case you haven't noticed so far, he's my boyfriend."

"Don't get snarky."

Behind Jacklyn, Lesley mimed a bored expression, then one of disgust. She finally sat on the counter, feet pressed against a shelf, and started juggling with four spice boxes.

"I'm not snarky, but you treat Nicolas like he's a runaway bum who's lucky to get a hot meal." She added oregano to the soup and reached for a spoon to taste it.

"Maybe not a man from the street, but truly not one with prospects. He can't even pay for the house. Did you tell him about our arrangement?"

Jacklyn was quiet, angered, and not for the first time grumpy with her mother. Lesley stopped juggling and made wide eyes.

"Jacklyn-darling, did you talk with Nicolas about the house?"

Jacklyn wished she had the strength to end the call and calm her nerves before she had to talk to her mother again. "No. Not yet."

"It's about time, isn't it? I always plead for order in a relationship. After all, he moved in as a matter of course and placed his . . . *stuff* as he pleased. Any interior designer would throw their hands up in horror seeing your terrible mix of furniture."

"And why should he not bring his stuff? I wanted to buy a house away from DC. It was my decision, and I'm happy he agreed with me and moved in." She tasted the soup, her hunger growing. "After all, he's got a longer commute to get to work."

Mrs. Hollander huffed. "Everyone who can afford it moves out of this stinking town. I urged you to search for a house in the countryside years ago. We would've paid it back then as we did now. You wouldn't listen."

"Please, not that same tune again. It's getting old." Jacklyn signaled to Lesley that she'd hurry to finish the call. "Mom, I've got to go." She stirred the soup once again, then turned off the stove. "We'll talk again when I know for sure whether Nicolas can come with us."

"Sure."

Jacklyn put down the phone while Lesley slipped off the counter and set the table, grinning like a shark.

"A taxing relationship?"

Jacklyn shook her head. "No, not at all, but my mom and Nicolas had a bad start. He accompanied me to my parents but was called back to Washington half a day later. My mom doesn't understand that being an FBI agent is as demanding as being a diplomat. Even I can't wrap my mind around it." She put the pot on the table and went back to fetch a ladle. "She's been married to my father for thirty years and travels with him wherever he needs to go. Sometimes they leave in the middle of the night, and she never complains about that."

"She's picking at Nicolas for doing his work?" Lesley shook her head. "But she tolerated your former lovers, didn't she?"

"Oh, yes." Jacklyn sat down and filled Lesley's bowl, trying to get into a better mood, for Lesley's sake. She didn't intend to ruin their girls' day. "You remember them, don't you? They had money, they owned companies, and they were bosses or at least top managers. All of them planned their days as they pleased and impressed my mom with their tailored suits and their disarming behavior. On some occasions, I felt like the nice decoration on a very large cake."

Lesley laughed. "Oh, boy, that's a misleading metaphor considering you spanked those men at night."

"Never at my parents' home!" Jacklyn took a spoonful of soup, and though it was delicious, she didn't enjoy it. Her thoughts were with Nicolas. "I hoped my parents would be happy for me that I found a man more my age."

Lesley broke pieces off the baguette. "Your father doesn't seem to have a problem with him."

"He wouldn't say a word even if he disagreed." She threw up her hands. "Remember—he's a diplomat. He mastered the art of saying less and thinking more. My mom's the one who does most of the talking."

"And the judging." Lesley smiled and showed her perfect white teeth. "Maybe you really should've taken a bum off the street to your parents' house. I would've liked to see your mother's face when you introduced him."

"Don't be ridiculous. I love Nicolas, and she doesn't see that. She sees account numbers and expensive suits and watches. And, of course, whether he's available whenever she decides to throw a party. In her eyes, he has a job of no importance."

Lesley cocked her head, frowning. "Do I have it right that you earn more money than he does?"

"Yes. One more point on my mother's list why she treats Nicolas with open scorn. She's the classical lady, wrapped tightly in the cloth of the old times when women stayed at home, raised the children, and knew nothing of the working world."

"But she worked when she met your father."

"I tried to argue with her about that, and she said that it was a *transition time* until she found the right husband." Jacklyn shrugged. "Don't tell me you know how to answer that."

Lesley laughed. "No, arguing with parents is never easy."

"How does your father handle your profession?"

Lesley beamed at her. "He's happy that I'm successful. My dad admits he never thought I could pull this off in his lifetime. I don't think he brags about my success in front of the neighbors—at least not in detail—but I don't care. I run a legal business, and that's much more than other people can say."

Jacklyn was quiet for a moment. Lesley's mom had run off with a local drug dealer when her daughter had been fifteen years old. Before that, Lesley had suffered her mother's drug addiction, outbreaks of aggression, and several uncouth lovers throughout her childhood. Lesley never talked about the *bad time* in detail, and Jacklyn assumed her girlfriend had been a victim of domestic violence in her younger years. It was only after her mother left without a note that the Department of Children and Families had made an effort to try and find her father.

"I wish my mom felt the same way."

In her exuberance, Lesley dropped her spoon, and soup splashed onto the tablecloth, making a glaring stain. "I've got an idea! I accompany you to that fancy dinner, and we claim that we're together and that you'll join my business as a partner. I could dress up accordingly. What do you think?"

Jacklyn choked when laughing and swallowing didn't go together. "Les, that's unfair while I'm eating!" She coughed and took a swig of water. "I don't know what would shock my mother more than Nicolas being an FBI agent—the part that we're a lesbian couple or the one where I take the whip and advertise my services in local papers."

They laughed themselves silly, drank wine, ate, and when their mood sobered, looked at each other.

"I don't know what I'd do without you, Lesley."

Lesley waved her empty wine glass. "Well, live healthily but with less fun." She reached for the bottle to refill their glasses. "Did I tell you that I've got a new pet in my dungeon?"

"I'm sure you're referring to one without fur. Thank you." Jacklyn drank, feeling the warmth of the alcohol kick in. "How is he?"

"Obedient."

Jacklyn rolled her eyes, close to exploding with laughter

again. "Okay, I kind of expected that. Anything else I should know about him?"

"He looks . . . like a wild lion. Beard, long, wavy hair. Raiden's a young dude, tall, broad shoulders, tattoos, large amber eyes. He's got good manners. I bet you'll like him."

"You intend to introduce me to your pet? How come?"

Lesley put down the glass and bent across the table to whisper, "I intend to share him with you. He's out for pain in capital letters. Humiliation, caging, flogging . . . you name it, and he wants it."

Jacklyn frowned. "Sounds to me the guy's got a problem. What's his profession?"

"He works for a company that builds recreational craft—*Taras Boats*. Yep, he's got decent money, he's a good swimmer, a better sailor, and—" She smacked her lips. "He sucks my toes like no one else could."

"Gee, Lesley, you let a pet come this close to your body? He must be really special."

Lesley shrugged. "Since you told me of the weekends you spend with Nicolas in a cabin far away from civilization, I thought about doing the same—take him there, lock him up, make him beg for my attention."

"You're a mean little bitch."

"Oh, no, my dear friend. You're the little bitch. I'm the big one. And I'll make you an offer you can't turn down."

"I'm listening."

"Are you all right?" Jason touched Nicolas's shoulder. "Hey, buddy, are you okay? Are you hurt?"

Nicolas wanted to reply that he should've stayed home, enjoying Jacklyn's hands as they massaged his sore and battered body, but instead, he nodded and carefully straightened in his seat. "Damage?"

"Car won't start. It's stuck, and I can't back up. We're gonna have to climb out through your side."

"Okay." Nicolas opened the door, which squealed in its hinges. A pedestrian approached and asked if they were all right. "We're fine. Thank you." The young man walked on, and Nicolas tried to take some deep breaths, but his lungs were too constricted to allow normal breathing.

"What's going on?" Matthew's voice asked in his ear. "Is someone hurt?"

"The sniper's still close by," Nicolas replied as he put his feet on the concrete. His legs were wobbly, and he held fast to the doorframe as he got up. He was dizzy, but as far as he could see, uninjured. "The car's probably totaled. We'll meet you at your position. What's the status of the truck? Any signal?"

"No signal, but there's a truck on route toward the dump. I'm trying to confirm it's the one we're looking for."

Nicolas hung his head. Sirens were getting louder, and at the back of the traffic jam, police cars and ambulances arrived, followed closely by a fire truck. "Katherine used the marksmen pretty damn cleverly. She knew exactly what she was doing." He helped Jason out of the car while he spoke with Matthew. "Do you think it's not our truck?"

"I'm not sure since we lost visual contact for a while, but I'm on it," Matthew replied. "Local PD and I are checking the intersection and all surrounding streets. Most of them have traffic cameras. I'm going back a few minutes, and then I'll know more."

"Roger that. Keep us posted. We're moving to the rendezvous point."

Matthew mumbled, "I'll be here."

Nicolas reached back into the car for the tablet and a bottle of water he'd kept in the glove compartment. "If he wants us dead, they've got a chance now."

"No." Jason straightened, groaning. He massaged and carefully moved his neck. "They could've killed Cardena and didn't do it. They don't want the murders of federal agents on their list. The sniper's task is to delay us, to take us out of the hunt." He started walking on the sidewalk. "He knows we didn't get here in great numbers. Standard FBI procedure." Jason thanked Nicolas for the water bottle. "We only stand a chance if we get a signal from the bugs in the prisoners' clothes. It was the right time to change transport. Fuck this woman! I wondered if she could do it, but she's outsmarted us again."

Nicolas matched Jason's pace. "We'll pick up their trail."

"Yeah, right. And tomorrow, Sullivan gets my head on a silver platter."

Nicolas looked back at the small monitor, but when he argued that the jammer wouldn't work indefinitely, Matthew was back online.

"The police found the truck that was used for the prisoner transport under the bridge at the junction of US five-oh-one and US four-sixty. Looks like the gangsters left in a large SUV or pickup truck. There were skid marks from another large vehicle, so I assume the truck we're watching is a ruse. Other marks indicate a quad leaving from the same spot. Its direction is so far unknown, but we're rechecking traffic surveillance as we speak."

One-hundred-eighty miles east, Francisco Chávez was driving his car and thinking about his job, his wife, and his child. He couldn't imagine that God had burdened him with such an insubordinate brat. Last night he'd demonstrated his superior position at home, first with words, then with his hands. His wife had cried he should leave the kid alone, but he couldn't, and he'd been too angry to stop when that ankle-biter dared to lift his little hands against him. If he disobeyed, he needed punishment. It was just like his own father had done to him in his childhood. Brats needed to learn the rules. In the end, Maria had taken their neighbor's car to drive to the hospital. His son had cried the whole time, and he'd been relieved when both mother and child were gone. Finally, he'd found the peace to drink his beer and watch his favorite show. Much later, she had returned and walked on tiptoes so as not to wake him. He had been awake, of course.

Francisco clenched his teeth and nodded to himself. His family would learn to accept his rules and that no shouts, complaints, or even whining would change anything. After all, he wanted the best for his family, and discipline and strict order in the household were part of it. They shouldn't doubt his decisiveness.

He kneaded his upper arm, groaning when the pain didn't abate. After the small accident at the buzz saw early in the morning, his boss had sent him to the hospital for first aid, and now his hand and his arm hurt. Two miles further down the road, the pain intensified and spread toward his shoulder and neck. He couldn't lift his arm anymore. In his fear that the doctor had done something wrong, he accelerated, thinking that once he was home he'd feel better. He kneaded his neck with his right hand and quickly put it back on the wheel when his left arm dropped to his lap. Steering with his right hand, he considered pulling over. His eyes hurt, and his mind appeared to be working more slowly than usual.

He looked through the windshield and squinted—the car ahead of him blurred to an unclear mass. The contours seemed distorted and the road swayed as if pulled by a giant. Francisco cried out when the increasing pain stretched hungry fingers through his skull, hampering both his sight and his hearing. His throat constricted, and his breathing turned laborious while at the same time, his heart raced. The more pressure he felt in his head, the less he saw the road. His eyes bulged, and he couldn't tell how fast he was driving as he couldn't read the display anymore.

Francisco steered the car to the left, as if he wanted to overtake the car in front of him, but he didn't stay there. Instead, he headed directly for the other side. The car broke through the rail and slid over the steep stone embankment into the river.

Quickly, the water pressed through the half-open windows, surrounding him, filling the vehicle until it was completely underwater.

Increasingly desperate but unable to move, Francisco dumbly regarded the spectacle of the rising water, unmoving as the water climbed toward his shoulders, his neck, and finally across his face.

"Washington PD reports they've identified the man who hired the gang members to kidnap Agent Hayes," Agent Lawry told Jason via headset. "His name's Herb Sanders. He's believed to have been involved in several assassinations over the past ten years. There has been no conviction so far. The man is a sniper, a former member of the German Bundeswehr. It's fair to assume he's not acting alone. We're searching for his accomplices as we speak."

"Thank you, Lawry." Jason slipped into Matthew's car and closed the door. He was breathing heavily and bathed in sweat from the quick walk. Nicolas took the back seat, his gaze directed at the tablet he held on his lap. "Anything else I need to know?"

"Air surveillance has reached the compound. Agent Fowler reports they're searching the area. The local police have also arrived on the premises. They brought dogs, in case infrared imaging doesn't work."

"Copy that." Jason let go of his breath slowly. He hadn't felt so bad in weeks, and the pressure to re-capture the Nelson twins tightened his chest. He looked at Matthew. "Tell me we won't lose them."

"We won't—" He stopped when a beeping indicated the trackers were online again. "Now, look here what we've got!"

Jason felt a burden lifting off his shoulders. "Where are they?"

"Lynchburg Salem Turnpike, heading west," Nicolas said. "Now turning on US six-forty-nine in New London."

"That's not far away." Matthew hit the gas, and the car jumped forward, pressing Jason into the seat.

"But where are they going?" Jason denied his urge to hold the door handle. He didn't trust Matthew to drive as safely as Nicolas did.

"There's the second signal," Nicolas said. "But this one just stopped." He called up the map. "It's a truck service station."

"So, they split up?"

"No, no, I don't believe that." Nicolas bent forward. "Matthew, the traffic cameras in the area. Now!"

"You could ask more nicely next time." Matthew faked an indignant tone but switched to the many cameras along the turnpike.

Jason went back to the minute the tracking device had come back online and detected a large red pickup. From the cargo bed, a white sack flew onto a transporter standing close.

"Someone's dropping the prison gear!" Jason laughed out loud and then stopped when he saw Matthew smile. "Where did it go?" He switched to the cameras along the route. "It could be heading for Bedford. What the hell is in Bedford?"

"There's a private airport a few miles off the turnpike." Nicolas grunted. "I don't like spoiling your mood, buddy, but they're fast."

Jason pointed at the image on the screen. "There's the second sack. At the curb of the service station." Jason wiped the bridge of his nose and called the Bedford PD to ask for assistance. When he finished the call, he felt like hitting the dashboard with his fists.

"What did they say?" Matthew asked.

"They say that the tires of their black-and-whites were slashed last night. They're doing repairs, but they can't send a car to the airport right now. Isn't that fucking funny?"

"Katherine *is* a genius," Nicolas mumbled.

"And we're like lapdogs jumping from one tiny biscuit to the next," Matthew replied. "It's about time that we got better at following her trail."

Jason hadn't wanted to believe Matthew was a ruthless driver, yet he stepped on the gas, turned on the flashing lights and siren, and chased the squad car over the turnpike. Jason held his breath and jerked when he heard Agent Fowler's pleasant and relieved voice in his ear.

"Agent Beckham, we've found Mrs. Cooper and her daughter. I repeat, we found Mrs. Cooper and her daughter. They're both alive. Dehydrated, hungry, in need of medical attention, but alive."

"Thank you, Fowler, that's really good news. Any leads on the kidnappers?"

"Both victims had been overwhelmed and drugged so they never saw their kidnappers. They woke up in the locked-up room. The kidnappers had left food and water, but not enough for the time of their imprisonment. Pardon my French, but they're vicious bastards. They would've left them here to die." Fowler paused, then said, "We're canvassing the vicinity—maybe they left something behind that's useful for the identification, but the area is huge."

Jason smiled at Matthew. "Well, now you can overrun them, if you like."

Chapter Nine

Herb Sanders's breathing relaxed when the pickup left the turnpike to turn into a cross-country road. There were no traffic cameras on this route, no police cars in pursuit, and no FBI vans with flashing lights behind him. The hardest part of the escape was over—the twins safely tucked in the cargo bed behind him. They hadn't made a sound, a good sign that they were following Herb's instructions. He hadn't expected such good behavior.

He slowed down to cross a small creek and switched on the communication to his passengers. "You can throw out the sacks now."

"They're already gone," one of the men answered in a bored tone. "We got rid of them long ago."

"You did—" Herb stopped, fighting to control his voice. "Where?"

"Way back. How the fuck should I know where? We can't see a damn thing in here!" The Nelson brother sounded indignant and then, out of the blue, laughed. "The cops will search in two different directions. I bet they're still wondering where we are."

"You threw them out right after you changed clothes, right?"

"Yep."

Herb hated the ring of triumph in the man's voice as he calculated when and where the clothes might have hit the road. "Onto two different cars?"

"Who the fuck cares? Drive on, man, we want out of this

coffin!"

Herb rechecked the mirrors. Katherine had picked the place to drop the prison garments because the sacks would tumble into the creek, soak with water, and probably destroy the tracking devices. She had demanded he make the detour because of the lack of traffic cameras, then head back to the main route and drive on to Bedford. Now, after the brothers' foolhardy actions, the police who were already searching for the twins would know about the tracking devices. He cursed viciously.

"I told you not to make a move! Why didn't you listen?"

"Don't you dare argue with me, you bum! You're just a lousy little sidekick our sister picked up! Do as you're told and stop fucking around! Drive, for fuck's sake!"

"Your sister told me where you should drop the sacks."

"So what? They're gone. Move on!"

Herb clenched his teeth and drove on, thinking of the FBI and their surveillance gear. By now, the HRT might've found the hostages, and the hunt for the Nelson twins would be driven with even more force. He swore he'd never again accept a job that included the transport of idiots.

Jacklyn and Lesley watched a few videos of Lesley's dungeon partners, sipped wine, and talked about lovers, past and present. When Lesley put down her glass, she turned to Jacklyn with a deep frown.

"Tell me, why you don't just order Nicolas to quit working? As I see it, you don't need his income to live, and he could be around twenty-four-seven. He wouldn't be in danger, and you wouldn't have to worry anymore, not to mention that he'd be here to serve us now." Her eyes twinkled mischievously. "In nothing but a chastity device and a black leather harness."

Jacklyn cringed on the couch. She thought about the dangers of Nicolas's profession every time he left the house. "He wants to work, and I won't interfere with his wishes."

"Seriously? But I see your worry every time he leaves. He could be injured or worse."

"He's already been injured, more than once. The last time when some shitheads tried to kidnap him."

"You see? That could be avoided. Tell him to quit." Lesley shrugged elegantly and pulled up her legs. "He should do it."

"That would be cruel."

"But it's necessary. Aren't you his mistress? He belongs at your feet. He should do what you want and not what he wants."

Jacklyn sighed. "Les, I love you like a sister, but you still try to push my relationship in a certain direction, and Nicolas and I don't want to go that way. We both work, and I knew from the start that he had a dangerous job. That's something I can't change. I wish I could, certainly. But he's a young man with ambitions. He's got a clear view of the world, and it's his job to solve crimes. I can't take that away from him."

Lesly pouted unconvinced. "But you'd give him so much in return."

Jacklyn couldn't help but laugh. "That's by your definition. No, Les, I let him work, and we play whenever we want and how we want." She lifted her brows. "It's not that we play master and servant every time he walks through the door. You know, we love to cuddle on the couch, we watch movies together, and sometimes we cook. This is so much more than an arrangement of sex and pain."

Lesley made a sour face. "And you think I should try the same."

"I'm not saying that. Do what makes you happy. That doesn't have to involve a lasting relationship. As long as you don't yearn to be with one man every day, don't do it. But why should I ruin my wonderful relationship by demanding Nicolas do something he clearly doesn't want to do? If I can't accept his work and its circumstances, why should he accept me the way I am?" Jacklyn shook her head. "I know that, years ago, I never dreamed about settling, but you said it last year—I'm no longer the youngest sapling in the garden. It's time to stay with one man and love him with all I am."

"Uh, that sounds so damn grown-up, it's on the brink of being boring." Lesley raised her glass. "Okay, then, stay with Nicky-boy, but, please, please, don't become a tedious friend."

Jacklyn raised her glass, too. "Well, you're here to tell me how I avoid it, aren't you?"

Nicolas gazed at the screen, searching for the red pickup when Agent Lawry's voice came back online.

"Hayes, there's been a caller, disguised voice, telling the FBI dispatcher that he's responsible for Dobson's murder. Claiming he was only the first victim and more were to follow. His words were *the deputy mayor was only the first one on my list. Be aware – the judge has come to town.*"

Nicolas frowned. "We already know there were two killers, and that this was a crime of hate. It's highly unlikely there'll be more murders of the same kind. I doubt that your caller is the real killer."

"Sullivan orders you to hurry up with the arrest of the twins so you can retake charge of the investigation. He's dissatisfied with your findings so far—"

"And what else is new?"

"So he wants you back on the case to organize security for potential victims. He didn't name the group of possible targets. That's up to you."

Nicolas was close to bursting with laughter. "What does he

want me to do? Order protective custody for all local Richmond politicians, for all famous men in Richmond, or shall I ask around who abuses his wife and kids—just to be more specific where to send a team?"

Lawry remained professional without a hint at the irony. "He didn't name a specific group, but he wants both Beckham and you back in Richmond, at your desk."

"Yes, I can imagine that. Keep me posted, please."

"Certainly will."

Nicolas smiled at her amused undertone, then turned to his colleagues. "The twins are off the grid, but I think we know where they're heading."

"Maybe." Jason glanced over his shoulder. "Or Katherine screws us again and the truck vanishes in a remote garage where she's got another set of motorcycles waiting for her murderous siblings."

"Don't be so negative," Matthew scolded good-naturedly. "State police and highway patrol have their description. If we lose them, another patrol will catch them."

"Eventually."

"Hey, they won't get away. Trust me."

Jason lowered his chin. "It's my head on a stake, not yours."

"Shall I pull over so that you can wallow in misery?" Matthew threw his hand in the air. "For an FBI agent, you're quite a wimp."

"I'm a wimp?" Jason couldn't have looked more flabbergasted if Matthew had presented him with the Nelson twins on a leash. "You'd never dare say that to Nicolas."

"Because he wouldn't act like you do."

"Hey, I'm sitting right behind you!" Nicolas patted the backrest of the passenger seat, but neither Jason nor Matthew reacted.

"You may be a good agent," Matthew said, "but you

lack . . . well, guts."

"I need my job. Don't you?"

Matthew snorted.

Jason went on. "All of this *lonely-cowboy-bragging* is hollow, because you need to pay rent, too. Don't deny that."

"But, still—"

"Still," Jason interrupted, "I'm the one who admits his fear and doesn't live and act in denial. If I lose my job, I'll sit on the street sooner than later. I haven't learned any other profession. Maybe you can hire as a stand-up comedian, but I want to be a cop."

"No one gets fired over a chase gone wrong." Much to Nicolas's surprise, Matthew remained composed. "And Sullivan's just like any other boss who wants to keep his people on their toes. This isn't about you losing your job, this is about Sullivan demonstrating his superiority, if there is any."

Nicolas watched Jason's expression turn from angry to thoughtful. "But he has the authority to fire me."

"Basically, he has the power to fire you, but he won't." Matthew's gaze was so encouraging that Nicolas thought his colleague was trying to calm Jason down just with his look. "He knows that you're a good agent. Hell, you solved a lot of cases in the past couple of years. He won't throw away that potential. So you can stop worrying and catch the twins before you find out about Dobson's killer, probably this evening. And then I expect you to invite me for a drink to celebrate."

In a way that Nicolas had thought impossible a few minutes earlier, Jason's mood brightened. He appeared motivated, looking forward to proving his value. Nicolas leaned back, shaking his head silently and hiding his astonishment by staring at the tablet again.

"The pickup's back on route, still heading for Bedford."

Matthew nodded. "Here we go."

Herb increased the speed of the pickup whenever it was possible without risking a collision. He checked the mirrors every few seconds and calculated his expected time of arrival but also possible escape routes. He thought of what he'd do with the money just to distract his mind from considering the worst outcome—that he might be stopped and searched. Even though he had a clean slate, the twins under the cover wouldn't vanish.

Herb couldn't stop thinking that the client's payment wasn't enough to cover the stress the unruly freight provided. His assumption that once the twins were out of prison, he'd simply drive them to the meeting point and live happily with the reward had been wrong in many ways. Looking back, Herb knew it had been a grave mistake to accept the lady's offer. Yes, she was very convincing. Yes, she was a great planner. Yes, she looked great, whatever her clothes. At no time did she mention that her siblings were the worst pains in the ass. Herb decided the twins needed to be busted out of jail, or the other inmates would kill them sooner rather than later just because they were so damn annoying.

Right now, they were complaining about the unnecessary detour and the long, hot ride. They were sweaty and miserable and wanted to know when they'd stop and change cars. Herb told them to stay put.

As fast as he dared, he turned into the service lane leading toward the private landing field, counting the minutes until he'd be rid of the passengers. He stopped the pickup but took a close look at the surroundings before he switched off the engine. He didn't detect any unusual movement of people, who tried to blend in but behaved too casually to be real. Cautiously, he left the car to open the cargo area. As grumpy as before, the twins crawled from under the cover, stood in the sun, and each took a deep breath.

Though they had only changed clothes, their looks had improved more than Herb had expected. Washed and properly groomed, both young men would look stunning, especially with their blue eyes and handsome facial features. Unlike Herb, they'd be the subject of the wet dreams of many women.

"What're you staring at, old man? Get going. Where're we heading? A plane? That's it? You're taking us out of the state by plane?" He made a gesture toward the landing field.

"We need guns." The second sibling stretched out his hand toward Herb, wiggling his fingers. "There were no guns in the sacks. Where are they?"

"Would you mind telling me your names?" Herb asked. "Or shall I call you Humpty and Dumpty?"

"Hey, old geezer, don't start calling us names, huh?"

Herb shook his head. "And I bet you didn't even get the pun. Your names, okay?"

"I'm Ben, and this is Theo."

"Thank you." Herb memorized that Ben was wearing the dark green shirt and Theo the blue one. That would suffice until they parted with him. "And to answer your question—I don't have guns for you." He didn't say that he wouldn't risk being shot in the back.

"No? Then hand me yours!"

"Most certainly not. And if you don't want to make a scene right here, we'd better get going. I need to talk to the pilot, and then we'll be up in the air."

"You know the pilot?" Ben asked as he matched his pace to Herb's. "Have you worked with him?"

"No. But he needs money and owns a small plane he uses whenever he wants."

Ben nodded, lips pursed. "Fine, whatever. He's a witness, though."

Herb took a deep breath. "He flies you out of here and won't ask questions, okay? He doesn't give a damn about being a witness."

Theo shook his head. "We won't take any chances. We won't go back to jail. You got that?"

Herb detected barely suppressed fear in both Theo's voice and expression. "I got that."

"Agent Hayes, this is getting serious." Lawry's voice was urgent. "The caller told us five minutes ago where we'd find another body."

"As much as I wish to be there, I can't. We're closing in on the fugitives in Bedford. They're heading for a landing field, and we've got to stop them before they can hijack a plane. You've got to take the lead."

There was a pause. When she was back online, her tone was clearly annoyed. "He's sending Clarkson, but I'm on the team."

Nicolas wished her all the best, but she was already offline. Jason turned on his seat, eyebrows raised and mouth open. "Don't say it."

"What I'm saying is—Sullivan is looking for a reason to blame us and make us look bad."

"Still, he won't fire you." Matthew glanced at Jason. "Have you never suffered setbacks in your career? Cases you couldn't solve? Witnesses that went AWOL? If the senior agents fired every agent who lost a case, the FBI would be filled with rookies." He shrugged, laughing. "That would be a sight. Sullivan and a band of rookies. That's like a blind man leading a group of deaf people through a minefield."

"The pickup stopped at the airfield. We're on target, guys." Nicolas's pulse quickened. "Step on it, Matthew, we can catch them before they board."

"What do you think I'm doing here? Twiddling my thumbs?"

"Looks like it."

"Up yours."

Herb calculated the FBI would be on his heels in less than twenty minutes through finding the pickup by checking traffic cam data. He never assumed his enemies were lazy or stupid. He had survived in his business for such a long time because he expected the police forces to be smart and fast. So far, he'd been faster.

Glancing back at the entrance gate frequently, Herb hurried the twins toward the small office. An old man wearing dark green overalls emerged, squinting against the sun. He was bald except for a narrow wreath of hair, which looked as if it was desperately clinging to the back of his head. He nodded when Herb waved to him briefly, put on a well-worn baseball cap, and shuffled across the gravel to greet them. His brown leather boots looked like they were as old as he.

"Hi, I'm Sam," he said, smiling and shaking hands. "You're a tad early, but that's all right. The plane's waiting."

Herb politely but firmly took the old man by his arm. "My apologies for being rude, but we really need to get going. The tank's full, I suppose?"

"Sure is." Sam turned his weathered face toward Herb, and a deep scowl replaced his smile. He tried to shake off Herb's firm hand. "No need to push me, young man. It's enough to tell me. I'm not that old."

Theo took Sam's other arm and dragged him forward. "Old enough to slow us down. Come on, douchebag, move your ass, or I'll shove a barrel in your mouth!"

Sam's eyes widened in shock, and instead of walking

faster, he slowed. He turned to Herb. "You told me I was flying you out of the city. You didn't say anything about guns. I don't—"

"Move it!" Theo shouted, and dragged him harder. Sam stumbled and was kept upright by Herb's and Theo's strong arms. "Get going! We're out of time!"

"I'll fly where you want to, but—"

"Shut up and move!" Theo screamed. "Where's your fucking plane?"

"Over . . . over there."

Sam looked at Herb pleadingly, but Herb refused to support him. The FBI was on their heels, no doubt. The sooner the plane left the ground, the better, even if that included rudeness. He held Sam fast by his arm until they reached the *Piper PA-30 Twin Comanche,* which looked old but well cared for.

"We're flying in this thing?" Ben asked. "What a piece of junk!"

Sam recoiled from Theo once more. "If you don't want to fly with me, that's fine. Just walk away!"

"I said, shut the fuck up!" Theo pushed Sam toward the plane.

The old man stumbled but regained his balance, gasping. He glared at the twins. "Milly's been faithful, more than any woman I had. So don't insult her." He clambered into the cockpit. "Sit and be quiet."

"The plane's got a name?" Ben snorted as he chose a seat and fastened the seat belt. "Yeah, right, and all your women were named Suzy."

"Here's the destination," Herb said as he handed Sam a map. "How long?"

Sam glanced at the coordinates. "An hour, less if you close the door."

Swearing under his breath, Theo pulled the door shut and sat down. "Now, get going!"

Sam put on his headphones, spoke to the tower, delivering them a different flight route, and waited for permission to take off. Herb used the second set of phones to listen to the conversation. Sam knew the employee, and they made small talk about the upcoming weekend until the plane rolled on to the runway. A look through the window confirmed Herb's premonition—a black FBI SUV rounded the corner almost on two wheels and sped through the open gate.

"Hurry up!" Theo shouted frantically from the back seat. "Don't you dare stop!"

The SUV changed direction and increased its speed as it dashed toward them, spitting gravel like confetti.

"There's the red pickup!" Jason exclaimed as the SUV rounded the corner toward the landing field.

"And there's a *Piper* on the runway!" Matthew clenched the wheel. "We'll stop them. Hold on!"

He stepped on the gas so that the car jumped forward. The passengers were pressed against the seats, and Nicolas held fast onto the tablet. The building to the left and the row of trees and bushes to the right were nothing but a blur as the car raced on. Matthew had his gaze set on the small plane that made a left turn to enter the single runway. The propellers were turning faster, and over the car's roar, Nicolas heard the twin-engine getting louder as the pilot accelerated the plane. He estimated they had less than a minute to catch up and block the plane's progress.

Matthew's jaw was set. Nicolas held his breath as he realized his colleague would go the extra mile and risk the vehicle and the passengers to stop the fugitives.

The car's right front tire exploded, and the heavy SUV went into a fast spin, rotating on its axle so rapidly Nicolas was thrown to the left and the safety belt cut into his chest.

The pain went deep like a chainsaw drilling through his torso.

Matthew tried to steer against the drift to get the car back under control, but by the time his maneuver had any effect, the SUV had slipped far to the right, almost colliding with a parked transporter. Matthew cursed viciously while Nicolas tried to stop his whole world from spinning around him. He found himself holding tight to the front seats, breathing raggedly. He tried to let go and straighten up, ignoring the fact that his chest hurt with every intake of air. When he tried to speak, he had no spittle for words.

"Are you okay?" Matthew asked, turning to Jason and Nicolas. His face was ashen, and pearls of sweat beaded his forehead. "Hey? Are you all right? Hurt?"

"I'm okay." Jason wiped his brow. He sounded breathless. "What the hell happened?"

"Shot. It was a single shot. I heard the impact, but it was already too late." Matthew looked through the side windows. "It means the second sniper is around, still trying to delay us."

"It means we're targets the moment we leave the car." Nicolas picked up the broken tablet. "Anyway, we've lost them." He pointed toward the runway, where the plane was lifting off. "And we don't know where they're heading. I bet they didn't leave the correct flight route with the tower."

"But that's not the end." Jason opened the seat belt and unlocked his smartphone. "The FBI's got a *Twitter* account."

Two bullets hit the car's hood like a wakeup call that the danger wasn't over yet.

Jason jerked, eyes wide. "He's still shooting at us. Why?"

Matthew undid his seat belt and reached for the door handle. "The engine died. It won't start again. We've got to get out of the car. If he goes for the tank, we'll blow up."

Jason tried to hold him back. "If we get out, he'll take us down like targets at a shooting range."

Once more, bullets hit the SUV, sounding like marbles

thrown against the metal.

Matthew shook his head. "We don't have time to discuss this. Get out on my side, so we have the car as cover."

They left the car, and Nicolas looked back the way they had come. Close to the fence was a row of bushes and young trees—the perfect cover for a sniper. Without a clear target, though, Nicolas's shots would be nothing but hopeful.

"We've got to get to the building!" Matthew set out with Jason while Nicolas covered their retreat. "Hurry!"

Nicolas assumed the sniper had packed up because he'd achieved his goal. He waited for another minute, but when nothing happened, he ran toward the entrance, where Jason was busy typing on Twitter.

"What're you doing?" Nicolas checked the surroundings. Aside from their riddled SUV, the area looked mundane.

"Asking for help. I'm sure the pilot didn't deliver his correct flight data, and such a small plane can stay under the radar. We need people to have a look at the sky for us." He finished typing and sent the message.

Matthew leaned against the wall of the reception building and calmed the secretary, who had hidden behind her desk when she heard the shots. He reported to the FBI HQ what had happened and concluded that they would follow the twins as soon as the HRT helicopter was at their command.

Nicolas heard Agent Lawry reply that she would reassign the chopper and send it to Bedford ASAP.

Matthew switched off his headphones and lowered his head. "I bet dollars to doughnuts the twins will kill both the pilot and their escape agent once the plane has landed. And if we aren't fast enough, they'll disappear." He shook his head. Sweat trickled off his forehead. He looked beaten and tired. "It's not what I signed up for when I took the mission."

"We've got a lead," Jason said, lifting his cell phone for Nicolas and Matthew to see. "The plane's heading west."

Chapter Ten

Nicolas used the waiting time to talk with Agent Lawry. "You searched the area?"

"Certainly." She sounded grumpy, annoyed, and tired. "We turned over every stone, so to speak, but—as you rightfully assumed—there was no body. The house has been deserted for some time. There were no signs of illegal entry. I can't imagine why someone wants to send us on a wild goose chase—aside from this being a crude joke."

"Is there any chance to identify the caller or the number he called from?"

"No. The techs are on it, but so far haven't found a clue. Whoever did this is sitting somewhere and is laughing his ass off. Pardon my French." She didn't sound regretful.

"What's the next step?"

Lawry snorted. "Clarkson and I will write the report for Sullivan about hours of investigation and nothing to show for."

Nicolas pitied her because he knew Sullivan would browbeat the team, even though that they weren't to blame. "Make it short and go home."

"I still can't wrap my mind around the caller's intention. Why did he send us to that remote location? Why did he want us to be there?"

"Maybe he wanted to divert you from another important spot." Nicolas had a sudden revelation but held it back. He tried to imagine Katherine while she waited for her siblings to be returned to her. What would she do to keep the FBI busy and as far away as possible?

"Do you have an idea, Hayes? I'm open to suggestions."

Nicolas stammered, "No, not really. I wish I had, but—there are a lot of crazy people out there who thrive on such a kick."

"Yeah, the loonies with nothing else to do other than ruin my day. What about your chase?"

"Jason—Agent Beckham's in contact with locals who are watching the plane fly west. We're getting new information every minute, so we'll know where they'll touch down."

"Best of luck, Hayes. You're gonna need it."

Nicolas knew what she was referring to—Sullivan would be in the worst mood after Lawry's report. If Nicolas and Jason let the twins escape, their boss would blow a gasket, and rightfully so.

"There's no gain without proper motivation," Nicolas mumbled when he put away the phone. He got up to fetch their equipment from the ruined SUV and handed Jason and Matthew their bulletproof vests.

"The chopper's coming," Matthew announced on the way out. "Do you have a direction for him, Jason?"

"Yes." Jason was eager as he strode toward the landing field, a bag with rifles and ammo in his left hand while he checked his phone. "Are you coming?"

Matthew turned to Nicolas to whisper confidentially, "Can we keep up with him?"

"I doubt it. He looks like he's gonna run faster than the chopper can fly. We better put him aboard."

Matthew laughed out loud but quashed it when Jason turned around, expecting another ironic remark, obviously.

In the helicopter, Nicolas noticed that neither the steep ascent nor the flight was good for him. He felt sick to his stomach and tried to think of anything else but the thin metal frame he was caught in. He couldn't remember ever feeling bad during a flight and wrote off his reaction to the pain in his chest and his poor condition in general. The tight vest added to his misery, and he was close to retching. For the fifth time that day, he wished he'd stayed home. He thought of Jacklyn's warm hands and longed for a massage and ten hours of uninterrupted sleep.

When Matthew looked at him, he said, "Lawry reported there was no victim in the house. The search was in vain."

Jason frowned. "So, it was a diversion. But by whom and why?"

Matthew lifted his hand. "How many details of the Dobson murder were released to the press?"

"Not many, only that the man was brutally murdered. The house's location was known, of course, and also that Dobson's bodyguard had been present at the crime scene."

Nicolas looked from Jason to Matthew. "Call it farfetched, but maybe Katherine did this hoping we'd follow the twins with fewer forces."

Matthew lifted his brows and shook his head. "Seriously, Nicolas? You're turning the woman into a genius who can do everything. I doubt she had the time and the courage to place a call to the FBI. I think it's a copycat, or it's a decoy."

"Even if she tried—our team was already on the way. In this case, Katherine miscalculated." Jason waved his finger *no*. "I admit it's too sophisticated for a teenager prank, but if I had to bet, I'd choose a copycat." His frown deepened. "I can't stop thinking, though, that there might be another murder with the same MO right around the corner." He lifted his gaze to Nicolas. "A lot of men are molesting their women out there."

"The last sighting was at Oakvale. They crossed the border."

Jason continued looking at his cell phone, waiting for the latest news. Some tweets were bogus, and some reports concerned small private planes further south, which had correct flight plans. However, Jason was content that his idea was working.

The helicopter pilot, Martin Reeds, nodded and adjusted the course. He was in his fifties, a veteran flying for the FBI's HRT. Jason had met him on several occasions.

"How long? Can we gain on the fugitives?"

Reeds replied with a wry smile. "We can't fly as fast as they do, but we're close behind them. The moment I know the landing zone, I'll have the local police standing by."

"Great." Jason leaned back and allowed his eyes to close for a moment. He was sweating despite the cool air around him. In spite of Matthew's attempts at calming his nerves, Jason didn't want to face Sullivan empty-handed. He couldn't deal with a setback. He had to succeed to feel accepted, to cherish the day and return home with a smile. Though Elaine would comfort him if he failed, he didn't dare think about the Nelsons getting away again. He would consider himself responsible for any crime they committed.

His father had taught him to be strong-willed, to march forward even if others stood back. Jason had followed that iron rule and berated himself during high school and college on various occasions because he wasn't the strongest, the smartest, not even the funniest student. Despite the setbacks and laughter around him, he hadn't given up once he'd had a goal—good grades or a girl he wanted to invite to a dance. He'd played basketball even though he was neither tall nor extraordinarily muscled. He had trained hard and won the admiration of the team captain—after months of struggling and jokes about his meager performance. He got better. He made himself better. He got faster and more agile. As a reward, he became a center player with a good feeling for the ball and the positions of his team members. No one had ridiculed him after his first season.

His elder sister had told Jason, with a condescending smile, he'd never make a good police officer because he was too straightforward and acted by the book too often. In retrospect, Jason considered her words reverse psychology. The more she mocked him, the more he wanted to complete the training successfully, and he had. But being a police officer wasn't enough. His father had higher expectations, and Jason was eager to fulfill them. Applying for the FBI academy had been the next step. To please his family, he had married early, hoping to start a family of his own but failed miserably. While he was cramming the learning for the exams, his wife had packed her stuff and left. She convinced him she hadn't done it for another man but to regain her freedom. She felt too young to be married for a lifetime. Though his wife had explicitly taken the blame for the ruined marriage, Jason felt downgraded and had begun to see himself as unworthy husband material.

In consequence, Jason had put all his time into learning, passed all his tests, and received the badge as an FBI agent. However, his performance during the first year was terrible. He couldn't stop thinking how much he had disappointed his parents and that he'd never become a good husband or a father.

The next text appeared on Jason's cell phone. "We've got a sighting in Pikeville, Kentucky. Looks like the plane's landing on a country road." He looked at Reeds. "I bet you can do the same."

"I'll take that bet."

Herb was reminded of Dwight's deficient performance under stress when Sam landed the plane. The old man sweated buckets, his hands shook, and the wheels touched the ground much too fast and at a steep angle. The plane bounced up and down before all wheels finally contacted the ground at the same time. Sam was lucky the road wasn't frequently used and was empty so he had time to bring the plane under control and stop it safely.

Sam wiped his forehead. His face was ashen, and his gaze switched from Herb to the twins. His voice shook. "I did what you asked. Now, get out and away from me."

"Not so fast," Theo replied. His voice was hard, and Herb noticed the siblings were back to their normal selves now that the immediate threat of recapture was over. "How do we know you won't give us away the moment we leave, hmm?"

"I won't say a word! I swear!" Sam's eyes were wide as he turned toward the siblings. "You pay me, and I'll leave. That was the deal."

"No good deal." Ben looked the pilot in the eyes. "You're a witness. You know where we left you."

"The FBI is on your heels," Herb interrupted Sam's stuttered reply. "We'd better get going. Get out."

Ben's cold glare turned to Herb. "If we don't kill him, he'll talk."

Herb lowered his voice and hissed, "If we kill him—do you think it's less conspicuous that the plane stays here, stranded like a ship? I say we let him leave and go our ways. He doesn't know where we're heading, and the police radar will follow the plane instead of following us. Do you get this?" Herb didn't wait for an answer but opened the door and made it clear that he wouldn't tolerate violence against the pilot. "Get out!"

Hissing and cursing, Theo and Ben left the plane. Herb watched Sam's expression light up when the door closed again. Without delay, the engine roared to life, and Sam turned the plane around so fast, Herb and the twins had to run out of the way.

"I should've killed that sucker!" Theo shouted over the noise. When Herb walked across the road and toward a small path into the woods, Theo asked, "Where are we going?"

Herb had the urge to turn around, pull his gun, and shoot the twins. He knew he wouldn't feel any remorse. In fact, his mind played with the idea all the way toward the thick shrubbery. There was no one in sight, no car, no man with his dog on a walk in the evening. He could kill the two men and walk away. The hideout in the woods would serve him well.

"Hey, shitface, where are we going?"

Herb's hand jerked toward the holster while his left hand clenched around the handle of his rifle bag. It was an effort to remain composed and think of the money he'd deposited in his offshore account. If it weren't for Miss Copper Head, he'd have turned and emptied a magazine into the men's bodies. "There's a cabin with food, drink, and a car waiting. We freshen up and move on ASAP."

"Oh, great! I hope you thought of booze this time. My throat's as dry as sand."

I could shoot you, and this would all end. Herb clenched his teeth and walked on.

At the end of the road, the small plane lifted off into a sappy, postcard-worthy sunset.

The pilot landed the chopper on the same country road the plane had just left. The three agents got out and ducked against the whirling wind of the rotor blades.

"That's the sheriff's car over there!" Jason pointed toward the flashing lights of a large black-and-white. "He says he can help us."

"He'd better." Nicolas grimaced. "I don't want this road trip to last all night."

Jason regarded his partner. Nicolas looked worse than after the street fight. Jason knew his work ethic had stopped him from staying at home. He always delivered for success, and Jason worked much better with him at his side. His guilty feelings as a friend said he'd misused friendship and Nicolas's dedication to his job. He should've sent Nicolas home after their car crashed on the highway. His injuries might get worse because of the additional ordeal he was going through. Jason decided to make it up to him later in the week.

The sheriff looked like an overweight copy of Brian Dennehy, including the gray hair and the mischievous look on his face. He greeted them with a tip of his head.

"You're the agents from the FBI? I'm Carl Spencer." They shook hands, and Jason brought the sheriff up to speed. "Okay, there're three cabins out of town that fit your description of what the fugitives need. I'll make a few calls and let you know where we have to go." He turned to walk back to his car. "Follow me, gents, I've got some food and drink in the back. I thought you would need it."

"Thank you, sir, that's very kind," Matthew replied, smiling.

"Yeah, right." Spencer waved them to follow.

Nicolas's cell phone rang, and when the helicopter departed, he took the call, listened for two minutes, and turned to Jason. "This was Tom. He dug into some old cases and told me Herb Sanders works with two men—Dwight Mueller and Leroy Jennings. Both are ex-military, sharpshooters, taking sniper jobs for money. The ATF dealt with them in at least twelve cases of assassination. In some cases, the ATF had leads, but none led to their arrest. The snipers are expensive but know their business. A search warrant is out for them."

"So Katherine hired locals for the job." Leaning against the car, Matthew chewed on a ham sandwich. He looked as contented as a cat after catching a fat bird. "And she spent a lot of money." He wiped his lips with the back of his hand. "I guess she saved all of the money her brothers robbed and spent it for the rescue mission."

"But that wasn't her plan." Nicolas uncapped a water bottle. "She wanted to disappear, and the twins' stupidity forced her back." He shook his head, drank slowly, and lowered the bottle. Matthew handed him a wrapped sandwich. "Thank you. If we catch them today, she'll be enraged and probably flat broke. Maybe that's the way we can catch her—she'll need another way to get money and leave the country for good."

"I want to catch her tonight," Jason said. "No more delays, no more hints and breadcrumbs. I want her in custody."

"Hear, hear." Matthew grinned. "The lion speaks."

"I'll get the info to HQ," Nicolas announced when he finished his sandwich. "Agent Lawry should have a look. By now, the snipers will be on their way out of the country or back to a hideout. We know one of them was in Bedford. It's a long shot, but maybe we can run the face recognition program, starting with the man's last known position."

Jason watched his friend walk a few steps away. When Spencer returned with the information that there was only one cabin rented to an unknown lady, he was exuberant. It was the first time that day that he felt confident they would close the case.

"I need a drink," Theo exclaimed once they were inside the cabin. "Badly."

"A drink and a shower. Where's our stuff?" Ben looked around. "Or have you forgotten to buy supplies?"

Herb wasn't in the mood for banter. He knew the twins wouldn't outrun the FBI forever. The agents would find ways to locate the plane even though Sam was already on his way back, probably flying low and careless, close to having a heart attack. If the FBI caught him, he'd sing like a bird in spring. It was also possible someone had seen the plane land and take off. If they were lucky, the twins had an hour to recover before they had to leave again.

"Your sister told me there'd be a bottle of bourbon, but I warn you—don't get drunk. We'll stay here for thirty minutes and then move on. Take a shower if you want to."

"Yeah, right." Theo was already on his way to find the bottle and glasses. "Did you rent this place?"

"Your sister did." Herb took a position at the window, overlooking the path they had come along. He unpacked his sniper rifle, intently watched by the twins.

"And you're our bodyguard?"

"I'd have left you in Bedford if the police hadn't been so close."

Ben and Theo emptied their glasses in one, long swallow. They didn't bother to offer Herb a drink.

"And now? What's the next step?"

"There're maps and directions on the table. Read them, destroy them, and see that you get away undetected." Finished with positioning the rifle, Herb turned to walk toward the back of the cabin. As promised, there was a small black SUV with license plates from Kentucky. "I'll find another way out of here."

"No, no, I don't like that." Deeply frowning, Ben waved his glass. "You come with us. I don't want you to get arrested and make a deal with the police."

Herb turned his head. "Are you nuts? No officer will ever offer me a deal, not even to cut a few years. Not with my criminal record."

"Still—"

Herb's anger got the best of him, and he walked back toward the window to look at the path once more, if only to keep his hands from throttling one or both idiots. "I was paid to take you to Bedford, put you in a plane, and leave for good. My partners secured that part of the escape. I don't intend to be stuck with you for days! Forget it."

Ben cocked his head. He was already on his third drink and let the bourbon turn in the glass. "Maybe you take the money and set us up, anyway. We don't know you. And I bet my sis doesn't know you, either. Don't take us to be stupid, sucker. We know you'd rat on us under pressure."

"I'll make my getaway, and you make yours. Got it?" Herb had the impression he was dealing with children. "Go, grab your stuff. We'll be on our way shortly."

Theo called out to his brother, and Ben imitated the firing of a gun with his fingers at Herb before he turned away, cackling.

Herb narrowed his eyes. The twins were whispering with each other, and he didn't like their sneakiness or the furtive glances. There hadn't been time to check on all details, and since he hadn't planned to accompany the twins to the cabin, he didn't know what Miss Copper Head had stuffed in the bags. He knew a moment later as Ben let out a loud hoot as he gleefully checked and loaded a handgun.

Herb lowered his head. If he didn't accompany them, his life would end in a cabin close to Pikeville, Kentucky. *What a bad way to go.*

The FBI agents, accompanied by Sheriff Spencer and ten of his men, set out toward a cabin a mile off the road. Pointing to the area map, Spencer explained that there was another, even smaller gravel road leading to and from the cabin. His men would block the exit on the larger country road and erect barriers closer to the highway, in case the fugitives escaped their first attempt at stopping them.

"They might try their getaway through the woods, but

that's BS. We've got the dogs out. If we don't catch these hoodlums, they will."

Matthew quietly whistled *Who let the dogs out*.

Jason thought of Katherine Nelson and wondered whether she was with the twins now, hugging them and celebrating their reunion. He imagined how he would enter the cabin, announce the FBI, and arrest the woman first. The triumphant thought carried him uphill even though his weary body protested. The small snack at the patrol car had been nice but not enough to satisfy him and give him strength. Like Nicolas, Jason wanted the day over, but not without the right result.

In the dying light of day, the cabin came into view. Matthew was up front, obviously eager to close in. Jason pondered about keeping him back when a hail of bullets forced the agents and the policemen to leap for cover. Jason could tell that they were two handguns and one rifle in play, the latter with a night vision device. The noise was numbing, but the hit rate was miserable—the policemen used the cover the trees provided and waited until the first surprising attack was over.

There was one window on this side of the cabin. Jason moved to the right to have a better view of the door. He was shot at again and heard the curses of the defenders. Obviously, they hadn't expected the police to find them so quickly.

In spite of the circumstances, Jason grinned when he reached Nicolas. "We have them cornered. They won't get away."

Matthew turned, frowning. "If you start sounding exuberant, I want a double shot of whiskey."

"Later."

Nicolas turned to the sheriff. "Tell your men to shoot at the window while we go and enter the cabin through the door."

"You want this over, huh?"

"The longer we wait, the harder it'll get."

"Well, that's fine by me." Spencer ordered his men to concentrate their fire at the window. "Shoot to kill, boys. They don't deserve any better."

Matthew took a deep breath as he looked at Jason and Nicolas. "For the record—this wasn't my idea, and the first round tonight's on Jason."

The cover fire granted Nicolas, Matthew, and Jason time to run through the shrubbery and hide beside the door before Jason pushed it open.

Nicolas swiveled around the doorframe, handgun leveled. "FBI! Drop your weapons and raise your hands!"

At the same moment, one of the twins appeared from behind the cabin. In a split second, Jason saw the muzzle flash and knew there was no time to eliminate the danger. The bullet's impact knocked Matthew off his feet and thrust him against the wall before he slipped to the ground. His eyes closed, and he didn't move. When the twin moved to target him, Jason pulled up his gun and shot instantly. He didn't take any chances. His bullets hit the man's chest, and when he fell, crying out, Jason shot him in the head. The Nelson twin lay on his back, motionless and with his eyes wide open.

There was more shooting inside the cabin, and Nicolas screamed, "Give up! Drop your weapons!"

"I'll never go back to prison!"

Shots followed, and Jason was about to turn around and see what was going on when three policemen arrived in support. They went past Jason in a rush, and then there was the sound of a short but fierce fight. Jason knelt beside Matthew. With sweaty hands, he felt for a pulse and was overwhelmed with relief when he saw that the bullet had hit Matthew's vest at chest level. He lowered his head, expelling his breath.

"Getting mushy on me, Jason-babe?" Matthew opened his eyes and grimaced with pain when he tried to move. "Don't worry, doll, I won't leave you so soon."

"Not without getting that drink. I get it."

"Fast learner." Matthew coughed and accepted Jason's help to get back on his feet. He stood with his head bowed, trying to catch his breath.

Jason turned to see Nicolas lead the second twin in handcuffs out of the cabin. A policeman escorted Herb Sanders, who was hissing curses. He was handcuffed in spite of a bleeding shoulder wound. His anger, though, was a mild nuisance compared to the twin's reaction the moment he saw his brother.

The Nelson brother fought with all he had to get away from Nicolas's grip. "You killed him, you motherfucker! You killed him!" He tore himself loose and stumbled across the porch toward his dead brother. Blood dripped from his wounded right hand. "Theo! No! No!" He fell on his knees and rested his face on his sibling's chest, sobbing and cursing. He resisted with all he had when Nicolas tried to pull him away. "Leave me alone, you son of a bitch! I'm gonna kill you, bastard!" Ben's face was contorted with rage when he rammed his body against Nicolas, causing him to stumble so that he banged against the porch post. When he tried to kick out, two policemen dragged Ben away. He didn't stop screaming that he'd kill them all.

Nicolas stood with his hands on his knees, gasping for breath. His face was ashen and covered with sweat. He appeared about to collapse at any moment, but Jason was there to lend a hand.

"What about Katherine? Was she inside?" Jason asked the sheriff who showed up behind him.

"No. But you'd better have a look at the stuff on the table. They'd been equipped with everything they needed to get away." Spencer mopped his sweaty forehead and straightened his hat. "If we'd got here an hour later, they would've been gone."

"Looks like we were lucky," Matthew rasped, still leaning against the wall, looking distinctly ill. "I . . . I think I'll take a rain check for the drink. Could someone carry me home, please?"

Spencer laughed heartily. "Son, we'll find you a ride. You bet on it. But let's take you to the medic first."

Jason entered the cabin. The stench of gunpowder was in the air, mixing with that of blood, alcohol, and unwashed bodies. He found a half-empty bottle of bourbon, candy wrapper, and an open pack of beef jerky. Maps were spread on the table, and Jason used a flashlight to read the instructions on the sheet of paper that was fastened between the pages. His heartbeat sped up.

"What did you find?" Nicolas asked, limping closer.

"Hopefully, their destination and rendezvous point with Katherine." Jason reached for his cell phone. "We won't make it, but the FBI office in Louisville can take over." He dialed the number of the dispatcher and told the leading agent of the Kentucky field office about the case and what had to be done. The agent was more than happy to cooperate. Jason had a hard time passing the case on after all they had been through.

"Don't be grumpy," Nicolas said quietly. "One dead, two arrested—that's not bad for a day's work."

"I'm sorry the chase went south so quickly." Jason wiped the bridge of his nose. Now that the attack was over, he felt tired to the bone. "I shouldn't have asked you to come to work."

"Yeah, that's right." Nicolas held fast to the back of a chair and closed his eyes. "I wasn't really ready for this."

"I'll help secure the evidence. Take a time-out and see a medic. I'll meet with you when we can go home."

Nicolas sat down and smiled weakly. "As long as I don't have to run anymore, I can give you a hand."

Katherine looked at the cell phone. Ten minutes had passed since her last glance, and she was more nervous than before. A gut feeling told her that something had gone wrong. Surely Ben or Theo should've called her, telling her that they were on their way.

When she heard the word *Pikeville* on the radio, she turned up the volume. The speaker reported a bloody shootout near Pikeville and that a criminal had been killed while two other men were arrested and taken to the sheriff's department for immediate transport to prison. The police reporter summed up that the combined forces of the FBI and the sheriff's men had surrounded the gangsters and quickly overwhelmed them.

Katherine checked the streets back and front, then gathered her belongings and left the cabin she had rented for two nights. She fled to the other side of the street, barely in time to escape the FBI search team that arrived with enough men and firepower to eradicate a gang of ten.

She ducked behind the house, angry, sad, and for the first time in her life, afraid that the FBI would catch her.

CHAPTER ELEVEN

Nicolas had Ben's screams of rage still in his ears when he unlocked the front door and put his keys on the board to his right. He dropped his backpack, took off his shoes, and felt his low blood pressure when he straightened. Though he'd tried to downplay his condition for Jason's sake, he was dead beat and yearned for his lady's embrace, words of love, and a good night's sleep.

It was close to four o'clock in the morning as he shuffled toward the living room. He smelled the fruity scent of wine on the air and saw two empty bottles and two glasses on the table accompanied by used plates and the remnants of a dish of potato chips. In the dim light of a small lamp, Nicolas detected his girlfriend curled up on the couch, dressed in short pajamas. He thought she was snoring softly, but when he lifted his gaze, he saw Lesley on the second couch, lying spread-eagled and with one foot dangling across the armrest. She wore her nifty black underwear and looked sexy as hell even though she wasn't trying.

Sighing, Nicolas took two blankets and covered the women carefully. Obviously, they were both completely drunk and wouldn't wake until morning—whenever their morning would start.

As Nicolas watched Lesley sleep, he wondered—not for the first time—if she was a good influence on Jacklyn or rather the evil sister who whispered naughty things in her ear. In Nicolas's company, Jacklyn never drank so much wine that she ended up senseless on the couch.

Right now, he wished Lesley gone so he could spend the next morning with Jacklyn alone, but he knew that any criticism or just a bad word about Lesley would ruffle Jacklyn's feathers. He wouldn't risk her bad mood at breakfast, not with the ordeal he had been through. He was too strung out.

Nicolas took a brief shower, changed into fresh underwear, and sank into his bed. He was asleep before his head hit the pillow.

When Nicolas entered the kitchen in the morning, Jacklyn stood at the counter, blowing over her cup of coffee. Her hair was tousled, her face free of any make-up, and she wore an oversized t-shirt—he knew it was his—and boxer shorts—not his. She looked lovely, innocent, and very young. He considered himself a lucky guy to be her partner.

"You came home late," she said regretfully. "I didn't hear you."

"Yeah, I know." He took the cup she offered. "Thank you."

"You look terrible. What happened?"

He glanced over his shoulder. "Would you mind telling Les to hurry up?"

"Tell her yourself. She's seen you naked. She wouldn't mind returning the favor."

"But I would." He looked at her, telling more without words.

Jacklyn complied. "All right." She stopped beside him for a kiss on his stubbly cheek. "You have to tell me what happened at work. I can see in your eyes that yesterday's events are haunting you. You can share your burden with me anytime."

Nicolas nodded and bit back that he wished Lesley hadn't stayed. He longed to speak with Jacklyn about the attacks, about their enemy's clever planning, and how Matthew, Jason, and he had screwed Katherine's resourceful plan. He knew, however, that he wasn't permitted to share details with her.

He sipped coffee, listened to the laughter and the small talk between the friends, and tried to calm down, to cope with the danger he'd lived through, and look forward. Putting Ben Nelson and Herb Sanders behind bars had been an intermezzo, a distraction from the murder case, and a nuisance in Sullivan's eyes. Nicolas expected their superior's pressure to intensify. Sullivan would breathe fire to find evidence that connected a killer to Dobson's murder. The public, represented by the press and the TV anchormen, wanted to know who had committed that horrible crime, more so with every passing day. The election campaign was underway, and nothing would stop it. Nicolas was convinced that the anonymous caller the day before had nothing to do with the killer, but he would neither omit him nor put too much weight to his statement.

Jacklyn returned and put a warm hand on his shoulder. Nicolas turned his head a fraction. The small movement hurt and made him remember all the large and small aches he had suffered during the mission. Though he had slept fitfully, he wasn't rested. He dreaded driving to work.

"She'll be out in five minutes and promised to be dressed." Jacklyn arched her brows. "You got something against Lesley suddenly?"

Nicolas wet his lips, trying to find the right words. It was so easy on the job and so hard with Jacklyn. He couldn't stand her stare. "I like Lesley, okay? But yesterday was damn stressful. My ears are still ringing from the shootouts, my body's bruised and battered, and I'm still bone tired. It's just not the right time for a visitor."

"All right. That's an explanation I can live with." She turned away again, and when she came back this time, Lesley was right behind her, blew her a kiss, and was gone.

"I didn't mean—"

"I know. Les understands. She didn't plan to crash on the couch, but she was way too sloshed last night to drive home." Jacklyn put both hands around her coffee cup to add quietly, "The girls' day got a tad out of hand." She cocked her head. "No comment? I mean, you find two girls sleeping on the couch in their undies and just go to bed? What kind of guy are you?" She smacked her lips, and when Nicolas didn't react, put a hand over his. "Okay, no banter. What happened yesterday?"

Nicolas didn't dare go into details, so he limited himself to a brief recap of the events without names or places and added that the agents had taken out the bad guys, but also suffered injuries and wouldn't be too happy moving around for some days. "What's for breakfast? I'm starving."

"You're in luck your hausfrau went grocery shopping yesterday." Jacklyn smacked his cheek and invited him to help set the table. "What about Jason? Is he okay?"

"He was the one most relieved after the hunt was over. He'll invite us for a drink tonight—if we can make it. We all need some days to recover, but that's not what we'll get. We've got the next case on the table, and in spite of our investigation, we don't have a clue of who's responsible." Nicolas sat down when Jacklyn served scrambled eggs and bacon. He couldn't remember ever being so hungry. He poured a second cup of coffee. While he ate, his mind calmed. "Sullivan will keep us on our toes. He wants the case off his desk."

"I assume you're referring to the murder of the deputy mayor. That case is drawing the media like jelly draws flies." Jacklyn held her cup to her cheek. She narrowed her brows. "I bet the killer's someone who knows the family intimately. So much hate—he can't be an outsider."

"We already checked the backgrounds of family and friends. So far, we've got nothing to go on. We're stuck."

Jacklyn put down the cup and came around the table to kiss Nicolas on the lips. "You can talk to me anytime you want to. I'll listen. I'll help you if I can."

He embraced her at the waist, burying his face against her bosom. "I so love you, Jacklyn, I don't have words to tell you."

She caressed the back of his head, then kissed his hair. "You can count on me, Nicolas, no matter what happens."

Katherine felt as if she'd been running all night.

It wasn't strictly true, and yet, no matter where she went or what she did, she expected the FBI to break down the door and arrest her. She had never been so frightened in all her life. The motel she had managed to reach in a stolen car didn't offer much comfort but had a TV set and a clean bathroom. She changed clothes, put on a wig, and pondered where to steal another car while the anchorman of the local TV station announced a stunning report.

She turned up the volume, mesmerized by what was on the screen. In a flurry of camera flashlights, her brother Ben was escorted by two police officers to the main entrance of the prison. His right hand was bandaged, and he looked as if he'd gotten into a severe fight. He shouted to the waiting crowd that FBI agents had executed his brother and tried, again and again, to tear himself free to get closer to the cameras. When questions were hurled at him, Ben shouted in a mad voice that he would see justice done and kill the bastards who had slaughtered his brother. The policemen dragged him away from the cameras and through the open gate.

Katherine stood rooted to the spot. She couldn't breathe. She couldn't take her gaze away from the scene. Ben fought to get free of the arms that were holding him until a third policeman rammed his fist into his midsection. Ben cried out, but gave up the fight and was taken into the building, howling like a wounded animal. The door closed, and an FBI agent began answering the reporters' questions. He looked arrogant and very pleased with himself as he summed up the chase and how the correctional forces played a key role in the arrest of the Nelson twins and their intermediary.

Katherine sobbed and slowly, when her legs wouldn't hold her up anymore, dropped to the floor. The remote control slipped from her weak fingers.

The anchorman continued. "After an exhausting pursuit that had lasted all day, FBI agents in cooperation with the Pikeville Sheriff's Department were able to arrest the brothers Theo and Ben Nelson, who had escaped from Baltimore Penitentiary in the morning. The brothers and their escape agent had caused several car crashes on their way to Bedford, where they stole a plane. But the FBI had already picked up their trail and finally stopped their getaway in Pikeville, Kentucky. During the shooting, Theo Nelson was shot and killed, his brother and a well-known undesirable, Herb Sanders, injured. Both men are in custody and awaiting trial."

Katherine's sobs got louder until she lay crying on the carpet. She realized she wouldn't see her brothers again. All that was left was her freedom, and a last deed she had to fulfill.

The important news channels broadcasted short versions of the arrest of Nelson and Sanders throughout the morning, and it was still an issue worth repeating when Nicolas entered the large office of the homicide division in Richmond. He couldn't believe his eyes—Jason had already brewed coffee and was sitting at his desk and copying his notes into the computer.

He looked up as Nicolas took off his jacket.

"Good morning."

"You look like death warmed over."

"And up yours, as Matthew would say." Jason leaned back and sipped coffee while staring at the screen to find the mistakes in his text.

"Didn't you go home last night?" Nicolas fetched a cup of coffee and sat down carefully. The injuries he had suffered seemed to affect his entire body—every movement hurt.

"I went home, took a shower, and changed clothes. I slept in a motel around the corner and hope the FBI will cover the expenses. It was easier. I've done most of the paperwork—as promised—so you can check it before I send it to Sullivan."

"Any news about Katherine?"

"Agent Lawry told me the anonymous calls concerning a second murder originated from southern Kentucky—so you might be right about Katherine trying to influence the chase. The team from Louisville hasn't caught her yet. They increased the search radius and alerted all police stations." He forced a smile. "There's news from Mrs. Dobson and Morrison."

"The bodyguard?"

"Security adviser. Agent Haskell, who was assigned to keep watch at the premises, told me that Morrison appeared quite friendly with the widow and that she, say, didn't push him away."

"We should talk with him again."

"Let me finish my notes, and I'm ready to roll."

Nicolas drove toward the Dobson estate, glancing at his partner. "I know why you didn't go to our office in DC—you didn't want to meet with Sullivan."

"You're clever."

"I know—I'm here with you."

"After all, he did want us to resume investigations yesterday. I consider it close enough that he's getting the report about our success. Did you hear from Matthew?"

"I know that he was treated at the hospital. He went home, probably. He's got a dog to take care of." Nicolas risked another glance when he stopped the car at a red light. "How did Elaine take the news about the chase?"

"She was great. She said she's very proud and also happy that I survived the day without severe injury. Do you hurt all over, too?"

"You bet. I won't be chasing anyone on foot for some days."

Nicolas turned the corner toward the main gate of the Dobson estate. The reporters were still present but in fewer numbers. He parked the car at the entrance and got out.

Mrs. Dobson greeted them in the dining room, polite but reserved. She was dressed in a black two-piece dress, black pantyhose, and matching high heels. Behind her, a lady rose from a place at the long table, wearing a formal black jacket and pants, combined with a white blouse. There was a striking resemblance between the women, and Nicolas knew he was about to meet Annie, Mrs. Dobson's sister.

He introduced himself, and Mrs. Dobson asked them to take seats. Upon an exchange of glances, Annie took over the conversation.

"As you can see, we're preparing everything for the funeral tomorrow and the reception afterward. I don't know how we shall manage it all, so, please, if possible, make this a short conversation."

"I understand the difficulty of the situation, Mrs. Dobson, Miss Hancock, and I don't intend to increase your suffering. Mrs. Dobson, you were seen with Victor Morrison."

"Well, he decided to stay at least until after the funeral. So if there're any gawkers or reporters who cross the line, he can interfere."

"I didn't refer to his tasks as a bodyguard. The observation we made was of a more private nature."

Mrs. Dobson blushed so quickly and so deeply that she didn't need to say a word. Annie took her hand in hers and looked at Nicolas, anger in her eyes and in her words.

"Victor is a friendly guy, and he's here to protect us. Whatever you think you might've seen—he's not courting her. And he clearly didn't do it while Buck was still alive."

Nicolas tried to keep the surprise out of his words. "You do understand that Mr. Morrison is still a suspect and that your statement includes the possibility that he committed the crime in order to protect you but also to have a chance at a romantic relationship?"

"There's no way he would do this!" Mrs. Dobson cried out, and tears trickled down her cheeks. "He couldn't! He could never do this! He's a man of honor. He's the good guy here."

"Compared to your husband, Mrs. Dobson?"

"Compared to the killer, who did this to Buck," Annie replied while Clare sobbed noisily and reached for a tissue. "You aren't insinuating that just because Victor exchanged some friendly words with my sister, he's responsible for Buck's death. That's insane."

"By your reaction, Mrs. Dobson, you admit that Mr. Morrison is here for more than providing security."

"I admit nothing," Clare said decidedly. "Why is it reprehensible for a man to be nice to a woman? Who are you to judge my relationship with Victor? Find my husband's killer."

"Where is Mr. Morrison now?"

"He's instructing the other guards at the guest room down the hall."

Nicolas and Jason got up. "I'm sorry for your loss, Mrs. Dobson, but as I see it, Mr. Morrison had a chance and motive to commit the crime."

"I told you he would never—"

Annie touched Clare's shoulder. "Let it be. They can't be convinced."

Down the hall, Morrison saw them coming and flinched.

"More questions? I'm instructing my team. Can it wait?"

"No." Nicolas gestured toward an empty room, and Morrison followed, sighing deeply. "As it turns out, you're involved with the widow."

"Involved? No. I'm not." Morrison frowned, then shook his head. "Listen, agents, I've been most cooperative in this case, but your insinuation is wrong. She's the client's widow, and I'm here to protect her until the funeral is over. That's it."

"I take it from her reaction that she sees more in you than just a bodyguard."

"Security adviser. She might—" He lowered his chin and wiped the bridge of his nose. "I can't help what she thinks . . . or assumes. I'm friendly, of course, because she's in mourning. I'm gentle with her, I take care of the security but with regard to the circumstances." He looked up. "Don't take this to be more than it is."

"We heard from the staff that you were present the night Mr. Dobson fetched his wife and son from the hospital after he had mistreated them. Is that true?"

Morrison nodded. Nicolas could tell that the incident haunted him.

"Apparently, her husband's action against Clark caused Mrs. Dobson to rethink her decision to stay with him until after the election. Is that correct?"

"I don't know about her thoughts or what she wanted. She stayed."

"Tell me about that night."

Morrison's eyes narrowed. "Are you trying to get a confession out of me like that? I had nothing to do with the murder."

"Humor me."

Morrison's shoulders sagged. "She'd taken Clark to the ER without Mr. Dobson knowing. When he found out, he was furious and ordered me to drive him to the hospital. I did. I accompanied him on the search, and when he found them both, he convinced her to come back home."

"She had a suitcase with her?"

"That's right."

"Did you think she wanted to leave her husband?"

"She might." Morrison put his hands on his hips, looking defiant. "And if you ask me if I'd have helped her—no. I was Mr. Dobson's security adviser. His family affairs didn't concern me. They *had* to not concern me."

Nicolas stared at him, and Morrison broke eye contact.

Jason cleared his throat. "It's obvious you had the time and the means to hire professionals to do the job and let it look like a crime of hate. And you had to be knocked out to not look guilty. The woman you called the real estate agent is still at large. She can't be found, and she hasn't reacted to the media alert. Fact is—if you wanted to kill Mr. Dobson, this was the perfect place and time to do so."

"We ask you to stay in the city," Nicolas said.

"I'll stay here, don't you worry, because I've got nothing to hide." After one last, angry look, Morrison returned to his meeting.

Nicolas turned around and followed Jason toward their parked car.

"You wanted to arrest him?" Nicolas started the engine and backed up.

"Yes, I wanted to arrest him, and you didn't. Why?"

"We don't have sufficient evidence. Even if he's more friendly with the widow than is respectable, that doesn't make him the murderer."

"But an accomplice."

"That, too, is doubtful. The CSU report backs evidence for two killers with smaller feet than Morrison's. We checked his financials—he didn't receive any extraordinary payments or have expenses that couldn't be explained. And his friendly behavior toward the widow can be just that—professional friendliness. We can't link him to the crime at the moment—at least not tight enough to present evidence to the DA." Nicolas smiled at Jason. "If we find anything, I'll let you arrest the bodyguard."

"Security adviser."

On the way in to the homicide division, Jason avoided bumping into a portly woman at the last moment. He mumbled an excuse, but she didn't react. She carried a paper bag in both hands, and her face, bruised and black-eyed as if she'd been in a car crash, didn't show any emotion. She looked straight forward and waddled toward the door.

Jason looked at her back, frowning. When he turned, Detective Bartow stood in front of him, hands on his hips, and followed Jason's gaze with the touch of a smile.

"And there goes another lucky woman, who won't get abused ever again. The second one this month. I'm glad there are stupid husbands out there, who get themselves killed sooner than later."

Jason's frown deepened. "What did you say?"

Detective Bartow huffed and pointed with his chin toward the departing woman. He put his thumbs into the waistband of his pants. "Well, did you think the deputy mayor was the only one around who battered his wife? Did you see the woman's face? All bruised and swollen? I've seen her hands and arms, too—lots of defense wounds. I bet she's been beaten twice a week and still stayed with that asshole." He shook his head. "There're too many poor souls who can't defend themselves. But some get lucky."

"You're saying there were more husbands found dead who abused their wives?"

"Can the surprise. This is Richmond, Agent Beckham, not some rural village." Bartow turned around and strutted back to his desk. He made a gesture as if dead husbands were his daily business. His tone was defensive. "We've got accidents galore, some stupid ones, too. I don't believe in divine justice, but in some cases, it's for the best that the men died."

"That's a harsh view," Nicolas said as he took off his jacket.

Bartow raised his bushy brows. "Seriously? Have you never thought that in some cases, a stupid accident for such a criminal is the best for all concerned?"

"There have been more of such accidents recently?"

"Is there a quiet time?"

Jason took the question to be rhetoric and was about to elaborate his point of view when the medical examiner, a man in his late fifties with hair as white as that of an idealized Santa Claus, approached Bartow.

"What's up, Sinclair? You look as agitated as my kids at Christmas."

Sinclair stopped as if he had just realized that Bartow was in the company of two FBI agents. He cleared his throat. "That's a strange if not totally out of place metaphor in this case. Not to mention that it's summer." Sinclair was overweight and obviously didn't work out. He spoke as if short of breath, and his face was an unhealthy red. His eyes narrowed. "I'm talking about murder, Detective Bartow. To your great disappointment, Francisco Chávez didn't die in an accident."

Bartow stared at Sinclair before his gaze flitted to Jason and Nicolas. He cleared his throat. "But the uniforms said he lost control of his car, the car went under, and the man drowned."

"That would be the obvious explanation, but I took the liberty of examining the lungs, and I found no water. He also didn't die of a heart attack, if you considered that a possibility. Instead, I found remnants of a drug in his blood that paralyzed him, which led to the loss of control over his car. Which means—"

"Someone wanted Mr. Chávez dead," Jason said and stepped forward. "Please, show me what you found. I'd like to see the report."

Sinclair made eye contact with Bartow, ignoring Jason. "It's a homicide, and it is *your* case, detective. Do you want to share the insight?"

"Why not?" Bartow made a face that was meant to be friendly, yet appeared sarcastic. "Why not use the immense resources of the great FBI?"

"Very well." Sinclair glanced at Jason and Nicolas, then back at Bartow. "I'll send you both the report."

Sinclair turned away, and Jason couldn't help but ask, "Do you remember other cases like this one that were declared accidents, say, in the last three years?"

"Are you kidding me?" Bartow huffed and shook his head. It was obvious he was angry and trying to get a grip. "Okay, just to be clear—every death is an unsolved murder case at first. As soon as the coroner says an accident or suicide caused it, we close the file."

"But are there other cases like that one?"

Bartow shrugged, and Jason felt the man's reluctance to reveal their investigations. "There are always suicides, unsolved cases of death, but also a lot of accidents. Do you know how many people die in accidents every year? Well, probably not, because you feds don't deal with simple accidents." His eyes narrowed, and his voice sounded gruff. "We don't go into detail in every case. There are real murder cases to solve, if you get my meaning."

Jason nodded, hands on his hips. "If you don't mind, I'd like to filter a query on unsolved cases of death and look into the file details. There might be congruencies with our recent case, and I'd like to be thorough. So—"

Detective Bartow puffed his cheeks, then, as if weighing the pros and cons of an FBI special agent rummaging through his cases, he nodded.

"All right, I think it's better that *I* go and fetch the files. Don't get me wrong—it's just that I know more about the backgrounds than the files will tell you. A query wouldn't help that much." He left his desk and walked toward the room with the archives. On the way, he rudely ordered a uniformed policeman to accompany him.

Nicolas lowered his voice. "He's pleased as punch that we're here."

"Stow the sarcasm. Police forces always consider the FBI a nuisance."

"No, it's more like supervision, and no one likes supervision." Nicolas leaned back on his chair and let a pen tumble from finger to finger. "It's like dealing with the internal affairs. And there's a rivalry. A lot of rivalries."

"It's stupid."

"That doesn't mean it's not real." He cocked his head. "What are you up to?"

"It's just an idea, and probably not even a good one. When we consider—just a mind game—that Dobson's death was not the first but the most recent murder, there could be cases of lesser violence that caused the death of bad husbands. We know that, in theory, serial killers start with a simple killing and increase the amount of violence over the years."

"So you think it's a serial killer whose targets are brutal men? Like that old case you mentioned? Leon Hill and his partner?"

"The partner was never found, and I don't think that he

started over. But remember the other case I talked about? The man was clubbed to death with a baseball bat, and, yes, he had hit and almost killed his wife before. Though the wife was treated at the Richmond Health Clinic, I see a connection. She had multiple fractures. From what I learned, she was a submissive wife who'd never have dared to leave him." When Nicolas's eyes widened, Jason continued. "I think there may be other unsolved murder cases that were declared accidents because they lacked that kind of violence." When Nicolas pursed his lips, Jason nodded, opening his hands on the desk. "And yet it's still possible a family member committed Dobson's murder. I just want to look both ways."

"All right. But—if I follow your train of thought—this recent murder doesn't fit. This man died yesterday, and the cause of death is a drug, no brutal beating in an empty house. Serial killers don't take a step back once they've found an MO that suits them." Nicolas turned his gaze toward Bartow and an officer. They carried two large piles of files and dropped them on Nicolas's and Jason's already cluttered desks as if dropping bones to hungry hounds.

Bartow tried and failed to keep the anger out of his voice. "Here you go. Last three years, Richmond area—accidents, suicides of men of whom we know beat their wives, kids, girlfriends. The whole bunch. Have fun."

Bartow turned away with a look that rivaled an erect middle finger, but in this case, Jason couldn't care less.

Nicolas already knew his partner was a bloodhound when it came to case details. Jason saw connections and congruencies others didn't see or ignored as unimportant. He remembered names and places and was so deep into every case that shaking him out of his work was as hard as pulling a golden retriever from a bowl of dog food.

"Jason? You need a break. You haven't eaten all day."

Jason put three sheets of paper side by side and compared the lines, his lips pursed and his gaze fixed on the words.

"Jason? It's about time you stopped and got something to eat and drink. The cafeteria is around the corner." Nicolas slapped the table with his flat hand. "Snap out of it!"

Jason stared at him. "You don't need to yell at me. I can hear you very well. What do you want?"

"To see that you don't die of thirst and hunger."

"Oh, that. But wait—I want to show you something before we go." He waited until Nicolas rounded the table. "This man was said to have died of a heart attack in his friend's garage. He had been an alcoholic for years, and he beat his wife if she didn't deliver the money she earned. The report says she worked overtime and came home late to drop into bed without checking whether he was there. When he hadn't come home by the next morning, she called the police. The friend, whose garage the man used, wasn't home that night, either, and discovered the body at noon. The wife identified him and walked away." Jason looked up. "Just like Mrs. Chávez did. The ME concluded that Mr. Garibaldi had had a heart attack, knocked his head on the sharp-edged table, and died. It was declared an accident. There's no report a full autopsy took place."

"Okay, then let's talk to Mr. Sinclair."

The medical examiner was grumpy as the Grinch, his resemblance to Santa Claus disappearing when confronted with the question about Mr. Garibaldi's cause of death.

"That one? It's clear as mud that he was trashed. I could smell the alcohol on him even though he'd worked with motor oil and whatever else! He fell and was dead. Why do you ask?"

"It's one of the files Detective Bartow delivered for me to

give a closer inspection. Mr. Garibaldi fits the profile—a husband who had abused his wife for years and made her work hard to get the money for his booze. Did you do a blood test? Because it's not in the report."

Sinclair grumbled into his beard. "I should've sent my findings to Bartow and not—"

"What?" Jason put on a friendly smile. "You didn't want us to know the results?"

"I wanted to do a blood test. I was about to do it." He shuffled toward the refrigerator. "The case is just two weeks old, and I had a lot do—in such clear cases, the chief urges me to let it go and do the important work." He took a test tube in his hand and shooed Jason away with a gesture. "Just go about your business. I'll tell you what I find out later."

Jason pursed his lips. "Does it take long?"

"Are you always such a pain in the ass?"

"That's my nature. Just ignore it. I'll wait." Jason turned to Nicolas. "I'm starving. Would you fetch something from the cafeteria, please? I'll meet you when I know about the result."

Nicolas lowered his chin and raised his eyebrows, but Jason smiled and waved for him to leave.

On his way home, Nicolas thought about the day's events.

Jason hadn't merely discovered that Mr. Garibaldi had been a murder victim, he had also found out that among sixty-seven cases of *accidents* and *suicides,* there were two more cases worth investigating. His exuberant joy at the results was in stark contrast to Detective Bartow's dismayed expression and Dr. Sinclair's open annoyance that someone dared to question his work. Hot on the trail, Jason followed the evidence, but hadn't found connections between the victims other than their violent behavior against women and children.

Frustrated, he had given up and gone home.

Smiling about Jason's eagerness to solve—maybe—a case of serial killings, Nicolas unlocked the door, dropped his bag and shoes, and went into the living room. Standing at the dinner table, Jacklyn was skipping through the pages of a catalog that had nothing to do with summer fashion but everything to do with nocturnal dungeon activities. Her clothes—a short champagne-colored negligee—indicated she was dressed for the evening without the intention of leaving the house again.

She looked up, obviously in a bright mood. "Imagine, Les offered me a part-time arrangement—twice a week." She opened and closed the gown, displaying shameless nudity beneath. "The money is good and easily earned. I just need some new clothes." She laughed. "Okay, what I call *clothes* in this context."

Nicolas stared at her, open-mouthed. He needed a moment to find an answer, then stammered. "But I don't want you to do that. Now that we both gave up our apartments, I've got enough money to pay my part of the mortgage. I told you so weeks ago."

She shook her head. "But I don't want you to."

"What's this kind of shit?"

"I won't let you pay for my house. Period."

He pointed at her, feeling as if he'd lost the argument before it had even begun. "Anyway, we're in a relationship, and you told me that the session in the dungeon with Richard and Harry would be the only time you'd do this because they're your friends. You're breaking your promise."

Jacklyn's eyes narrowed, her bright mood seemingly blown away. "I can do what I want. I don't need your permission."

"This is not about permission." He tried for a calming tone of voice. "You can't simply change the rules and expect me to tolerate them."

She glared at him, and her words were as hard as nails.

"Get on your knees!"

Nicolas blinked. He opened his mouth but closed it again as the words stuck in his throat.

Jacklyn raised her eyebrows, and when he nodded, she repeated her order.

Though Jacklyn was smaller than Nicolas, he felt her staring down at him. She reduced him to the level of any man she had ever whipped. He was but one of many she had brought to heel, and like all the others, he was unable to resist. Nicolas went down on his knees.

It was a challenge, a new game of excitement, and his frustration lasted only seconds before driven out by the ultimate thrill of sexual expectation. His mouth was dry. He gritted his teeth, curled his lips, and narrowed his eyes.

He didn't want to obey.

His analytical mind, schooled in police work, told him to stay strong, to resist, and tell her that she was going too far. She could play dominant the whole evening, and he still wouldn't give in. It was his right to deny her wishes. She couldn't play with him as if he were a toy, bought to please her.

None of these thoughts were formed into words to come out of his mouth.

Jacklyn stepped around him and pulled down his jacket forcefully. Nicolas didn't protest.

His doubts vanished. He wanted to obey, and he knew he was safe and loved.

Jacklyn's behavior reflected pure sexiness. She was the woman he'd dreamed of. The onslaught of lust washing through him squashed his defenses. He followed her with his gaze, suffering like a swimmer close to drowning. He wanted to be saved. The jacket hit the floor. Jacklyn reached around, took off his tie, and pulled the shirt hard so that the buttons sprang off. She ripped the shirt off his body, and with it, she stripped him of his free will, piece by piece. Still, he remained where she had put him. The tumultuous desire in his mind grew stronger. And yet he had to say *no* or risk losing every argument to her in the future.

Her favorite pair of handcuffs dangled from her hand. Nicolas stared at the metal, Jacklyn's red nails, and at her face, unable to move or speak. He sweated, waiting for her command. She dropped the handcuffs between his legs and strutted toward the bedroom.

"Come when you're ready."

Nicolas's lips parted, but the words still stuck between his mind and his vocal cords. He knew what she expected of him. It was a part of their game that she demanded him to be in the mood for whatever she wanted to do with him. He stared at the handcuffs, then closed his eyes to review the conversation.

The turmoil between his mind and his loins grew stronger. He panted as he turned the handcuffs around, and it took him a few minutes until the lower part of his body won by arguing that it was a bad idea to keep his mistress waiting. He left his clothes on the floor and walked toward the bedroom. She stopped him on the threshold.

"No entry without cuffs. If you—"

Looking into his mistress's beautiful face, Nicolas closed the handcuffs around his wrists. The anticipation—seeing her in a leather bra and garters, black pantyhose, and high-heeled boots—fired his lust. He wanted her to work on his member, cause him pain, and then drive him toward an orgasm that would make him forget all his aches and worries. He was so fixated on being satisfied by her that he felt the urge in his loins as a violent pull.

"You changed your mind, Beast. Very well." She smacked a crop into the palm of her hand. "On the bed, on your elbows and knees."

"I'm—"

"Shut up! I know what you are, and it doesn't concern me. If you resist my order, I'll punish you all the harder." She smacked his butt when he took up position. "Don't you dare move away from my hand! Hold still!"

She forced a gag between his teeth and thus rendered him speechless in every way.

Jacklyn spanked his buttocks and foot soles with the crop, but it was minor discomfort, adding to Nicolas's growing arousal. The ring she put around his scrotum was tight and heavy—just the way he liked it. She added a chain that led from the ring to one of the loops at the lower bedpost. He could hardly move forward when Jacklyn started rubbing his penis, but this, too, was exciting. Nicolas tested the chain's tautness over and again, grunting with satisfaction while his hard erection was in his mistress's hand. She extended the teasing game of letting him wait for her next move until his thighs trembled on the brink of orgasm.

When she finally allowed him to come, he felt as if he was in the center of an avalanche, and the release was much more than just the physical letting go of his ejaculation. He was panting with exhaustion and yet so utterly satisfied he wished it could all be repeated even though his strength was fading. He sank onto the blanket and closed his eyes.

Jacklyn relieved him of the gag and kissed the corner of his mouth.

"Hmm, you were wonderful."

Nicolas whispered, "And close to a heart attack."

"That's your interpretation." She freed him from the chains and handcuffs. "I know what you crave."

Nicolas didn't dare look into Jacklyn's eyes. She read him completely and actually knew better than he what he longed for. This was another frightening thought—Jacklyn had found a way to understand and anticipate—even provoke—his sexual wishes. It was amazing. He wondered whether she read every man the same way.

Slowly and with considerable effort, he got up. "Damn you, Jacklyn, that was great."

"I know." She looked smug, and he loved her for her alluring, very feminine arrogance. With a flip of her hand, she threw the crop toward the nightstand and started opening her boots.

"You know that I didn't want to give in." He cast his gaze down. His mind still reeled and was disheartened by the fact that his sex drive had overwhelmed his common sense, his need to have his desire fulfilled without thinking about the consequences. "I didn't—"

"Don't say it." She closed the gap between them, stood on tiptoe, and kissed his lips sensuously. "I love you, Nicolas. You're a wonderful man and an extraordinary lover."

"Wow. That's a great compliment coming from you after you subdued me so completely."

After more kissing and fondling, she took a step back, and he saw an uneasiness flutter in her eyes.

"Was it too much? I had no intention—"

"You knew how I would react . . . that I would fight against it."

"Yes. You thought—"

"I lost."

She flinched. "No, not really. Don't look at it that way. It's just the other way around. Our game stepped up. I had the impression that you agreed, that you wanted it. Was that wrong?"

"No." Nicolas lowered his chin, and once more, the two incompatible parts of his mind got into an argument without a winner. He breathed, and it came out a helpless laugh. "What's next?"

"Whatever you're up to." She looked benevolent and yet demanding.

Nicolas shivered, still digesting the whirl of feelings that led to questions he couldn't answer. His trained mind told him he was being manipulated and hovering on the edge, about to tumble into the abyss of addiction. His heart countered that he was in a developing relationship of his own making. Nothing happened without his consent, and his heart was happy. Nicolas hadn't ever felt this amount of satisfaction before, and he yearned for every touch and every command of his lover.

He wanted to be under her power.

The revelation implied that there was no limit, no frontier, no line he could draw that would never be crossed. Jacklyn's ability to read and wield a man's mind was unrivaled and boundless. If he stepped back, he might see how far he had fallen, and he feared what he would learn about himself. Nicolas already knew he would never go back to a relationship without elements of bondage. His uneasiness arose from the fact that Jacklyn granted him what he craved like no other woman ever could while his craving was of her making.

"So serious?" Jacklyn ran her fingers through his hair. "Is anything amiss?"

"I realized that I pretty much depend on you."

"And that's how it should be." She kissed his cheek, then turned and left the room with her hips swinging seductively.

Nicolas stared at the cuffs discarded on the covers. After all the introspection, all the doubt and misgivings, one incongruous fact leaped unbidden into his mind—he hadn't received an answer to the questions why he shouldn't pay the mortgage and why Jacklyn wanted to take up a job as a mistress again.

Chapter Twelve

Nicolas watched Detective Bartow approach Jason's desk, looking like he was on the verge of being angry. "Okay, you found more cases which—in your eyes—are not clear accidents. Now what? Will you treat these cases as serial murders in connection to the Dobson case or shove them back on my desk?"

Jason stood up to tackle the detective without blinking. "You said your captain wants you to work on the important cases, so, leave the files on my desk. It's probably just a waste of time, anyway."

Bartow pursed his lips and narrowed his eyes. Nicolas could tell the detective understood that the involvement of the FBI in Dobson's murder hadn't been the bureau's idea in the first place. The homicide division had to live with the consequences.

Bartow lifted his hands and stepped back. "Okay. I'll leave the cases with you."

Jason glared at him but settled with a nod and sat down to resume typing his report.

Nicolas let out his breath when Bartow was out of earshot. "You pushed him."

"He didn't investigate as thoroughly as he should have. The ME neglected evidence. I don't think they're both completely overworked, so they have no excuses. They missed the key points."

"Still, you have nothing more than a hunch. Maybe the death of Mr. Glandale was committed by the same killer, but the rest . . ."

Jason shook his head. "I can't change the fact that the false Miss Olbridge hasn't shown to enlighten us. Maybe she left the country."

Nicolas frowned. "The men have a connection—the abuse of their wives and kids. What about the women? All of them had an interest in getting rid of their partners."

"Let's see what we can find about them. I already tried to call Mrs. Garibaldi, but she wasn't home."

"Where are we going?" Matthew asked, approaching the desk. He rubbed his hands and smiled broadly. "Yeah, you missed me, right? What's up?"

"You're the one I was looking for," Jason said, returning the smile. "You're so great with women that I expect you to find the right words to talk to two widows who won't admit that they had anything to do with the deaths of their husbands. I want to prove the opposite."

"You were looking for me?" Matthew opened his eyes wide and pointed to his chest. "For me, who took a bullet for you? I'm honored."

Before Jason could protest, Nicolas asked, "How're you feeling?"

"Like a train hit me, but I'm all right."

Jason understood Nicolas's warning glance and continued. "Concerning the Dobson murder, we're stuck. Family and friends have alibis or no motive at all. There are no leaks, no money transfers. We have Morrison and the widow under surveillance, but they both deny a romantic affair, and according to Nicolas, we can't prove Morrison's involvement in the murder. So I turned to the other murder cases—they have one thing in common—the widows were abused for a long time. I know from the photographs that Mrs. Madison knew about the support-group at the St. Mary's Medical Center in Richmond. She had a flyer on the kitchen table. For now, that's a link to Mrs. Dobson, though she denies having been there. The nurse at the hospital, though, confirms she saw her with a suitcase walking toward the room of the support-group."

Nicolas waved a hand. "We won't get a court order to search the support group's files based on those facts. The DA respects the privacy of such organizations to protect the victims."

"Besides the widows, we can ask their friends," Matthew said, lifting a hand. "We can ask if they sought support and check their backgrounds."

"It's obvious the killer wanted to make it look like accidents, and I bet he succeeded in many cases." Nicolas pointed toward the steep pile of files. "He helped the women out of their misery. There's no doubt about that. But how did he choose the victims? How did he get to know about them?"

Matthew nodded. "You want me to use my charm and get the right answers out of the women? I can do that."

"If my theory applies, the women may have met somewhere, joined the same club, had the same hobbies. Who knows? There has to be a connection."

"Or they even visited the same support-group at St. Mary's, but we can't learn any more if they all keep their mouths shut. Well, first I'll ask Mrs. Madison what she did there." Matthew leaned against the desk on the other side of the aisle, much to the chagrin of the detective sitting at his computer. He frowned. "The killer works with methods that can be called *low key*. He wasn't out for spectacular killings but for causes of death that wouldn't be investigated too much."

"That's right." Jason lifted and dropped his shoulders. "Sorry, it's only a hunch. And the murder of Dobson doesn't fit that MO. That bothers me, too."

"Who's with me on this? Nicolas?"

"Sure." Nicolas took his jacket and, glancing at Jason, left the office behind Matthew, who sauntered out, singing *The One I Love*.

Six hours later, Nicolas admitted that even with Matthew's fine-tuned voice and subtle questioning, they were no closer to solving the cases than when they'd left the office.

The first widow, Mrs. Madison, complained about police harassment and that she had answered all the questions three months ago. She was in a new relationship and didn't want to be reminded of the *bag full of shit* that she called her former husband. She repeated that he had been drunk as always and had collapsed in the bathroom where he—to his misfortune leading to his death—had toppled over a rug and fallen into the full bathtub. The ME concluded the man had drowned. She admitted she had sought help with a support-group, but claimed the meetings with like-minded people hadn't helped her at all. She refused permission to exhume Mr. Madison, claiming the case was closed, and she wished the agents a good day.

"We barely got past a kick in the butt," Matthew said on the way back to the car. "It's clear she's happy to be rid of him. What do we know about her?"

"She has no money to pay a hired killer." Nicolas slipped behind the wheel. "But she has a tall and muscled son. I saw the pictures of him on the shelf in the living room." They exchanged glances. "The police report ruled him out as a suspect. He had an alibi."

Matthew shook his head. "Could be false. Do you want to check on him? Shake the tree?"

"We can try."

Mr. Madison junior's alibi stood up to further inquiries, and Nicolas and Matthew drove on to Mrs. Newark. She was astonished the FBI showed up on her doorstep, but invited them in, offering coffee and cookies, and chatted about her deceased husband as if he hadn't been a bruiser who had repeatedly beaten her senseless. Nicolas assumed that eight months were a sufficient time for her to overcome her grief as well as her anger. Mrs. Newark looked healthy, and the apartment reflected the hobbies of a sporty woman—she owned a treadmill, a yoga mat, and several light-weight barbells. A shelf was filled with books and DVDs about a healthy lifestyle. There were no pictures of her deceased husband anywhere.

In retrospect—so she told Nicolas and Matthew—Mr. Newark had been a troubled soul who couldn't be blamed for his misbehavior. He'd had a bad childhood and little fun in life. He hadn't deserved to die of electrocution. In Mrs. Newark's eyes, her husband should have lived to find a way to improve his behavior.

Nicolas covered his confusion by asking her about the accident. Mrs. Newark reported that her husband had been working in their garage, and the chain saw's power cord must have been damaged by age. Upon touching it, Mr. Newark had been electrocuted and died within seconds.

"Did you seek help with a support-group before the accident?"

Mrs. Newark lowered her chin, then, as if it didn't matter anymore, shrugged. "Yeah, I tried that. They're kind people and offered help to deal with my problems, but . . . I couldn't do what they wanted—leave my husband."

"Was it the one at the St. Mary's Medical Center?"

When she nodded, Matthew cleared his throat. "Did you make friends with anyone there?"

"No, not really. Like I said, they couldn't help me, and I didn't like Mrs. Nyeburn. She's quite arrogant, but that's only my two cents."

"We had a look into your financials, Mrs. Newark, and

there's a five thousand dollars cash withdrawal listed one week prior to your husband's death. Would you please explain this?"

Mrs. Newark's cheeriness was replaced by open scorn. "Why are you concerned about my money?"

"Please, tell us what you did with it."

She sat up straight in her chair and looked at Matthew with growing anger. "I lent it to a friend. And that's all I'll tell you about it. I know a lawyer, and if you want to ask more questions, I won't say a word without her at my side. Now, leave me. The case was closed months ago."

"We would like to exhume your—"

"He was cremated."

"Another one bites the dust." Matthew slumped on the passenger seat and drummed the rhythm on the dashboard. "Summing up—"

"Don't do it." Nicolas started the engine and filtered into the traffic.

"Yes, they each had the chance to commit murder and make it look like an accident. Maybe the women knew and helped each other." His face lit up to a bright smile. "Like in *Strangers on a Train*. You know—"

"Yes, I know. The perfect crime. It doesn't exist. But there's one aspect that we have not yet sufficiently addressed—the hospital."

Nicolas learned from Jason in a short telephone call that two hospitals were involved concerning the possible murders they were investigating. One of them was the St. Mary's Medical Center Mrs. Dobson had chosen to have her son treated at. Jason also reported that Mrs. Garibaldi had been treated at the same ER. She had admitted she knew of the support-group, but stated she hadn't visited the support-center. She claimed that no one could help because whatever she had tried in the past years, her situation had worsened. Jason added that Mrs. Glandale had never contacted the support-group at any hospital, stating she'd been too frightened to do anything that would anger her husband. She confessed tearfully she had tried to leave him, but he had found out and beat her more than ever.

"So, Mrs. Madison came here, too, both to be treated and to join the support group," Matthew said quietly. "And Mrs. Newark and Mrs. Garibaldi knew about it." He approached the counter, showed his ID, and asked to speak with the doctor who had treated Mrs. Madison.

Obviously enjoying Matthew's charm, the nurse told him that they needed to talk to Dr. Llewellyn and where to find him. The ensuing conversation revealed that Dr. Llewellyn had recommended the support-group in the hope the woman would decide to leave the bruiser and escape the punishment.

"But she didn't. She couldn't let go. She claimed that she had no money, didn't know where to go or what to do once she left him. She was afraid he'd follow her and harm her even more. It's the same argument I've heard many times before. The women are stuck, they get hurt, but they're afraid to leave even though staying might kill them in the end." The young doctor ran a hand through his thick brown hair. He stood with his head bowed and flinched as though the memory caused him physical pain. "I urged her to seek the help of a lawyer. Mrs. Nyeburn works at three medical centers, at least. She offers help and says that there are always ways to start a new life." He shrugged. "Maybe she did."

"She obviously did." Matthew couldn't keep the sarcasm out of his voice. "She's in a new relationship and wasn't depressed at all."

"That's good." Dr. Llewellyn lifted his head, but the hurtful expression remained. "Don't get me wrong—I'm a doctor, and I stick to my oath, but the death of Mr. Madison was no loss she should waste her time mourning."

"That's what they all say." Matthew cocked his head. "Do you know if Mrs. Madison found a soul mate and confided in him or her about her misery?"

"I assume she exchanged information with the other members of the support group, but all of them are in the same boat." He shrugged again. "She didn't tell me about her friends, if there were any. Her husband took care that she didn't leave the house for too long or too often. He was a terrible man."

Matthew thanked the doctor for the information and turned to Nicolas. "I'd like to talk to Mrs. Chávez."

"And roam into Detective Bartow's territory? That's not a good idea."

"Let's check what he found out first."

Detective Bartow had already finished the preliminary report about Francesco Chávez's death. He listed the events of the day of his murder in detail and concluded that the deadly dose of drugs must have been given to him an hour or an hour and a half prior to his death.

"That leads us back to St. Mary's Medical Center." Nicolas looked up into Bartow's unhappy face. "What did the staff say about Chávez's treatment?"

"He had cut himself with a saw. His boss sent him to the ER, and the wound was treated and bandaged. He received a shot against tetanus because he couldn't recall when he had the last one. Then he stopped at a bar, drank two beers, and drove home." Bartow shrugged, then shook his head. It was obvious he hated being stuck with a case he couldn't solve. "The doc and the nurse claim they did nothing else, and there was no evidence that they lied. They didn't know Mr. Chávez or have any private connection to him. They were shocked to learn about Mr. Chávez's death."

Jason flipped through another file on his desk. "Mrs. Newark had been treated in the St. Mary's Medical Center, too, but only once, because that day she had an appointment with her dentist, and he urged her to seek medical attention."

Matthew looked from Jason to Detective Bartow. "All right, folks. I'd like to go back to that hospital and have a chat with the staff at the ER. Maybe there's a voodoo group practicing in the basement."

On the way home, Nicolas learned that one of the two remaining snipers, Dwight Mueller, had been arrested. The police had monitored the route from the airfield in Bedford to his hideout via traffic cam footage. He had resisted arrest, but local police forces in association with two FBI agents overwhelmed him in the end.

Nicolas was whistling a tune when he entered his home, but the song died on his lips at seeing Jacklyn and Lesley in clothes which—even combined—wouldn't dress a child.

"Excuse me, but what would've been your plan B if I had brought home my partner?"

Lesley strutted on high heels in his direction, her hips gently swinging and her very upright gait clearly showing off her pert breasts. "I was hoping you'd bring someone with you that I could play with." She pouted, giving him the eye. "Now, what shall I do? Amuse myself?" She put a hand between her legs.

Nicolas had trouble finding his voice. "I'd prefer you didn't." He made eye contact with Jacklyn, looking for help. "I assume you've got something planned? Shall I just leave again?"

"I'd prefer you didn't." Lesley giggled and pulled Nicolas forward by his tie. "We do have plans, and your participation is required."

"Are one of you gonna ask me if I *want* to join in?" Nicolas claimed back his tie with a hard tug. "I might want to watch TV and just relax."

"You can relax." Lesley had her hand around his tie once more, and this time her grip was stronger. Her eyebrows twitched. "As long as you please us."

Nicolas was still at odds with the situation. He took off the tie and left it with Lesley. "Jacklyn, would you mind— "

"The question is—do you mind us playing with you?" Jacklyn stepped closer, waiting for his decision. "We're in the mood. Are you?"

Nicolas swallowed the superfluous question of asking whether this was what it looked like. They were like cats around him, and he was the cream they wanted. The metaphor made him smile, and Jacklyn's assuring glance told him he had nothing to worry about.

"If I don't have to do anything else than relax—I can do that."

"Hmm, sounds good enough to me." Lesley and Jacklyn made eye contact, and Nicolas began to realize he had given up control of the evening. "Take a shower—you need it—and then join us here again."

"I hope your plans include dinner," Nicolas said on the way to the bathroom. "Otherwise, I might get grumpy rather than interested."

"Just relax." Jacklyn waved a hand. "We'll take care of everything."

Nicolas wasn't surprised he ended up in handcuffs and with a blindfold tight across his eyes. He was surprised the women ordered him to lie down on his belly in front of the couch. He heard them settle behind him.

"That's good, my wonderful beast. Now, if you excuse us— " Jacklyn popped some earphones on him and adjusted the volume so the latest pop music kept him out of the women's conversation.

Nicolas was tempted to laugh out loud, but he suspected that might ruin the mood. He rested his head on his crossed hands and let go of all thoughts. He was peaceful, quiet, whatever the music.

Lying on the floor without seeing what the women did or hearing their conversation—*I'm a rug, for God's sake!*—he felt tranquil. He was calm and content with the situation. Lesley's and Jacklyn's feet rested on his back and buttocks, and he relaxed as they massaged his muscles by flexing their toes and pressing down their heels. He grunted and exhaled with bliss. He didn't doubt Jacklyn anymore. She managed to keep him under her heel—in this case literally—and serve him and his wishes at the same time. He couldn't tell if Lesley had the same intentions, and he found he didn't care.

Jill Nyeburn leaned back on the comfortable armchair, a coffee cup in her left hand. She was dressed in light blue pants, an eye-catching raspberry red blouse, and matching high heels. She crossed her legs as she finished her monologue about work ethics—that every patient had the right to be treated fairly and with great care, whatever their standing in life. Even though she wasn't a doctor, the nurses sitting around the large table in Jill's office clung to her words, drinking in the wisdom she provided. She was their friend, their instructor, and in more than a few cases, the wise counselor of every nurse at the hospital. They knew and cherished her support and came to her with a variety of problems that she was always willing to solve. In return, she heard the gossip and received information about doctors and patients alike.

"Are there any further questions?" Jill looked from one nurse to the next, challenging them. "Don't tell me my little speech covered all aspects." She put down her cup and lifted a finger to wave *no*, accompanied by a benevolent smile. "I might come to the conclusion that you slept all through my words and are happy I'm done. Don't forget to take a cookie on the way out. At least they're good." Laughter followed her words. The nurses stood, put back their chairs, and took their cups to the shelf where the coffee maker stood.

"Thank you for the inspiring words, Jill," Kathy Warner said, her freckles shining deeper while she blushed. "It's always a pleasure listening to you."

"It's my pleasure that you come to listen. By the way, what about Mrs. Binkley? How is she today?"

Kathy's smile died. "She was released yesterday. It was her wish. Or so she said. I saw her husband in the corridor. He must've come to drive her home."

"Oh, the poor woman." Jill shook her head. "Couldn't you do anything? Convince Dr. Lubock to let her stay here for another day or two?"

"I'm afraid not. And she claimed she had to take care of her two kids. She wouldn't want them to stay with her husband for too long since the neighbor is afraid to care for them—because of the husband, of course." Kathy made a face. "I'm sorry, Jill, she wanted to leave."

"I see." Jill gently touched Kathy's shoulder to lighten the young nurse's mood. "You did what you could."

"Thank you." Kathy turned away.

"What about the pregnant woman, Mrs. Claridge, who got here three days ago?" Jill stopped Nurse Tessa on the way out.

"She's still here." Tessa was tall and lanky, and only a few people knew she had the strength of a horse if need be. She was the daughter of a rich couple and could've spent her time playing tennis or horseback riding. Instead, she had chosen to work for society. Jill had learned that the nurse donated most of her salary to the women's shelter in Richmond. Tessa beamed at Jill and said with pride, "I convinced her and Doc Esterman that she was far too weak to go home and be burdened with housework. She can't use her right hand, anyway. A complicated fracture that'll hamper her for six weeks. Her husband argued, but we stood firm against him, even when he got angry. Her pregnancy weakens her, there's no doubt. And the fact that Mr. Claridge uses his fists—they have to be the size of cantaloupes—against her, doesn't help the situation, either."

"Very well done," Jill praised.

The nurse blushed.

"Keep up the good work, even if it's hard. We have to protect the victims as best as we can."

"I know. We all do what we can." Tessa put back her cup and ran after Kathy, who was already in the corridor.

"We need to find a way to protect the children, too." Jill pulled a notepad from her desk and scribbled down a few lines. "The women would be more easily convinced to stay if we had a backup plan for their kids."

Nurse Melissa Roberts was the last one to get up. She smiled in reply to Jill's friendly gaze and pushed back a strand of brown hair behind her ear. In her early thirties, she was the most highly trained nurse Jill had ever met. Her face would look hard if it weren't for the large brown eyes that conveyed sincere friendship and understanding.

"You're already planning an extended service?"

"Yes. I realized that more or less every wife with kids refuses to leave her husband because she doesn't know what would become of her children."

"A kindergarten? Like the ones they have at the women's shelter?"

"Something like that, yes."

"You're coming to the *Tae Kwon Do* lesson tonight at eight, right?" Melissa asked. She straightened her ponytail. The lab coat's sleeves slipped up and revealed muscled forearms.

"I'll be there, as always." Jill took the tray with cups and began to put them in the dishwasher. "Do you have news?"

"Mrs. Woolsey will be at the next meeting. I convinced her that if she doesn't leave her marriage soon, she may be crippled in the end. If I read her notes right, she was close to losing the function of her right arm two years ago. It seems to me that her husband let her heal to start hurting her all over again. The thought of leaving him makes her shiver, and I don't think she's got the strength to sever the bond without help. She still believes he might change if he joined a self-support group to control his aggression."

"So many of them believe they will. Poor woman. I hope I can do something for her."

"Yes, I hope so, too." Melissa sighed. "Don't be late."

Jacklyn took away the earphones and ordered Nicolas to get up on all fours. He sensed movement around him, and then Jacklyn slipped under him so that he felt her warm skin against his.

"Hard and horny, hmm? Oh, my wonderful beast, I fear your time to relax is up."

Upon her sensuous touch, his hard erection started throbbing. His lower body trembled when his glans touched her vulva. She guided him inside, and he held his breath, speculating what her next move would be. This wasn't their usual game. This was new and exciting. Jacklyn moved up and down, granting him a glimpse of the satisfaction he was going to experience.

Nicolas felt Lesley's presence. She stood beside his right calf and slapped his butt with a paddle hard enough to sting, but not hard enough to cause harm.

Nicolas twitched. A shower of lust shot through him. He

understood the women's intention and would have smiled if he had dared.

Jacklyn pulled him down to intensify the contact. "Slowly," she warned.

His arms quivered with the effort. He thrust into her, wanting more, dying to increase his pleasure. He clenched his teeth. There was no way to force a climax. Jacklyn knew well what he craved for and would deny it if he was too eager.

Lesley hit him again. Nicolas groaned. The pain was welcome, adding to the pleasure, pushing him along the road to satisfaction. He hadn't expected such a ride, and he had to admit it was more thrilling than playing with Jacklyn alone.

Jacklyn lifted her legs to wrap them around his waist. "Go on."

Her weight didn't bother him, and the angle for his thrusts was much better like this. Nicolas wanted more.

He needed fulfillment.

He felt the climax building inside him.

He was so close.

Lesley hit him harder, but the pain didn't reach him anymore, and it didn't stop him.

Jacklyn moaned deep in her throat. "This is so good. Hold it."

The last two words cut into him like a knife. His hot pulsing cock wanted release. He wanted two more thrusts. That was all.

Lesley closed a ring with a chain around his balls and tugged. The sensation was almost too much to bear. Nicolas grunted, not daring to argue by telling Lesley she shouldn't overplay her hand. She gave in an inch, but still, his craving wasn't dimmed. Quite the opposite—the more Lesley did, the harder he wanted to come.

Jacklyn dug her nails into his shoulders. Even without seeing, he knew she was biting her lower lip. Her trembling grew stronger, even with the little movement he was allowed. Jacklyn bucked under him and screamed out loud. She clung to him rigidly, as if trying to hold him tight with her vulva.

"Harder!" she demanded.

Disregarding the tug on his balls, Nicolas pushed forward, deeper into her, exploring the space as if he'd never been there before. There was no holding back now. The orgasm rolled through him, thunderous in its intensity. For a few seconds, he couldn't make sense of anything. Couldn't tell whether Jacklyn cried or if Lesley slapped him again. He was bathing in a shower of lust that was worth every pain and every elongated minute they stretched out of him.

How he loved to be alive!

CHAPTER THIRTEEN

Like every summer, Melissa Roberts was housesitting the large estate her friends called their home. Victoria and her rich husband, Desmond Morgan, had bought the place four years ago and didn't trust any electronic burglar alarm or security service. They relied on a trustworthy person to check the rooms every night to be sure potential invaders knew there was someone present to defend their belongings.

Melissa was that person. She loved that even the critical, analytical, and no-nonsense businessman Desmond trusted in her abilities. Vicky would've left the house behind and returned without regret, even if it was cleaned out by a gang of drug addicts. But Desmond cherished his wealth and watched over it like a dragon watched over a pile of gold. Melissa and Vicky had spent evenings laughing about Desmond's tendency to list his riches the way most people listed the ingredients for a fine recipe.

Vicky and her husband had left two days before for a trip to the Caribbean to spend some of the money Desmond had made with his construction company. Melissa leaned back on the thick, cushioned sun lounger by the pool. The training with Jill had been excellent, as always. Her girlfriend had picked up the sport in high school and taken a break during her marriage. After the death of her husband, she had searched for ways to compensate for her anger and frustration and gravitated back to her martial arts training. Besides *Tae Kwon Do*, Jill had tried *Kung Fu* and kickboxing. She was an amazing student.

Melissa smiled and closed her eyes. The warm air brought the sounds of the neighborhood toward her.

Being a good observer, Melissa had no difficulty in learning about the closest neighbors within two days. The Millers to her left were old and almost deaf. Their conversations were loud and turned around the weather and the choice of plants to buy from the local store. The Norads across the street to the right liked to show their wealth and spent a lot of time driving their cars—three at that time—in and out of the large garage. The engines howled every time as if to announce a great revelation. They arranged barbeques and chatted with friends about automobile brands, horsepower, custom-made parts, and leather upholstery—prices not included. Melissa owned an old *Honda Civic* and was regarded with silent scowls, as if her old car reduced the value of the Norads's *Mercedes, GM,* and *Lexus.*

On the other side of the street lived Jill Nyeburn. The house was the biggest, with much glass, sharp edges, well-trimmed hedges, and manicured arborvitaes. The garden consisted of a lawn every golf pro would envy. Anyone with the guts could jump from the porch on the first floor into the large, oval-shaped pool. Though an intriguing concept, it had never been attempted. No one sat in the beautiful garden, either.

Melissa sighed. Her mind traveled back in time, and she remembered one of the quarrels Mr. and Mrs. Nyeburn had fought on the patio.

The subject varied between *You work too much* and *My family expects us to have children*. Donald was bickering for the umpteenth time that Jill should take care of her health and do something about her fertility. When she barked that she loved her work and wouldn't quit during her lifetime to become a housewife, Melissa heard the smack of a nasty slap to Jill's face. Jill cried out, called him an *asshole without brains or manners,* and reached for a vase. Melissa heard the porcelain explode into pieces on the stone floor. Another slap had followed, and Jill must have hit a chair. Something tumbled to the ground while Jill cried out again, louder this time. Then the big glass door was closed with a swing. Donald rambled about the *frigid, ignorant bitch* he had married, rammed his fists against a shelf so that another pot with flowers crashed on the floor, then opened the door again to vanish inside, announcing he would teach her manners.

Melissa opened her eyes and wiped away tears. Even now, she trembled with horror about what she had overheard that night. She took comfort in the fact that Jill was much better now—without the bastard and with a job she loved. Jill was Melissa's role model—a woman who had gone through hell to come back with more strength and determination. Jill had shown courage, where others had faltered and given up.

Melissa looked up to the evening sky that turned from gold to purple and lifted her cup of herbal tea to toast the brave woman she called her friend.

It was a good night.

Matthew received the report of Dwight Mueller's interrogation and whistled softly.

While Sanders had kept his mouth shut, Mueller was out for a deal to cut his time in prison by half. The DA was willing to accept it if Mueller offered substantial information. Mueller confirmed the three men had been working for a woman referred to as *Miss Copper Head* because she had never revealed her true name. She had made the plans for the liberation of the twins and had also told them how to escape. Mueller was convinced the woman wouldn't leave the country if there was one sibling still alive that she could try to get free.

Matthew shared the report via email with Jason and Nicolas. He had the feeling that Katherine Nelson wouldn't be taken into custody easily.

Jacklyn was still in high spirits after the shower. She slipped into comfortable pants and shirt and hugged Nicolas on the way through the bedroom.

"Thank you. You were an outstanding beast tonight. I love you so much."

"My pleasure." He kissed her forehead. "No matter how often we play this game—I can't help but wonder why you chose to become a mistress. It's not a job I'd expect from the daughter of a diplomat."

She leaned back in his arms and gently caressed the curve of his ear. "No, not really. But as a diplomat's daughter, I lived to see a lot of men. I noticed their power, their hunger, their possessiveness, and their blatant arrogance. They held important and influential positions, and they knew how to use them excessively. More often than not, those men were accompanied by shy, devoted women, who didn't say a word. They didn't protest when they were scolded in public. I witnessed how the high-ranking member of the diplomatic corps backhanded his wife. She said *thank you* and bowed to him. I swore I'd never become a man's floozie, a toy, a willing follower. I swore I'd rather live alone than bow to a man's obsessive wishes."

"Did you ever suffer . . ."

She frowned. "Do you want to know whether I was raped? No. My father took care of my mother and me. We were guarded when we left the hotel or residence, no matter what country we visited. No, I never became a victim . . .close to, but, no, it never happened. But those events showed me that

I'd never want to be the inferior partner, no matter my strength or whether I could defend myself. That being said, you'll understand my position when it comes to bondage games."

He kissed her lips. "I do. So it's the part of utmost control that arouses you like nothing else could."

Jacklyn grinned. "You're a clever agent. I know why the FBI chose you."

After more fondling and kissing, they made it downstairs again. Lesley had showered, dressed, and ordered Chinese take-out food for three in the short time they were gone. In casual, tight jeans and a midriff shirt, she looked like a mature student and not like the owner of erotic shops and a dungeon. Nicolas marveled at how versatile Lesley truly was.

She sat down, pulled up her legs, and clapped with the chopsticks. "Come on, girls, I'm hungry."

"Me first!" Nicolas sat down, pulled all the food boxes to his place, and guarded them with his long arms. "That's mine. What do you want to eat?"

"Ha!" Lesley attacked him with the chopsticks, and when he sent them flying across the table, she got up to work her fists on his arm and shoulder. "I'll get my share, don't you worry! Never underestimate a hungry mistress!"

Nicolas was close to dying with laughter. He hadn't known she possessed a playful streak, and when she pretended to bite off his nose, he relented and generously offered her two boxes and some rice.

Both turned their heads, astonished to find Jacklyn already eating.

She shrugged. "I love to see a good fight, but right now, I'm starving. I guess I lost a pound or two in the last hour."

"What about me?" Nicolas asked and claimed back the food. "I had the hardest part."

Lesley and Jacklyn exchanged glances, then burst out

laughing. "Yep, undeniably—yes!"

Jason looked up from the desk as Nicolas entered the large office. "Wow, look at you! You fucking know how to use your virility. You're radiating satisfaction."

Nicolas frowned and took off his jacket. "What do you mean?"

"You look so damn rested, as if you've been on vacation. That woman's good for you. Definitely." He shook his head. "Go, get yourself a cup of coffee. I can't stand your obnoxious, self-satisfied expression for more than a few seconds, or I'm gonna puke."

"All right." Nicolas helped himself, and when he sat down, Matthew arrived. "And how are you today?"

Matthew opened his mouth, closed it, and narrowed his eyes. "You're much too chipper this morning. Did she do you right?"

Jason chuckled and pointed a finger at Nicolas. "I told you."

Nicolas knew it was useless to pretend he wasn't in high spirits. "You got me. Yeah, I had a great evening. Anything about our case?"

"Not much to keep you in your great mood." Matthew summed up his conversation with Mrs. Chávez and the ER crew he had questioned. "The ladies and gentlemen working at the ER are professionals, and if one of them prepared drugs to kill Mr. Chávez, he or she knew well how to hide any evidence. The drug found in Mr. Chávez is available throughout the hospital—nothing special that someone had to smuggle inside or that could be traced to one employee. About Mrs. Chávez—she knew of the group, and Nyeburn and Billingham had both tried to convince her that there was a way out of her marriage. Mrs. Chávez explained to me that God had wanted couples to stay together until death parted them, not any other way. And she wouldn't have left him, even if the kid got hurt again. I read in her eyes that the idea of acting against God's wish horrified her." He shook his head. "If you ask me—the connection is the Medical Center, and I bet the support-group, is in the center of it all."

"Agreed." Nicolas took a deep breath. "I mulled this over, all night." He ignored the knowing look shared by the other two and their barely quashed guffaws and continued, "Tell me, what shoe size did the CSU find?"

Jason called up the file on his computer. "A nine, maybe a ten."

"We already assumed that they wore overshoes to avoid usable footprints. What if they have small feet—women's feet?"

"Are you insane? Or did you catch too much sun? Remember the brutality?"

"We haven't found the false realtor. And the real one was knocked out by a cake she got. This was well planned and executed with a lot of knowledge about the circumstances and the drugs. What if the woman was one of the killers and had an accomplice?"

Matthew grinned. "Are we back to *Strangers on a Train*?"

"Maybe. Let's play this—"

Jason held up his hand. "No, wait. I want to know where this idea comes from."

"No, you don't."

Jason nodded, emphasizing his words with a broad grin. "Now, I want to know for sure."

Matthew lifted a finger. "Me, too."

Nicolas huffed and waved away their curiosity. "Two women. They know the abused wives. They know the circumstances and that the wives won't leave their husbands, especially not the wife of the deputy mayor. And it explains why the swings with the bat were so low."

"You mean we should have another look at the hospital staff? We've been through them, and nothing showed. Nada."

"They won't be easily spotted. A nurse, for example, could provide a person outside the hospital with information and let someone else do the wet work. I bet there are a lot of angry women who'd love to act out their revenge. Just think of it—the women claimed they attended the support group but didn't consider the meetings helpful. But they profited immensely—their lives changed for the better after their husbands' deaths."

Jason rubbed his eyes. "I don't want to imagine two women committing such a brutal murder."

Matthew lifted his butt off the desk. "That doesn't mean it can't be. The false realtor is the key. I'll show her picture around again at the hospital and also at the shops in the street."

He left, and Jason turned around, eyes wide and demanding. "Now that he's gone, tell me about the source of your idea."

"The stylish connoisseur enjoys and remains silent," Nicolas replied smugly.

"Oh, come on, buddy, that's not fair. No, if you don't tell it's a special kind of torture, you're putting me through."

"Torture—interesting word."

"I want to know what you did that left you thinking about the size of women's feet." Jason kept staring at Nicolas. "And you can bet your next nocturnal activities that I won't back off."

"What about your wedding date? Any news?"

"Ah, you son of a bitch, don't change the subject. We set a date in November, if you really want to know. Invitations are in the making." Jason tapped the desk. "Come on. Share it with me."

Nicolas bent forward to go on secretively with a wink. "It

was a great night. Jacklyn massaged my back with her feet."

"And you?"

"I didn't massage hers." Nicolas grinned. "I'd break her ribs if I tried."

"We're convinced that the staff of the support group and some members are involved in the murders we uncovered," Jason said, trying to keep a hold on his temper.

Senior Agent Sullivan, on the other side of the line, huffed. "You were sent to investigate the mayor's murder, not to snoop around in old cases of the homicide division."

"There might be a connection, sir."

"Ah, another of those famous hunches of yours, or should I say infamous?"

"Yes, sir, the evidence tells us these cases might be connected. The women had information about the support group, and most of them were members until their husbands died."

"But the MO doesn't fit." Sullivan was grumpy. "Why did they bash the deputy mayor and not the others?"

As always, the boss was trying to find the flaws in Jason's cases, but after all, that was what he was paid for. Still, it didn't endear him to Jason, and because Sullivan couldn't see him, he rolled his eyes knowingly.

"You just said the men were killed and their deaths were cloaked to look like accidents. Dobson's murder was—"

"A screaming mess," Jason replied, sighing. "Yes, sir, I admit we're still looking for the one clue that will explain the connection."

"What about the other criminal who sent Agent Lawry on an irrelevant chase?"

"Nothing so far. I'm convinced it was a copycat, sir, who tried to sound important."

"All right, then, proceed. Inform me about your progress.

Daily."

Jason put down the receiver and looked into Nicolas's expectant face. "We'd better make progress soon, or Sullivan will hand the case to someone else."

"Well, at least you haven't lost your head yet." Nicolas grabbed his jacket. "Let's go see Mrs. Dobson again."

This time, Mrs. Dobson's expression hardened the moment she became aware the FBI had returned for yet another questioning. Her sister Annie was at her side, and her anger showed immediately.

"Why can't you leave her alone, damn it?" She crossed her arms and planted her feet apart as if to keep Jason and Nicolas from crossing the hall. "Or did you come to tell her you found her husband's murderer?"

"No, not yet." Nicolas tried for a soothing tone. "Please, Miss Hancock, Mrs. Dobson, let us take a seat so that we can talk."

"We buried him yesterday," Mrs. Dobson said meekly on the way to the dining room. She flinched. "It was awful. All those speeches . . . glorifying Buck as if he'd been a saint. I want this situation over. I want to make peace with myself and take up my life again. Don't you understand that?"

"We do." Jason pulled a chair out for her, then for Annie. "We hope that you understand that Mr. Morrison is still a suspect, and if you want his name cleared, you'd better tell us about the night you took your son to the ER at St. Mary's. We know you had a suitcase with you. We have a pretty clear idea of what happened that night, but only you can tell us the truth."

Mrs. Dobson lowered her chin, and Nicolas saw tears trickle down her cheeks. Annie provided a handkerchief, glaring at Jason as if he tore open old wounds. Both agents waited patiently for Mrs. Dobson to find her voice again.

"I wanted to leave Buck—for Clark's sake. Buck had been so angry, so . . . beside himself. First he threw me against the old cupboard, and then, when Clark tried to help me get up, he pushed him away . . . down the stairs, like you'd do with a burglar. My son . . . he cried out, and that cry . . ." She broke down, weeping uncontrollably.

"Fine, agent, is that what you wanted?" Annie looked close to spitting at Nicolas as she took her sister in her arms. "He was an asshole. Isn't that enough? He's six feet under now, right where he belongs. Whatever else does she need to tell you?"

"Did you intend to return home that night?"

Mrs. Dobson shook her head. "I was so afraid. I knew they wouldn't keep us overnight at the hospital, but I didn't want to come home. I talked with a nurse, and she took me to Mrs. Nyeburn. She had offered a safe haven before, if ever the situation at home became unbearable. And that night . . . with Clark being injured so badly . . . I still remember his cry when he hit the floor." She shook her head. "I'd had enough. I wanted out, but I didn't know how. However, in the end, I had no strength to resist Buck. His argument was believable. And he seemed to honestly regret his actions. You must understand—I didn't want to ruin his career, his life. He'd worked so hard for this election, and Fitch always stressed that the public appearance was everything. One wrong move could ruin everything."

Jason made eye contact with Nicolas and waited for him to nod.

"Mrs. Dobson, what was the reaction of Mrs. Nyeburn and of others present at that time?"

Mrs. Dobson looked up, irritated. "Mrs. Nyeburn argued with Buck for a minute, but when I declared that I'd leave with him if only to avoid a scene, she gave in, claiming that she had a different opinion but wouldn't interfere with my wishes." She shrugged. "Some nurses might've seen us, but I don't know their names."

"Thank you, Mrs. Dobson." Jason put away his notebook. "If you remember anything else, please, feel free to call us."

"Do you think Mrs. Nyeburn has something to do with my husband's murder?"

"We don't know yet." Nicolas frowned with sympathy. "We'll keep you informed."

"The net tightens," Matthew summed up their investigation after Nicolas's and Jason's report. "The support group hired some unknown persons to find out about Dobson's whereabouts that morning and made arrangements to kill him in cold blood." He snapped his fingers. "And suddenly Mrs. Dobson is out of her misery and can raise her son as she pleases. Not to mention that she inherits a lot of money."

"She was faithful to him until the very end." Jason leaned back on his chair. "I don't believe she initiated her husband's killing. And Annie? I'm not sure whether she contacted someone she trusted. If so, we don't have the smallest lead."

"Let's put Nyeburn under close surveillance." Nicolas made a call to the agents of the department and explained the situation. "Let's see what she does after hours and who she calls while at home."

Nicolas smelled a rich and flowery perfume on his way into the hall. He knew Jacklyn couldn't be home already. She had explained she had to work late, relying on Nicolas's and Tom's bar meeting as they did almost every Friday. But then Tom had canceled their meeting, so Nicolas had driven home. He left his badge and gun on the table in the hall and walked toward the dining room.

In the kitchen, Jacklyn's aunt, Georgette, was busy emptying paper bags. She turned with a broad smile. As usual, her wardrobe was colorful, exclusive, and reflected her young soul much more than her age.

"Oh, I know, I shouldn't be here, and I know you didn't expect anyone at your home, but, hey, here I am! I thought I could do something useful before I drove to my hotel. I bought something to eat for the two of you." She embraced Nicolas. "Ah, all those muscles! Do you work out whenever you aren't working on a case?"

"Sometimes." Nicolas took off shoes and jacket, still nonplussed by Georgette's presence. "Did I miss something?"

"No." She handed him a glass of orange juice. "I'm in DC for a few days, and after my meetings, I decided to drop by. Jacklyn left a key for me in case I had to let myself in." She stretched her arms out. The wide sleeves of her blouse reminded Nicolas of angel wings. "See? Here I am."

Nicolas sat down at the table she had set for two. "Yes, I can see that." He wanted to ask her a question, but she was faster.

"You're looking good. This relationship is good for you." She put a glass of water on the table and rested her hands on the back of a chair. "And for Jacklyn, too, of course." She gave him a knowing look.

"Thanks." He drank and ran a hand through his hair. He was tired but tried not to show it. "How are you?"

She made a dismissive gesture. "Oh, I'm an old lady who tours the world as long as possible. I closed a nice deal today, but that was boring business. You know, the usual things." Georgette went into the kitchen to fill the refrigerator with the groceries she'd bought. "But don't talk about me. I'm here to see how you and Jacklyn are getting along."

"We're fine, thank you."

She turned her attention from the fridge to look at him.

"When you two met, I couldn't explain why she chose you—young, good-looking dude, but I learned that she trusts you very much. She tells me every time I call her. I mean, you could wrestle her to the ground if you wished. And you wouldn't even break into a sweat."

"I'd never attack my lady."

Georgette's look was sly. She closed the fridge with her butt. "I know all about this dominatrix-adventure. I think I was the only one she confided in when she started that job."

"She changed jobs."

"I know that, too." Georgette rejected Nicolas's helping gesture and opened a bottle of red wine. "Don't try to digress. You're her lover, and I bet you submit to her."

"Why?"

She handed Nicolas a full glass and set the bottle aside before she sat down. "Otherwise, she wouldn't be able to stand this relationship." She let the wine turn in her own glass and sighed contentedly. Her large golden earrings twinkled in the sunlight beaming in through the window. "Believe me when I tell you, son, that your relationship with her is the longest I've known her to have. She's had lovers, yes, but she got rid of them once the thrill was gone." She waved her hands high in the air. "You know, first, you thrive on a wave of lust, but after a while, the glamor is gone, and you ask yourself whether there's more in the relationship than great sex . . . and it turns out there isn't."

"And she left the other guys?" Nicolas took a swig of wine even though his stomach was empty. He felt like he needed the booze to cope with Georgette's surprising revelations.

"Yes, all of them. She claimed the thrill was gone when the gentlemen wanted to settle down with her. One of them announced his retirement plans three months after they got together."

"He was that old?" Nicolas could not imagine Jacklyn in

the arms of a man twice her age.

"No, he was a filthy rich company owner who thought he'd won a lottery prize. He wanted to marry Jacklyn on the spot, and you can bet your meager salary he would've carried her away—in the figurative sense." She lifted and dropped her hand. "He wasn't that strong."

"She walked away?" Nicolas found out his glass was somehow empty.

Georgette refilled it with a knowing glance.

"From a marriage?"

Georgette snorted in a not very ladylike manner. "She rolled her eyes, complained that the guy was boring in capital letters, and angered her mom and dad because they had been happy about that connection. In her defense—the filthy rich putz had asked her parents first."

"How stupid is that?"

"I said he was rich. I didn't say he had a brain." She lifted her glass in his direction. "This is to you, Nicolas, because you managed what others couldn't do—you've satisfied her for more than three months."

"More than two years now." He took another swig of wine and felt the alcohol kick in. "She never mentioned that she'd been close to marrying one of her lovers."

"Are you out to marry her?"

"That question again?"

"Forgive an old lady for asking."

"We haven't talked about it, and I'm in no hurry."

"Well, that's good for now, but you can't dodge the question forever."

"If she can, I can, too."

"Ah, are you insinuating that her parents want to push her into something?" She waved her finger, making the large diamond ring sparkle. "They won't try. You aren't that rich. And they've lived with her long enough to know that Jacklyn doesn't allow herself to be pushed into anything."

"Are they really looking for more money in the family? I mean, they're rich. Why do they care?"

Georgette took a deep breath and looked at him as if teaching a young buck the reality of the world. "Money marries money. If my sister had anything to say, she'd find my niece a rich guy with good manners without regard for age or looks. But Jacklyn always had a mind of her own. She doesn't give a shit for what her parents want. You're good for her."

Nicolas smiled. "A submissive man?" He drank another swig of wine. The alcohol made him feel good. "I bow to her and let her spank me."

"And during the daytime, you're an excellent police officer."

"Special agent."

"Whatever. What I'm saying is—you aren't helpless in real life. You know what you're worth. Jacklyn plays fantasy games with you because you're strong, and you're a damn good player. That's what counts. Happiness, Nicolas, is so hard to find. Forget what my sister wants or that she judges you by your income. No one changes her." She put her hand over his on the table. "Promise me that you'll never be ashamed of your position in this fantasy that you both love."

Her words touched Nicolas. "I'm not ashamed. I agreed to her games in the first place. I admit that I'm still like an apprentice she needs to teach the moves."

She nodded. "And she's taking you further on that road. Remember to stay honest. You don't have to accept any move she makes if you don't want to. She would never violate your rules."

"My rules? I don't think I have any."

"Oh, but you do." She emptied her glass. "Jacklyn stresses that she watches you closely, always aware of your expression. Though she's eager to play, you don't have to worry."

"Good to know." He lowered his gaze. "Sometimes, she's so deep in her fantasy world that I feel like I'm just a guy she met somewhere to have fun."

Georgette frowned as she cocked her head. "No. She'd never do that. She's in the game, yes, but she doesn't treat you like a toy. You mean too much to her."

"Enough that she shares me with Lesley."

"Not in the true sense, right?"

Nicolas was astonished at how easily he talked with this elderly lady about his sex life. "No. She's a watcher and the one with the paddle. Or the whip. That depends."

"Lesley is a hardcore dominatrix." Georgette smacked her lips as if disagreeing with Lesley's way of life. "She thrives on the pain of men, wants them under her heels twenty-four-seven. If you ever meet one of her subs, you'll be surprised what a man allows to be done to him." She shook her head. "I'm not saying she's overstepping a line here, because all of the men in her dungeon agree to that treatment. But I think she enjoys her power very much. She's a good friend, though, a lioness if strength is needed. She'd never back off if Jacklyn needed help." Georgette lifted a hand when Nicolas was about to protest. "The help of a woman. A female support." Once more, she patted his hand. "For all other matters, you're the one." She checked her watch, stood, and sighed. "I'll be on my way. I'm going to meet a long-time customer who wants to invite me for dinner at some fancy food palace. I bet the servings are so small I'll have to search for them under the lettuce. I'm happy that I had a decent lunch."

Smiling, Nicolas stood and accompanied her to the door. "Your car?"

"Parked at the curb." She took her handbag as he opened the door. "I don't mind walking a few steps. Keeps me healthy. And you are a true gentleman, who—" She stopped, the words hanging on the air, forgotten.

In front of them stood a black-haired woman. Her powdered face, though beautiful in many ways, was contorted with rage. Her look alone would have made any person step back, but the gun in her outstretched hand caused Nicolas and Georgette to recoil immediately.

"Hands up and back into the house! Now!" the woman ordered.

Nick recognized the gun as a *Beretta 87 Target* with a ten-bullet capacity. It was a weapon with an easy pull, and at this close range, a .22 bullet would kill instantly.

"Oh, my—" Georgette put her hands on her heart, stumbled back on weak knees, and reached for the table rim, crying out in pain.

Nicolas tried to stop her fall, but the woman yelled at him. "No! Step away from her, or I'll shoot!"

Georgette dropped to the floor with yet another pitiful cry, and didn't move anymore.

"I must—" Nicolas made another move in her direction, concerned whether Georgette had suffered a heart attack.

The woman slammed the door shut and made a step across the unconscious woman. "Away from her! Go!"

With his hands raised, Nicolas went backward from the semi-darkness of the hallway into the sunlit dining room. He tried to see Georgette, but the shadows were deep. Behind him, someone smashed the glass of the back door. There was the sound of careful steps on the crunching shards as the woman's accomplice entered the house. Nicolas desperately wracked his brain for a way out, a means to stop the attacker, but she was keeping a safe distance, and from her furious expression, he knew he'd best not provoke her. His hopes of getting out of this situation alive began to dwindle.

"What do you want?" he asked.

"You. Dead. Slowly."

He stopped as his butt hit the table. "I don't—"

"Don't claim you don't know me, you bastard! You killed my brothers, and now your time's up."

Nicolas couldn't do more than whisper, his gaze moving from the gun to the woman and back again. "Katherine Nelson." She had a finger around the trigger and waited for him to make a move. Her gaze was murderous. Instinct told him he had to fight or risk losing his life when she was done talking. "Your brothers didn't leave us a choice. They fired at us."

"Don't you dare defend yourself!" she screamed, then tightened her finger around the trigger. "You killed him in cold blood!"

Nicolas twitched, fearing that anger would overwhelm her and she'd throw her plan to the wind and shoot his face. He broke into a sweat, failing to find any words to soothe her. Out of the corner of his eye, he saw a broad-shouldered man in jeans and leather jacket move into the room, cautiously scanning the corners as if he expected trouble by another person. Though Nicolas didn't take a look, he expected the man to be armed.

Katherine grimaced, showing her teeth like a wolf. She obviously perceived Nicolas's distress and was enjoying it. "I killed your partner, Montagna, that miserable bugger. He didn't see me coming, and he stank of fear just like you do. Oh, how he whined to let him live."

Nicolas tried in vain to hide his shock. "You killed Matt?"

"Oh, yes, I did. I tied him to a chair and killed him slowly—a hundred small wounds—just like he did with my brother on the parking lot. I watched him bleed out, real slow. He cried like a girl, begged me to spare him, but I didn't."

Nicolas had trouble breathing. He had seen enough dying people to imagine Matthew bleeding his life out on the floor of his apartment. "Oh my god. That'll take you to death row."

"Shut up!" Katherine threw caution in the wind and made a step forward. "You miserable sucker! You'll crawl before me, bleeding and groaning, and then you'll die, just like your partner."

As she moved forward, Nicolas was quicker. He grabbed Katherine's wrist with both hands and turned the weapon away from his body. A bullet flew with a crack, and it missed her crony by only inches, making him dive for cover to the right, leveling his gun as he fell. Nicolas wrested the *Beretta* from Katherine's hand, and it tumbled to the ground. He pulled her around as a shield against the man's shots. Katherine let out a hate-filled scream and tried to bite his nose. She put all her weight into the attack, seeking to unbalance her opponent and wrestle free. Nicolas stumbled against the table but kept his balance, breaking Katherine's wrist with one hard jerk of his hand. She cried out, her fury turning to pain for a second, but still tried to escape his grip. In her rage, she was much stronger than she looked, and he had no choice but to slam his fist against her temple. Nicolas hit her again and stood for a second over her unconscious body, gasping.

Two shots twanged horribly close to Nicolas's ear. He looked up, afraid the accomplice had him cornered. Instead, he watched the man break down on the carpet, groaning. The gun slipped from his hand, and Nicolas hurried to push it away. Blood oozed from a wound at the man's chest. Irrationally, Nicolas thought about the soiled carpet and what Jacklyn would say seeing the mess.

"Georgette?" He squinted into the hall, where she knelt on the floor. "Are you all right?" He crouched beside her, astonished that she held his *Glock 22* in both hands. "Give it to me."

Georgette looked up as he took the weapon from her. "Is he dead?" Her voice was void of any emotion. "And what about her?"

Nicolas helped her stand. "I knocked her out. He—I'd say you got him."

"Good." She smoothed her skirt and pushed back a strand

of stray hair, though it had little effect on the overall mess she had made of her hairdo. "He didn't deserve any better."

"You—"

"I told you I was an army pilot. I know how to shoot, sweetheart."

"But you—"

"I broke down, yes. I'm an actress, too." She made a face. "And you're bleeding. He almost got you."

"What?"

"Your cheek. I think you need a medic." She stopped his hand as he was about to touch the wound. "That was close."

"Yes . . . yes, it was."

Two policemen in uniform stormed through the broken door and stopped when they saw the lifeless body on the floor. "I'll be damned," the first one mumbled, a young Latino with a crew cut and a slim goatee. He lowered his weapon, sighing and shaking his head.

Nicolas put away his gun. "I'm glad you're here."

The young officer made a face. "A little late, huh?"

"The situation's under control," Nicolas replied, shrugging. "You couldn't know—"

"We had the job of protecting you. Didn't really work out well."

Nicolas frowned. "You were assigned to be here?"

"Yes, we were." The Latino looked like a teenager who'd missed an important test at school. "And these people are—"

"Katherine Nelson and one of her flunkies. I don't know him."

"He's dead?" the second officer asked and looked from Georgette to Nicolas.

"Yes, shot before he could shoot me." When Nicolas put a hand to his burning cheek, his fingers came back bloodied. He stopped himself from thinking about how close he had been to being severely wounded. "I'll give you my full statement later."

"All right."

The police officers pulled Katherine Nelson to her feet as she slowly regained consciousness. She glared at Nicolas, but as she was about to speak, the officer pulled her arms across her back, forcing a scream of pain. He locked the handcuffs locked around her wrists, disregarding the injuries.

"We'll take it from here, sir." They pulled Katherine through the front door and her delayed curses ebbed away.

Two black-and-whites appeared at the curb, and within two minutes, the house was filled with cops, asking questions about Katherine and her unknown accomplice, who had died unceremoniously by a shot to his heart.

"You don't take prisoners, do you, Georgette, hmm?" Nicolas asked quietly.

"Like I said—army, but not the *Salvation Army.*" She had turned pale. "I'm shaky on my feet. If you don't mind—"

Nicolas escorted her to the table in the dining room. He brought her a glass of whiskey, and she gulped it down.

"Better?"

"Leave that one with me." She waved a trembling hand as if the bottle would fly to her if she wished.

Nicolas put it in front of her. "But your date—"

"I'll cancel dinner. I can't sit at a fancy restaurant tonight and eat while I think of you and that you almost lost your life to that bitch and her crony."

"You saved my hide." In the spur of the moment, he kissed her brow. "Thank you."

"Oh, you old charmer!" She turned to embrace him, and he felt her trembling. "I could never have explained to Jacklyn how you'd died even though I was around." She cupped his face, careful to avoid the wound. "She needs you, Nicolas. As much as you need her." She let go, sighing, and reached for the bottle. "And I need a lot of booze to calm my nerves. My,

I haven't been in a shootout for thirty years!"

Chapter Fourteen

Nicolas had been relieved to learn that Katherine had lied about killing Matthew to make him crumble. In the morning, he hugged his colleague like a long-lost friend. Matthew—never at a loss for words—quipped that his dog would've eaten her raw for breakfast.

While Jason grimaced with sympathy about Nicolas's bandaged cheek, Matthew joked that he looked like a dog after a brawl. Though the banter was inevitable, Nicolas refused to dwell on the episode, refused to think that there had been less than an inch between an injury and a deadly hit—a slight move to the right, a stumbled step, and the result would have been grossly different. He didn't dare think about the possibility of Georgette's death, either. He was still amazed by her actions.

Katherine Nelson's arrest was worth a report on the prime-time news shows, and Senior Agent Sullivan took the praise for the finally successful investigation without going into details. Nicolas wasn't mentioned.

He turned down the volume of the anchorman's morning summary of the events and looked at Jason. "Tell me, were those officers sent to protect me?"

"Because I knew that Katherine would be after you and Matt." Matthew lifted his head, and Jason answered in an impatient voice. "Yes, you had a bodyguard, too, even on your walks with your dog."

"You care for me. I'm flattered."

"Don't make fun of me. Both of you had targets on your

backs, and maybe your protectors kept Katherine from coming after you."

Jason's indignant anger blew away Matthew's smile and made him lift his hands in defense. "Hey, I'm grateful, okay? I really don't want a bullet in my head." He pointed at Nicolas. "And you look as if you came damn close."

"You don't say." It was meant to be sarcastic, but Nicolas knew he wasn't convincing anyone. The medic had explained that he was lucky to get away with a burn wound instead of a bullet in his cheekbone. The painkillers were good, but when they wore off, Nicolas tried to avoid any facial movement.

"How did Jacklyn take the news?" Jason asked.

Nicolas looked into his empty coffee mug. "Not well. She was torn between worry and anger, maybe frustration, too, that a hardcore criminal could walk up to our doorstep to kill me." He took a deep breath. "I couldn't soothe her, and not even Georgette's copious report of how she fought off the crony lifted her mood. She's talking about selling the house and buying another one far away from the city, but she knows that it's all make-believe. Just the shock talking. No one is safe if a killer is determined to get to you."

Matthew shook his head. Disbelief was in his voice. "Jacklyn's aunt killed the second guy?"

"Yep. She was pretty shaken up afterward but took it like a trooper. Without her, the situation would've been worse."

"What a badass woman." Matthew nodded in appreciation. "But the assault doesn't look as if it went the way Katherine planned."

"No. I thought about that. Usually, I meet with Tom for a drink, so Katherine would've had time to enter the house and lie in wait for me. Or for both of us. I bet her plan included Jacky." A shiver ran along Nicolas's spine. The more he thought about Katherine's devilish plan, the more his mind obsessed over the deadly consequences. She would have taken Jacklyn hostage and killed her while Nicolas watched. Nicolas knew he wouldn't have been able to stand that, and he couldn't get rid of that picture in his head. "But then Georgette was there, and I think Katherine feared that I was going to leave with her." He shook his head, then stood up to fetch more coffee. "She couldn't know I was about to walk Georgette to her car and that I'd have been back inside alone within minutes." He poured another cup, thinking of Jacklyn's frightened expression and how restless she had been throughout the night. He hadn't slept well, either, for obvious reasons. "If Katherine had waited, she'd have caught me alone and—"

"Don't think about it," Matthew interrupted. "She's in custody. Her partner is dead. You made it."

"Yeah." Nicolas sat down at the desk and switched on his computer. He wiped the bridge of his nose. "Any news on Dobson's murderer?"

Matthew helped himself to a cup of coffee and luxuriated in the first sip with a contented sigh. "I showed the drawing around—no one recognized the false Miss Olbridge at the hospital or at the shops on the street. Some said they might've seen a woman similar to her, but no one pointed a finger and identified her." He frowned. "By now, I'm convinced that the woman is a make-up artist. Otherwise, it would've been far too risky to show her face to Morrison because, obviously, she wasn't out to kill him."

Jason turned away from Matthew. Anger was in his voice. "Now that we know of Mrs. Dobson's attempt to leave her husband and that she asked Nyeburn for help, we're concentrating on the lawyer and the people working for her, for example, Mrs. Billingham, and also the two assistants at her lawyer's office. So far, Nyeburn did nothing out of the ordinary. Not surprisingly, considering the meager evidence, the

DA has refused permission to tap her phone, so we're going to have to rely on our observations."

"If she gets wind of this, she'll be yelling for a court order to stop us from following her."

"Then we'd better hope our people stay out of sight."

At the round table in Jill Nyeburn's office at St Mary's, Melissa described Mr. Delaney's situation and his reaction to her offer. Six nurses, as well as Jill and Mrs. Billingham, were present, listening intently when Melissa reported that the young man suffered at the hands of his wife and didn't dare ask for help because he was too ashamed.

"My offer for him to join the support-group was rejected because he thought he'd be ridiculed." She looked from one face to the next. "We have to work on our reputation. There're more men like Mr. Delaney, who need help but fear they'd become the center of bad jokes and disbelief. The police officer was an asshole, but Mr. Delaney's assumption that the support-group was for women only was worse. Jill, what can we do?"

Jill put down the cookie she was nibbling as she listened. "We can try and extend the service—offer separate meetings for men and for women to assure the male victims that they're taken seriously. Though there are very few men at the moment, we might increase the numbers that way. I could ask my male colleagues if one of them is willing to take over clients who don't want to talk to a female lawyer." She shrugged. "That's what immediately comes into my mind. Other suggestions?"

"As always, you've got great insight," Nurse Tessa said, nodding rapidly. "It would be great to include this in the flyer and put it where men can find it."

"At bars and nightclubs?" Nurse Kathy said and was rewarded with supportive laughter. "Local car repair shops? Local gyms? I'll offer to take a walk and place them on the counters. At prime time, of course."

When the laughter subsided, Jill used the silent moment to ask for the usual rumors and reports from the ER and other wards. Like a sponge, she took in all information, scribbled notes, and drank coffee. She was happy to be surrounded by nurses who were dedicated to their jobs. If it hadn't looked unprofessional, she would have hugged the nurses and the male nurse who had attended the meeting.

After the staff left, she checked her calendar. She had two appointments with clients, one of them a woman in treatment at the Richmond Health Clinic. Afterward, she would prepare for the group meeting in the evening. Not for the first time, she wished she could do more to help people in need.

Clarence Woolsey—*Wookie* to his friends—had never seen a woman like her, and he knew a lot of women. He loved women, the more, the merrier. He preferred the curvaceous ones, women with a lot of bosom and real fine hips and bottom. In his imagination, he had two on each arm, and they were mesmerized by his looks, his charm, and his ideas of what he wanted to do with them. In reality, women despised him the moment he told them what kind of sex practices he preferred. The prostitutes at the usual corners laughed in his face if they had a powerful pimp behind them. Others turned away from his untrained body, his blunt chat-up lines, and his idea of entertainment, which included bamboo staffs and lots of rope.

Woolsey wondered if the hot number in front of him, standing on his porch with a dazzling smile, would stay for a one-night stand. He wet his lips at seeing her voluptuous body, the feminine swing of her hips, and her well-formed, long legs that ended in perfect feet with painted toenails. Yearning grew in his mind and in his pants, becoming almost overwhelming within a minute. Maybe he could convince her with a knock against her temple—hard enough to break her resistance but soft enough that she would regain consciousness quickly. Once he had her tethered, he would do with her whatever he wanted. The prospect made his pulse speed up.

"Hello, Mr. Woolsey, I'm Jenna Mitchum. I'm with the mayor's office, and today I'm conducting a public opinion poll. I've got a few questions for you. It won't take long. Do you have a few minutes to spare for me?" She flashed an ID card briefly in his face.

He made an inviting gesture and led her toward the dining nook. His brows twitched, and his lips curled into a hideous smile. "Many minutes, if you wish. Sit down. Do you want a drink?" He wiped his mouth and pulled up his pants. He quashed a smile of satisfaction as his gaze dropped to the coiled rope under the bench.

"No, thank you." She stood beside the bench, and he saw that she wore short white gloves. At that moment, his blood rushing through his veins and his whole body tightened to attention, he considered her the most adorable woman he'd ever met. He must have her.

He cleared his throat, hoping she wouldn't detect his arousal pushing at his pants. "So, what's up?"

She looked at the paper on her clipboard. "Voter satisfaction. You're a listed voter, so I presume you voted the last time?"

"Yes, I did." Mr. Woolsey stared at the lady's powdered face and full red lips. Her eyelashes were long and black, her eyes of a fantastic green. With the dark red two-piece outfit and high heels, she looked like one of those impressive cover girls—a startling beauty in her mid-thirties, perfumed with seductive charm. He swallowed nervously. She smelled so good. He wanted to rub his naked body against hers.

"Great." Mrs. Mitchum smiled convincingly.

Mr. Woolsey waited for the perfect moment to attack her. The woman was of average height, but he didn't trust in his ability to wrestle her to the ground without being hurt. She looked too sturdy to try that. He looked around the room as inconspicuously as possible, trying to find a suitable weapon. He didn't want to damage the goods—if he hurt her too much, he'd have less fun.

"My first question concerns your way of life. What's your job?"

He returned his gaze to her beautiful face and decided it would be a shame to ruin her perfect cheekbones with a club or the heft of a wrench. He needed something else, something with a flat side but heavy. "I'm a mechanic. Car repairs." He pointed at the ladder in the hall with the toolbox on top. "But I do all kinds of repairs. Whatever is necessary." His brows twitched again as he lowered his voice. "The ladies call me a handy . . . man."

Mrs. Mitchum laughed merrily. "That's good! I'm sure you really know what to do with your hands." She cleared her throat. "Would you mind fetching me a glass of water?"

"No, not at all." Mr. Woolsey was under the impression that this woman saw him as the attractive man he was and not as a mid-forties dude with suspect fetishes and whose best days were behind him. With swinging steps, he went into the kitchen down the hall and came back with two glasses and a pitcher of water. Careful as he was, he had added two slices of lemon, as he had seen in TV advertisements.

He almost dropped it all when he saw how Mrs. Mitchum had changed. Instead of the elegant outfit, she now wore white plastic overalls, and rubber boots had replaced the high heels. She'd covered her hands with pink gloves. However, her smile was intact.

"Oh, there you are already, quicker than I thought."

"What the hell— " He put down the glasses and the pitcher, angry about the enforced change in his plan, for he had hidden a meat tenderizer in the small of his back. He wanted answers and stepped forward to shake them out of her.

As he did so, a heavy object hit the top of his head. He fell to the floor, and his last thought, bitterly running through his head before oblivion took him, was about all the women he would not get the chance to conquer.

Jason sighed. The profiler's results were inconsistent, and he had to admit regretfully that there was no way to determine the origin of the killers by the way they had committed the murders. Poisoning would point to female killers, but the brutal murder of Buck Dobson went against that. Cloaking the murders as accidents indicated a clever killer, while the attacks with baseball bats revealed sheer uncontrolled aggressiveness. The profiler had concluded that Jason and Nicolas might be dealing with more than two killers, a fact that increased the difficulties of solving the case. He concluded that the Glandale case and the Dobson murder fit a scheme, but the rest did not and that Jason should sort them out before contacting him again.

The agents on stakeout had reported that Nyeburn had entered the Richmond Health Clinic and hadn't left it again. Because of Jason's order to undertake the surveillance as discreetly as possible, they hadn't followed her into the building but had eyes on her car in the garage.

Frustrated, Jason listed the times and circumstances of the murders once more in the hope of finding something that stood out. When the much-needed revelation didn't happen, he looked out of the window. The afternoon sun bathed the buildings in bright light, and he realized he had spent hours at his desk. His thoughts turned to his upcoming marriage with Elaine and how it would be to start a family. He pondered whether he'd be a good father. Could he manage his job and his duties as a parent, or would he end like many of the men he worked with—divorced because the women had high expectations an FBI agent couldn't fulfill? He remembered Nicolas's report about his first love. The woman had left him because he hadn't been home for days or weeks. She had wanted a marriage with a man who was there for her.

Jason made a face thinking of Elaine's exuberant monologue about the marriage preparations and what they had to do—the many choices they had to make for the guest list, the meal, the decorations, and the location. She wanted his input and his participation, and yet here he sat at a desk in the Richmond PD office without knowing when he'd be home again.

He picked up the phone to call his fiancé.

When he came home, Nicolas was determined to get answers to his questions concerning the mortgage, even if it only to distract his mind from the brutal attack the day before.

Jacklyn welcomed him from behind the dining room table. Her smile seemed forced. "You're late, and I was worried sick. I don't know if I can stand this, Nick," she confessed quietly. "Really, I can't get it out of my head that you—" She turned away to look at the locked door toward the rear porch where wood had replaced the glass. "Throughout the day, I thought about what happened, and I came to the conclusion that moving away wouldn't change a thing."

"I agree with that." He took off his shoes and put down his gun and badge. "It would be a shame to pay for the house and move away so soon. By the way—"

"Yes, the house. The mortgage." She turned back, nodding.

"I'll tell you later. But there's more. Much more." She sighed deeply.

"Yes, why you want to work as a mistress again." He went into the kitchen. "That's something *I* can't get out of my head."

Jacklyn took a deep breath and put her palms together in front of her face. "I want to talk to you about so many things, but—" She bit her lower lip, and he read hesitation all over her face. "I don't know how."

"Why not?" He filled a glass with water and drank it slowly.

"It's not an easy subject."

Nicolas put down the glass and embraced her, but she was rigid in his arms. "What do you want to tell me?"

She shook her head and freed herself from his arms. "The events . . . and whatever else happened . . . I can't think clearly, but I need to talk with you." She stepped back toward the table and sat down. A single tear trickled down her cheek. "I'm so damn confused."

He opened his arms to her invitingly. "Jacky, please, whatever happened—I'm here to help you."

She bit her lower lip. "You're the best man who has ever come into my life. Seriously. You're caring, you're honest, you do for me whatever you can, and you love me the way I am. I've never felt so safe with anyone. And that's why it's so hard to tell you." She fetched a tissue and blew her nose. "You told me long ago that Harry Fuller is a bad guy."

"Did he come to your practice?" Nicolas clenched his hands into hard fists. "Did he hurt you?"

"Maybe he wanted to, but no." She looked up at him.

His heart broke at seeing the misery tinging the beauty of her eyes. "Jacky—" He wanted to step closer but knew instinctively that it was the wrong moment for intimacy. He retreated toward the kitchen counter.

"He came to my clinic just before I opened. He told me he'd been out of town, but now that he was back, he wanted to repay me for the prank I'd played on him." Jacklyn's smile was full of sadness. "I should've known that a man like him wouldn't be a good loser."

"You tricked him in Lesley's dungeon, I assume?"

"Yes. Richard was rewarded with a session for his help against Harry's attempt at cheating on me with the house I wanted to buy. Do you remember? And Harry . . . well, he wasn't invited and therefore got very pissed."

"What happened then?"

Jacklyn needed a moment to find her voice. "Harry pushed me into one of the parlors, closed the door, and accused me of misusing my position as a mistress, claiming that a mistress would never play pranks and that it had ruined his trust in every mistress he'd ever meet. He was so angry." More tears followed her words. "He had me cornered. I didn't know what to do, but then I kicked his jewels, and he broke down to his knees."

"Good." Nicolas wanted to embrace and kiss her and make her feel better. She looked like a bundle of misery crammed inside a beautiful woman. But when he made a step in her direction, he knew by her glance that she wanted him to keep a distance. "Did you call the police?"

"My secretary did. She recognized him, and she knew he wasn't welcome. When she heard his accusations, she dialed nine-one-one." Jacklyn snorted self-consciously. "I fled the room and locked it from the outside until the officers arrived."

"Great. Let's celebrate your victory."

She seemed not to hear him. "He was so close to me. He was so close and so full of rage. If he'd been prepared any better, I would've . . ." Jacklyn let out her breath shakily. "Right now, I can't handle that I won against him. Kind of."

She looked Nicolas in the eyes. "But I still think that he could've hurt me."

Nicolas hung his head, wishing he'd been there to help her. "Did you file charges?"

This time, Jacklyn needed even more time to answer. Her voice was small. "To be honest—no."

Nicolas breathed loudly. Keeping his flaring anger in check was much harder than he had thought.

Jacklyn lowered her gaze to the tissue in her hands. She continued even more hesitantly. "The officers told me that I could press charges and that he'd be taken into custody, but since he's got no previous criminal record, he'd be out of jail within two days."

Nicolas had a bad premonition. "So, what did you do?"

"I told the officers to take him out of my rooms, and Richard filed a motion that he may not approach any nearer to me than a hundred yards."

"Do you think a piece of paper will keep him from harassing you? That's like fighting fire with a water pistol!" Nicolas held tight to the counter rim, but he couldn't keep the anger out of his voice. "He's a weasel! He'll wait for you somewhere and attack you when you don't expect it. Damn it, Jacky, such men can't be stopped by an injunction. He must be put into jail! He's been stalking you for months, I bet. You must get rid of him."

Jacklyn looked from his face to his impotently flexing white knuckles. "You're angry with me."

Nicolas's shoulders sagged as he shook his head. "Yes, I'm furious, but not with you. This man's a threat and must be treated like one."

"But he was my friend once. I don't know what took him so long to face me, but it doesn't matter. I just couldn't—" Her voice trailed off. "Richard recommended the injunction. Yes, it might not keep Harry from appearing on my doorstep in the first place, but he's not a ruthless brute."

"You sound pretty shaken," he reminded her.

"On the other hand—Harry was shocked by his actions. I saw the terror in his eyes when the police arrived."

"So, you'll forgive him?"

"Get rid of the sarcasm. No, I don't forgive anything, but I knew it was useless to throw him into jail. He suffered a lot. His son's been convicted, ten years in prison. That's hard to swallow for a father."

Nicolas bit back the response that ten years wasn't nearly enough for the foul murders the son had committed, but the jury hadn't been convinced by the evidence that Fuller junior was responsible in all cases. If so, he would've been sentenced to life.

"Don't try to justify his actions. You can't believe he'll be just the friendly guy from the neighborhood the next time you both meet."

"I can handle him." She lifted her hand to stop his protest. "But that's not the only thing I thought about today."

"I guess so." Nicolas felt like a caged tiger. It was hard to stand and do nothing. "And what else did you want to talk to me about?"

She made a face but didn't get up. "I'm getting to that now."

Matthew entered the yellow-painted house at the end of the cul-de-sac, and the front door was hanging open. The interior was neat. Furniture and knickknacks spoke of little money but a classy female touch, making the best of what was available. The somewhat faded photograph of a brightly hopeful wedding couple hung on the wall of the small corridor that led toward the living room and the dining nook on the right side.

Detective Bartow welcomed him with a grim smile. "There you are, Mr. FBI, I've got another dead husband for you." He gestured toward a body on the floor. "Meet Clarence Woolsey, husband of Thelma Woolsey. As the clues indicate, he was about to change the lamp when he was hit by a hammer directly on his head. Messy business. He died instantly."

Matthew pursed his lips and took in the evidence. Mr. Woolsey lay between the ladder and the table, a bloodied ball-peen hammer close to his shoulder. There was a large bloody wound on the top of his head the size of the hammer's square side. Blood had oozed into the carpet under the table. Mr. Woolsey wore sweatpants and an undershirt, neither socks nor shoes. At first glance, this seemed to be the scene of an accident with fatal consequences.

"Take a closer look," the detective said with an all-encompassing gesture. "The killer was clever, but not clever enough."

Matthew didn't like being put to the test. He kept his displeasure to himself and set to work. "Did he fall off the ladder and the hammer followed?"

"He might, but it's not likely."

Matthew walked around the body to look from another angle. "Even if the hammer fell off the toolbox, it wouldn't have caused a deadly blow to his head. That's not possible." He crouched to examine the hammer. "Hmm, a hammer will always fall with the heaviest part first, but the blood is on the square side, not the top." He looked up and met Bartow's grumpy stare. "This was staged. It's a case of murder."

"Now that we've cleared that up—do you want to pursue this murder case as part of *your* investigation?" Bartow made a step back and raised his hands, palms out. "If so, call your colleagues, and we'll leave."

Matthew knew enough about the rivalry between the FBI and local homicide divisions to try for a complacent tone. "I'm grateful that you called me. I know you weren't obliged to. But you're right—the FBI should take over the investigation. Considering the cases we're already looking into, this fits the killers' MO. If we assume this was staged to mislead the police, the killers made an effort, but this time they were sloppy. They should've known about the hammer and that the weight wouldn't kill a grownup man."

"Right." Detective Bartow scratched his head. "What eludes me—he was carrying a meat tenderizer pushed into the back of his pants. Any ideas, why?"

Matthew looked more closely at the body. "None." He curled his lips to a small smile. "I admit I haven't seen anything like this before."

"Fine. Whatever. If you don't mind, I'm gonna talk to his wife. Do you want to accompany me?"

"Where are we going?"

"St. Mary's Medical Center." When Matthew twitched his brows, Bartow grinned. "Exactly what I thought."

"All right, what else is on your mind?" Nicolas tried to loosen his grip on the countertop. Reining in his anger right now was harder than on a workday.

"I don't want criminals on our doorstep." Jacklyn looked up, sorrow in her eyes. "I can't stop thinking that this woman would've killed you and my aunt in cold blood."

"It's not a daily occurrence. Bad guys aren't always knocking on my door."

"It's not? If you remember—the serial killer kidnapped you two and a half years ago right around the corner from my apartment."

Nicolas was rendered speechless and lowered his chin to avoid her stare. Jacklyn was right. The serial killer had spied on him and kidnapped him to hamper the ongoing investigation.

Jacklyn sighed. "See? It's not like the bad guys respect your privacy. If Katherine Nelson knew about our home—who else might? The suspects in this case? Or in the next one?" She closed her eyes. "Nick, I want to be with you. I want to be your lover, but I don't want to look over my shoulder, wondering if there's a killer wanting to take me hostage or shoot me if I don't cooperate. I'm not that strong."

"I've dealt with many criminals over the years, Jacky, and the Nelson sister was one of the worst."

"Maybe." She looked up to him again. "I don't care. Nick, I want you to think about quitting the FBI."

"Quit working?" Nicolas bit his lips to stop the words that wanted out. He didn't want to accuse or hurt her. It was an effort to calm himself down when all he wanted to do was to roar that she knew about his job from the beginning. "The answer's no. I love my work. You know that."

"But it's dangerous—for both of us. You get hurt frequently. Just look at your face. It was pure luck you weren't killed."

"Agents like me work for the safety of all citizens. And sometimes the criminals are armed and shoot at us. That's the risk all agents or police officers accept. Our work is dangerous from time to time."

"Much too often for my taste." Jacklyn's look was pleading. "I want to be safe. I want *you* to be safe, and that won't happen as long as you serve in the FBI."

Nicolas forced his voice to remain calm. "You knew about my profession from the beginning. It's no secret that I've always wanted to be in police work. And the salary's good."

"But we don't need that money."

"No, don't start down that path." He shook his head. "Jacky, you can't pay all of our expenses—the house, the cars, our vacations. We need both incomes."

"I've got enough money for both of us, believe me."

Her conviction made him uneasy. "You're telling me your physiotherapy clinic makes so much money?" He shook his head. "No, I don't believe that."

"It's not just the clinic." She put her palms together and looked him in the eyes. "My parents made a donation. It should've been my dowry, but I convinced my father that was so old-fashioned. So, four months ago, he put the money on my account." She shrugged. "It's a nice sum, and I invested part of it. The other part can be used for our daily needs."

Nicolas's frown deepened. The prospect of living without the daily grind might've been tempting for some of his friends, but not for him. The thought was excruciatingly awful. "If I quit working—what would I do every day? Clean the house? Go and buy groceries?"

"What would be so bad about being the man at home?"

"I can do that once in a while, but it's not fulfilling. Jacky, please, understand that I won't quit, regardless of your financial situation."

Jacklyn sighed deeply. "All right. I understand you love your work as I love mine, but I needed to tell you of my fears."

"Agreed." He pushed off the counter. "You know what? I think I'm going for a run. I need to loosen up."

Jacklyn nodded and remained pensive at the table when he went to change clothes and leave.

Chapter Fifteen

Matthew stood with his head bowed in front of the hospital door that separated him from Mrs. Woolsey. A minute ago, he had left the room. He couldn't stand looking at her split lips, swollen eyes, and bloody cheekbones. The doctor had listed the injuries in a litany of ways to hurt the human body. She had suffered a complicated fracture of her right arm and abrasions as well as contusions all over her torso, arms, and legs. Matthew had seen victims of car accidents who looked better than Mrs. Woolsey.

He yearned to leave the corridor for a smoke.

Detective Bartow had tried to speak to her, but when he mentioned her husband's name, she had closed her eyes and turned her head away. She hadn't reacted to the news of Mr. Woolsey's death or answered any questions concerning enemies or people who wanted to harm him. In fact, she hadn't shown sadness or glee. She appeared to be a lifeless shell still going through the motions of living but cold and dead inside.

Matthew couldn't blame her. If she had found the strength, he suspected she would walk away and never look back.

"You don't see something like that very often, hmm?" Bartow asked quietly as they left the building. He waited patiently for Matthew to light a cigarette. "I know what you think—the woman was taken to the hospital, and someone took revenge on the husband. I agree with you. But I also agree that the husband didn't deserve any better."

Matthew drew on his cigarette, relishing the smoke filling

his lungs. He exhaled as he watched the detective unobtrusively. "Are you saying you wished the killers had done a better job so that this would be an accident—file closed?"

"Don't you?"

Matthew felt the strain ease, now that he was outside and the nicotine was in his body. "No. The victim's former actions cannot justify murder. It doesn't work that way. Mrs. Woolsey had to press charges against him so that a judge would've decided the verdict. The law must be upheld. That's the only acceptable way."

Detective Bartow huffed, then looked back toward the parking lot. "A lot of shit goes on in this world, agent. If we assume all these murders were committed by the same men, they're doing the women a favor."

Matthew didn't comment. A part of him agreed with the cruel justice the husbands had received. The other part rebelled and reminded him of his duties as a special agent. Mr. Woolsey's sudden death made it all the more urgent to discover and arrest the perpetrators before there were any more.

"We'll find them," he said.

"Yeah, right." Bartow blew his nose as they walked toward the parked cars. "Do I get a copy of your ME report?"

"Sure. I'll keep you in the loop."

"Thanks."

He sounded sincere—maybe he didn't consider all special agents to be a pain in the neck.

After a long run, Nicolas returned home after nightfall, expecting Jacklyn to be in bed since they both hadn't slept the night before. He left his running shoes in the hall and walked through the dimly lit living room to fetch fresh underwear when he saw her sitting at the dining table, a bottle of wine and a glass in front of her.

He stopped. "You're still up?"

Her smile was sad. "I knew I wouldn't sleep if I tried."

Nicolas stood at the other side of the room, not knowing what to do. He had vented his anger out on the run through the park—long and fast without regard to muscle aches or his growing tiredness. He wanted to exhaust his body and clear his mind to stop thinking that his lover had allowed Harry Fuller to remain a free man. As he sweated the last half mile, his plans had turned to a quick shower and getting to bed, with the hope he would see their confrontation differently after a good night's sleep.

Jacklyn poured another glass but didn't drink. "I should've known that you love your work—I love mine, too. But it was worth a try. I'd prefer you to have a safer job. I guess a girl can dream, but she won't get everything she wants." She drank and put down the glass, sighing. "What shall I do? I don't want to lose you, but at the moment, I'm trembling when I think of tomorrow and the fact that you're hunting another serial killer." Jacklyn shook her head and looked down at the tabletop.

Nicolas helped himself to a glass of watered-down juice. "You're shocked that she invaded our privacy. That's understandable. Her behavior isn't the rule. Most criminals stay away from the police for as long as possible. They prefer running away over attacking us." Nicolas took a deep breath. "I'll call a locksmith and tell him to change the locks, re-secure the house."

"Okay." She emptied the glass in one long swallow. When he was about to leave, she got up and approached him. "Please, wait."

In the dim light, Nicolas couldn't see her expression to interpret what she wanted, but he saw that she hesitated, she wasn't sure. In all probability, the bottle on the table was empty.

"Are you still angry with me?" She stopped in front of him with her hands in the back pockets of her pants.

Nicolas knew her well enough to know she honestly regretted her actions. "No, I'm not angry. I want you to be safe, Jacky, and Harry might be a threat. Maybe not tomorrow, but he might come up with a plan."

"I told you—"

"And in time, I'm sure I'll understand." He cupped her face for a small kiss. "I'll take a shower and go to bed."

Jason ran both hands through his hair, sighing deeply. "There's been another murder?"

Matthew nodded. "He was hit on the head with remarkable force—the killer murdered him with one precise blow. This indicates the killer was strong but also skilled. The ME thinks the killer knew exactly what he was doing."

"Do we know of the whereabouts of Jill Nyeburn and Mrs. Billingham at the time of the murder?"

"Nyeburn was at the Richmond Health Clinic, Billingham was leading a group meeting at St. Mary's."

"Is that confirmed? Do we have witnesses? Did anyone see both women?"

Matthew narrowed his eyes. "The surveillance team followed her to the clinic and waited until she came back to her car. That's it."

"How much time between arrival and departure?"

Matthew checked the information. "Four hours. She spent the afternoon meeting with clients, so I was told."

"They didn't have eyes on her all that time? She had enough time to drive to Tuckahoe, kill him, and drive back, right?"

"Yes."

Jason already grabbed his jacket. "Let's see whether the

woman has any other profession besides advising people on legal matters."

Mrs. Nyeburn's secretary had an angel's face and an equally pleasant voice. She told Matthew and Jason a story about the most hard-working lawyer in Richmond and that Mrs. Nyeburn deserved a medal for her ongoing help for poor abused women and men in bad relationships. She stressed that Mrs. Nyeburn never missed an appointment and had been working the day before. She couldn't confirm, though, that she had seen her between her arrival and departure, but stressed that two clients had come and gone.

"This doesn't help us much," Matthew stated outside the hospital in the parking lot. He blew out smoke and leaned against the car, squinting against the sun. "Is it possible she left and came back? Maybe she had a car parked at the back of the building."

"She met with an accomplice." Jason stood in front of him, arms crossed, frustrated. "Mrs. Billingham has twenty witnesses who state emphatically that she didn't leave the room while the group met. So she isn't the one we're searching for. Who is it? A male nurse? Another woman? One of the women she relieved of her violent husband?"

Matthew frowned and lowered his head to be on eye level with Jason. "You're convinced the lawyer's one of our killers? Remember, we don't have anything against her. She's virtually a saint."

"Her reputation's one thing, but we should check the time frame of all the murders we've detected so far." He opened the driver's side. "Then we compare them to Nyeburn's appointments and other obligations and see what turns up."

Nicolas blocked every question concerning his late appearance at the office or why he was in a bad mood. Jason gave in, realizing that his curiosity was a nuisance. He brought his friend up to speed.

During the following hours, the agents compared dates and time frames of the murders they had on the list to the working hours of Mrs. Nyeburn, much to the chagrin of the angel-like secretary. She sent a copy of her employer's appointments over the last twelve months, stressing that any assumption of Mrs. Nyeburn being anything but a wonderful and honest lawyer was stupid and prevented the FBI from finding the true murderer. She added that there might be more appointments in her private life that wouldn't show on her business schedule and that this outstanding woman deserved a private life, which she didn't tell her assistant, of course.

Nicolas and Jason created a fact sheet with the dates of the murders and Nyeburn's whereabouts if the information was available. They stepped back from the desk, taking a deep breath in unison.

"It's possible." Jason scratched his head. "I don't know how we can find corroborating evidence, but she has no alibi for at least two murders, including that of Dobson."

Matthew joined them. "You look so serious. What's up?"

"As it turns out, Jill Nyeburn could be one of the killers." Jason sighed. "What did Mr. Woolsey's neighbors say?"

"Most of the neighbors were at work, but one old woman told me she saw an old dark blue *Honda Civic* park in front of Mr. Woolsey's house at the time of the murder. She didn't see the license plate, but she was sure it was a *Honda*."

"Great. And how many dark blue *Hondas* did you find?"

Matthew grinned knowingly. "You don't want to know. Fact is I concentrated the search on all members of the staff of the St. Mary's Medical Center and the Richmond Health

Clinic. There were only three cars registered to nurses or cleaning staff. Guess who owns one?"

Jill Nyeburn leaned back in her chair and closed her eyes, exhaling slowly. In her left hand, she held a glass of sweet cherry liqueur, in her right, her cell phone. She let the memories of the night of her husband's murder drift through her mind as scrumptious as the brandy. It had been the best night of the entire marriage.

Jill chuckled to herself and sipped the sweet stuff she loved so much.

It was a shock, to begin with. The killer had entered the house silently through the porch door, moved upstairs and into the bedroom. Donald stood at the foot of the bed, taking off his shirt and arranging his pajamas in his precise way. He had preferred to sleep completely covered up even though it had been oppressively warm. *Always a man of utter correctness, no matter the subject.* The hooded and masked killer came up behind him, raising a knife to sink it into Donald's broad unprotected back. Mesmerized, Jill had watched how easily the shining blade penetrated the undershirt and the flesh beneath. Donald cried out in pain, but then the blade cut through muscles, sinews, and fat twice more, and the cry stopped abruptly. Donald fell onto the bed linen. His dead eyes remained open, but his demands and threats were gone forever. Blood oozed from the wounds, soiling the white undershirt and dripping onto the bedsheet.

I didn't expect that to happen. She remained in her position on the bed, leaning against a thick pillow. Under different circumstances, she would have cried, yelled, panicked, but instead this time she had watched the killer clean the blade with baby wipes, an act she found hilariously funny. She started chuckling and couldn't stop. Maybe this was her version of panic—the conclusion that the killer wouldn't clean the blade if he were out to kill her, too. She looked from Donald to the killer and back again. *Should I feel regret? Sorrow?* She couldn't tell why she didn't feel fear or—to be precise—why she felt nothing at all.

"Take a valium or two if you haven't done so already," the killer said matter-of-factly, and Jill realized it was a woman. The revelation caused her pulse to race even faster than the murder had.

She nodded slowly. "Yes, I will."

"Mix them with whiskey or whatever you like."

"Cherry liqueur," Jill said and chuckled again. "Do you want a drink?"

"No." She put away the blade that fit perfectly under her long black jacket. Jill wondered whether the woman had a sheath sewed into the lining. "Tell me where you hide your money and jewelry. I'll take it and drop it somewhere."

"All right."

"Are you okay? Can you handle this?"

"Yes." Jill took a deep breath, wishing the sweet liqueur was already in a glass and in her hand. The longer the surreal situation lasted, the more she knew she needed alcohol to cope with it. But she wanted to tell the stranger that she was still clear-headed. "The killer came in, stabbed my husband, and robbed the house. I was too confused and dazed by the painkillers and the valium I had taken, so I couldn't call the police right away. I'm also beyond myself with grief and don't remember any features of the killer at all." She looked up, astonished at her coolness.

The killer nodded. "I knew you'd understand. I'll be in touch."

"How do I know who you are?"

"You already know me."

Jill had watched the other woman collect the money and a few bracelets, four sets of diamond earrings, and a valuable necklace made of forty rubies, Donald's wedding gift. The killer had left the house the same way she had come. Jill took the pills and the drink, roughed up her hair, cried a lot, and after an hour, made a hysterical call to the police to stammer about a murder and that she didn't know why she was still alive while her beloved husband was dead.

Savoring both her liqueur and the memories, Jill put down the glass. That night had been the beginning of an extraordinary friendship. To stay believable in the role of the mourning widow, she waited half a year to dedicate her work as a lawyer to abused women and men and start the therapy places and self-support groups. She was astonished at the feedback and the praise—even by the sitting mayor—for her outstanding service to the city. There were by far more citizens in the greater Richmond area who had serious trouble with their partners, whether it was lovers, husbands, fathers or simply the lusting neighbor. Many of the victims ended in hospitals, and unfortunately, a few of them in the county morgue before they were able to leave their brutal partners.

Jill Nyeburn had a mission and the perfect partner to fulfill it.

"Miss Roberts, you drive a 1992 *Honda Civic,* is that correct?" Nicolas asked politely after introducing Jason and himself.

Melissa Roberts scratched her head and yawned. She was dressed in short pajamas and freaky pink socks with pig faces on them. Her eyes were puffy from sleep, and the mass of hair tousled on top of her head. "Sorry, what did you say?"

"Is that your car in the driveway?"

"Yep. I'm sorry, I had a nightshift, and it didn't go well."

She checked her watch. "You woke me after two hours. So, please, say whatever you have to say so I can go back to bed."

"May we come in?" Nicolas asked with his best-disarming smile that he had learned from Matthew. Without looking, he knew that Jason was rolling his eyes. "We have a few questions."

"All right." Miss Roberts turned to shuffle into the living room.

"You're housesitting?"

"Yep."

Nicolas frowned. An idea knocked on the back of his head, but he had no time to dwell on it. "Do you do that on a regular basis?"

"Yep." Miss Roberts waved a hand. "Whenever the rich couple needs a watchdog."

"Where were you yesterday afternoon around five o'clock?"

She yawned. "I did some shopping, and then I had a nightshift. I already told you."

"When did you leave the house?" Jason asked as he pulled out his notebook and a pen.

Miss Roberts took a deep breath, frowning and looking at the clock on the wall. "At four, maybe earlier. I didn't check the time."

"Where did you go?"

"Walden's first, then a drugstore, and after that, I spent some time window shopping before I had to check in at the hospital. I'm still looking for a summer dress with more fabric than a bikini. It's hard to find one these days."

"Do you have the receipts?"

She gaped at Jason, then shook her head. "Don't need them. No one gives me back a buck."

"Your car always parks in the driveway?"

"The garage is full." Miss Roberts grinned. "My friends left by plane, and all the cars are still here."

Nicolas nodded. "Are you allowed to drive them?"

"Do I look as if I want to? No. I like my car. Desmond owns a *Jaguar*, a *Porsche*, and an old car . . . a *Bentley*. I wouldn't sit behind the wheel even if I knew how to drive one of them." She sighed. "Why do you want to know about my car?"

"Because it was seen at the home of a Mr. Woolsey, who was murdered yesterday."

"No. No matter where Mr. Woolsey lives, it wasn't my car that was seen." Miss Roberts shuffled toward the kitchen and poured a glass of orange juice. "Is that all, agents?"

"Not quite. Do you know Jill Nyeburn?"

Miss Roberts stopped with the glass half of the way to her lips. Her tone was sarcastic. "Is that a trick question? Of course, I know her. She's a lawyer, and she runs a self-support group at St. Mary's."

"Do you have any contact with her outside of the hospital?"

"Yes." She drank and wiped her lips. "We take *Tae Kwon Do* lessons together."

"How long have you been training together?"

"About two years." She emptied the glass and put it in the dishwasher. When she turned, her gaze and tone were impatient. "Agents, as I told you before, I'm tired. I worked a long and hard shift, and I've got another one tonight. I really want to catch some sleep."

Jason cocked his head, then took a casual look around. If he had hoped the nurse would leave damning evidence, he was mistaken. "We know it was your car at Mr. Woolsey's home. What were you doing there?"

"I wasn't there." Miss Roberts didn't flinch. "If you don't have any other questions, please, leave."

Outside in the sunshine, Nicolas stood beside the car, pondering.

"I see that you came to the same conclusion—you think she's the accomplice." Jason looked smug. "Or am I wrong?"

Nicolas snapped his fingers. "Now I know. Nyeburn's estate is on the other side of the street. Just look! The hedges are high, but they were smaller three years ago. I think that you can look across them from the veranda of the Morgan's home upstairs, don't you think?"

Jason frowned and hesitated with his answer. "You're saying that Roberts and Nyeburn indulged in small talk across the hedge about murdering people?"

Nicolas grinned. "We know Roberts has been doing the house sitting since the Morgans bought the house four years ago. She must've been witness to arguments between Jill Nyeburn and her husband."

"They were known as a reclusive couple."

"But it was hot. It was summer. They had the doors open. What if Roberts listened to the argument and decided to hire someone to help Jill get rid of Donald?"

"We don't know if—"

"We do. Roberts has been working for ten years at St. Mary's. We also know that Nyeburn was treated at the same hospital prior to her husband's death. I checked that," Nicolas said when Jason made big eyes. "The information was hard to come by, but I convinced an elderly nurse that she was doing something good. Though the crime report doesn't state it, Nyeburn was a victim of domestic violence—two broken ribs and several bruises in sensitive areas. I learned on the basis of confidentiality that she claimed she had fallen but didn't deny when the nurse insinuated that not all of the injuries derived from a fall."

"Why do I think that you've thought about this scenario before?"

"Because you're a good agent. You did so much research it's a marvel." Nicolas slipped behind the wheel and started the car while Jason got in. "Roberts hires someone to kill Mr. Nyeburn and confesses to Jill later. Instead of delivering her to the police, Jill and Melissa become friends, and the nurse supports the lawyer on her . . . revenge trips."

Jason pursed his lips and remained quiet for a while. Nicolas's thoughts returned to Jacklyn in a loop, and he missed Jason's next words.

"I said, is it possible that there is no hired killer in this case?"

Nicolas glanced at his partner. "Roberts is Nyeburn's partner?"

"Roberts was house sitting. She heard the fights and decided to take matters into her own hands." Jason made a sour face. "All right, that's hard to swallow. I can't believe that I said it. Two nice women—" He shook his head. "One with pink socks. They can't be the ones killing the men, can they?"

"And what about Deputy Mayor Dobson? Do you think they killed him, too?" Nicolas shrugged. "According to the timeline of Nyeburn's appointments, it is possible."

Jason stared at the dashboard. "All right. I'll call the DA and ask for search warrants for both homes and Nyeburn's offices. I hope he doesn't slap me down through the phone."

CHAPTER SIXTEEN

Melissa lay awake, staring at the light blue ceiling above her. She knew it had been a mistake to take her car if she couldn't park it out of view. But she had been in a hurry when her partner called. She put her hopes on the fact that the FBI agents didn't know the license plate. Otherwise, they would've arrested her on the spot.

She let out her breath with a deeply felt sigh. There was no way she could go back to sleep. Her thoughts returned to the first night she had met Jill Nyeburn.

Melissa knew the night was perfect. The neighbors to the left were on vacation in Idaho. The neighbors to the right spent their time watching loud TV in the bedroom. On the other side of the street, only the Norads could glimpse into Jill's and Donald's bedroom, but they were too absorbed in a barbeque party with friends on the other side of their house. Melissa heard peals of laughter and knew they would stay there for at least another hour, chatting about cars and expensive journeys to the end of the world.

After crossing the street, Melissa pulled up the hood and the mask in the shadow of the arborvitaes and slipped through the open glass door. Upstairs, Donald Nyeburn was telling Jill about the next day's meetings and that she should stay home and rest. He expected to be home early so that they could go on with their family planning, as he called it. Jill answered she had a full day herself, at least five clients, so she would be home late. Consequently, Donald repeated his litany about Jill's duties as a wife and that he – as the dutiful hus-

band—had rights that she better not dare neglect. When she remained quiet, he repeated his demands louder and with more verve, finally shouting that he wanted children to have heirs.

He didn't hear Melissa climb the carpet-covered steps toward the bedroom. He was about to change into his pajamas when she drove the five-inch blade between his third and fourth rib. He was dead before his body hit the expensive cream-colored bed linen. Donald stared at nothing—all malevolence finally gone from his eyes.

Melissa didn't say a word, and Jill was too stunned to do more than stare. She had watched her husband's murder without any reaction. It was off, irritating, frightening. Jill looked up, and if there was anything to read in her beautiful features, it was relief, even a twisted kind of gratefulness. The second they locked gazes, Melissa had known she had met a soulmate.

Her thoughts came back to the moment. She turned on to her other side. *Jill will know what to do.*

As with every day, Jill Nyeburn had chosen her outfit carefully. Even though it was warm outside, she wore a knee-length gray skirt and a burgundy-colored blouse with a decent décolleté. The shoes indicated she had thought about them—they matched the blouse perfectly. Although she had no appointments with clients today, she wanted to look the best she could. She was about to sit at her desk when Mrs. Billingham came up to her to place a pile of files on her table.

"Oh, the poor Mrs. Woolsey! That's a real tragedy!"

Jill looked up, astonished. "What are you saying?"

"I just heard the news—the police were here to investigate, but she couldn't answer—her mouth is too swollen to speak. They wanted to know if she knew of any enemies that her husband had."

"What happened?"

"He's dead! Oh, didn't I say that?" She put both hands to

her bosom. "Mr. Woolsey is dead, and the police assume he was murdered."

"Murdered? That's terrible." Jill sat down, hiding her bewilderment as best as she could.

Mrs. Billingham didn't appear to notice. "Terrible, yes, for a life is lost." She made the sign of the cross. "But on the other hand—did you see Mrs. Woolsey? She was close to dying, I bet, when she was admitted."

"Yes, she's a poor woman." Jill forced her most soothing smile. "But she will heal, I suppose?"

"She'll heal faster now that she's free from the terrible threat that was called her husband." Mrs. Billingham huffed, replacing a hand on her bosom. "Forgive me, but I hope there's a special place in hell for him—with all the other sinners who brought misery about their partners."

"Did the police say how he was murdered?"

"No. I just heard it from Tessa. She saw the FBI agents yesterday."

"FBI? Not the homicide division?"

"Rumor's out there's a serial killer in town," Mrs. Billingham said confidentially. "And the FBI has taken it all over—not just to investigate the murder of Mr. Dobson." She shook her head as if she couldn't imagine any man would kill another. "There might be more—not that brutal, but murders nevertheless."

"I see." Jill smiled but didn't look up.

The elder woman turned to leave. "I'll tell you more once I hear something."

"Yes, thank you. That would be kind." Jill waited for the door to close, then pulled out her cell phone, but before she dialed, she lowered it again. She realized that if the FBI was investigating, they would get a court order to tap her phones very quickly. So she left the office and used the phone in the nurses' room at the other end of the hallway.

The district attorney made it clear he did not think much of an investigation into a serial killer if the main suspect was one of the most respected lawyers in the Richmond area. Jason's clever explanation and the evidence changed the DA's mind—at least partly—but he was still adamant that the search warrant was restricted to the Nyeburn estate and shouldn't be misused to destroy the lady's property or invade her privacy too much. Her offices and clients' files were off-limits. No argument that Jason desperately tried to muster changed his mind.

Jason was sweating when he put down the receiver.

"We'll get the paper for Nyeburn and Roberts, but if we aren't careful, he'll rip our hearts out and eat them raw for lunch."

"That's what I like about you. You've got such a vivid imagination when it comes to possible punishments. Chill, man, we got this!" Matthew clapped his hands. "I'll call a team so we can start right away."

Jason despised Matthew's eagerness. "The DA was explicit—if we break anything or don't do this by the book, he'll put this on us."

Nicolas whistled through his teeth, then got up and put on his jacket. "The judge doesn't want a lawyer to be a criminal. Let's see what we find out."

While Jason led the team at Nyeburn's house, Nicolas chose to help the second team at Robert's home.

"What do you expect to find, agents?" Mrs. Nyeburn asked, and something in her tone caused cold shivers to run up and down Jason's spine. "A bloody murder weapon?"

"Well, if you could provide it right away, it'll save us time," Matthew answered with a friendly smile.

Nyeburn allowed the agents to move into her rooms. "I'll be in my study. And I'll hold you responsible for every damaged piece. I've got several valuable portraits, vases, and sculptures. Be careful. Be very careful."

Jason had the distinct impression the DA had called her, even though it was against the rules, but there was no way to prove it. He followed her, taking out his notebook. He was angry that this search could never go as he had planned. *Birds of a feather flock together*. How could he do his work properly if the DA obstructed it in this way? "Mrs. Nyeburn, I've got a few questions concerning your whereabouts on several occasions."

She turned to him with an arrogant look. "Your persistence is getting on my nerves, Agent Beckham. I've already told you and your colleagues everything I know, and I can't prove where I've been for every period you named, especially not when they were months ago. Do you still know where you were a month ago, on a Monday, at seven PM?"

"That's not the question, Mrs. Nyeburn."

"It's a question you can't answer, that's what. It's circumstantial. You compared my secretary's calendar to the dates of several crimes and came up with some correlations. It doesn't mean that the deviations or unoccupied periods of time can be used to claim that I have anything to do with a murder. I do more than leading a law firm. I spend time at home, I work out, or I drive to *La Grotta* for dinner. Just for example." She cocked her head, her look still adamant. To Jason, she looked like an ancient goddess—beautiful but distant and superiorly aloof. "You've got nothing, Agent Beckham." She lifted her hand when he wanted to ask another question. "Please, agent, stop right there. Your questions lead to nothing, and I'm no longer willing to answer them. You won't find any evidence here, no matter what you're looking for. So, I ask you again, leave me alone. Do what you have to do, then leave my home, and don't forget to close the door behind you."

Jason watched her settle behind her desk, considering whether her coolness was because she had nothing to hide or because she was confident she had hidden her equipment elsewhere. She might have known that the DA would never sign a search warrant for her offices, and what would be easier than hiding incriminating material where no policeman was allowed to look? Jason's agents walked through the rooms opening cupboards and boxes, looking behind paintings for a safe. For two hours, they worked diligently. Jason hoped they would detect a connection to one of the murders, may it be a wig or a costume, or a bag with plastic wrapping as used at the site of the Dobson murder.

They had no luck.

Nyeburn owned a lot of clothes, shoes, bags, and her home was elegantly decorated with pieces of art. They checked receipts and books, looked behind cupboards, and searched for double bottoms in drawers. The agents found that although the house exhibited wealth and taste, it didn't hold any evidence that the lady was a killer.

Jason noticed that there were no pictures of her deceased husband anywhere in the house. Then he realized there were no photographs at all—not of Nyeburn or of her parents and friends. There was nothing personal to her. If he hadn't known the owner, the furniture looked as if it belonged in the showroom of a store.

Clenching his teeth so hard his jaw hurt, Jason was forced to apologize to Mrs. Nyeburn for the unwelcome invasion of her privacy, expecting a harsh reprimand, but it didn't happen. She sent him away with nothing more than a bitter look. The agents packed up and left, shaking their heads and asking Jason how he could possibly think the lady was a serial killer when all she did was help poor people in need.

Jason called Nicolas and got the disheartening news that Melissa Roberts's mundane one-bedroom apartment was as clean as an operating room and that the nurse, too, had either explained her whereabouts at the times of the murders or claimed she couldn't remember. Because there were thousands of dark blue *Honda Civics* and they had no license plate details, it was impossible to justify her arrest by the supposed presence of her car at the last crime scene.

Disappointed, Jason decided to call it a day and drive home. It felt like he was hitting his head against a wall, and he needed Elaine in his arms to soothe away his disappointment and frustration.

For more than a week, Jason and Nicolas followed Nyeburn's and Roberts's daily routines between leaving their homes and returning. The team watched them take up work, drive to a *Tae Kwon Do* studio, fetch clothes from a dry cleaner, and pick up take-out from a Chinese Restaurant. Aside from the martial arts training, the women didn't meet for any private conversations. No other suspects were detected—the nurses and doctors at the hospitals were bewildered to be subjects of a murder investigation, and they regarded the agents with bitter scorn.

Jason's mood dropped further down the depressing road to hell. Senior Agent Sullivan announced he would bump them from the case and send in another team of investigators if there was no progress. Once more, Jason feared he would lose his job. He rejected Nicolas's invitation for him to go to the hospital and interrogate Mrs. Woolsey, who was finally able to speak. Nicolas and Matthew hoped she might help the agents with some insight about her connection with the self-support group at St. Mary's. Instead, Jason remained at the office to sift through the evidence they had so far and to compare the women's statements to the dates of the murders. He still hoped he had overlooked a clue that would connect either the lawyer or the nurse to at least one of the murders.

When he returned with his fifth cup of coffee, he looked at the crime scene photographs of the Nyeburn murder three years ago and stopped short, almost dropping the cup. He put it down quickly and spread all photographs of Nyeburn's bedroom on the desk. His heart beating in his throat, he pulled out his cell phone.

Although he had been determined to participate in the interview this time, Matthew couldn't bring himself to enter Mrs. Woolsey's hospital room. Like a schoolboy, he mumbled an excuse and turned away when Nicolas opened the door. He felt miserable to let his partner down, and he didn't expect him to understand his behavior. As he hurried toward the exit to light a cigarette, the main doors opened wide, and a stretcher with a middle-aged woman, who was constantly whimpering, was pushed in, followed by a second. Matthew got a glimpse of a boy of about three years with a bleeding head injury. The medics were shouting information to the receiving doctor. Matthew picked up from their words and the sense of barely contained panic that the boy was in critical condition.

A nurse came running, pushing Matthew against the wall.

"I knew this would happen! Damn this man!" She took a look at both victims and stifled a cry. "Oh, Mrs. Binkley, why didn't you leave when you still had time?"

Mrs. Binkley replied between sobs that she had tried. "What about my boy?"

"He'll be okay, Mrs. Binkley. He'll make it. Don't worry."

Matthew watched the stretchers go on their way to the ER

but held back the nurse by grabbing hold of her arm when she was about to follow.

"Let me go!" the nurse demanded harshly and freed her arm. Her freckles were prominent, standing out on her flushed face. "I'm needed in there!"

"Just one question. Is Mrs. Binkley a victim of domestic violence?"

"Who're you? A lawyer hungry for a case?"

Matthew showed her his badge.

The nurse stared at him, furious. "Great. Mrs. Binkley was in the ER about two weeks ago—beaten by her husband. We urged her to leave him and take the kids, but she didn't dare. When her husband came, she went home with him." The nurse snorted. "And now you can see what happened. Go, catch him, G-man. Do something useful!" She hurried away.

Matthew pulled his cell phone out as Nicolas came running down the hall.

"We've got to arrest Mr. Binkley," Matthew said, then told the uniforms on the phone to head for Mr. Binkley's home immediately.

Nicolas was out of breath. "What's up?" he asked on the way to the parking lot.

"Two victims, mother and son. Looks bad. If we're fast, we'll catch the bastard before he's got time to leave town."

"If not, our killers have another victim. I get it." Nicolas slipped behind the wheel and started the engine.

"Why were you running? Did Mrs. Woolsey tell you something useful?"

"She wanted to leave her husband and had already made an appointment with Nyeburn for assistance. The lawyer had told her that she'd get a place in a safe house if need be." Nicolas accelerated the car across the intersection, obviously hoping that the flashing red and blue light and the siren would magically discourage the other cars. "She confessed that she told her husband about her decision. Guess what he did."

The car skidded across the blacktop to take the corner, barely missing a small transporter.

"And the lawyer knew about it firsthand." Matthew held fast to the door handle and tried to dial the number of the surveillance team with the other hand. He was informed that Nyeburn was at a client's home and that the nurse had recently started her shift. Matthew urged them to watch closely and tell him once they left their current positions.

Five minutes later, the cell phone rang. Matthew listened and made a face.

"Uniforms arrived at the Binkley home, but he wasn't there. They're asking neighbors where he might've gone, so far without result. They're combing the area and the local bars and searching for his car."

"If his wife speaks up this time, he faces at least ten years in prison."

Matthew played with his phone, then dialed again.

Nicolas glanced at him. "Have you got another idea where that shithead might be?"

"I'm calling the hospital. I want to know how they're faring." Matthew listened intently, and when he ended the call, his gaze dropped to the floor, and he drew in a ragged breath. His voice was heavy with emotion. "He's dead, Nick. The boy died minutes ago—major head trauma. Now we're searching for a killer."

In one of the conversations Jill had had with Mrs. Binkley, the lady had explained that years ago her husband Robert had left their home at irregular intervals to take a ride to his brother's cabin near Cumberland to chop wood. The occupation had helped him deal with stress and bouts of aggression. As the years went by, he had to change jobs, and the depressive events increased in number. Chopping wood had no longer helped, and though Mrs. Binkley wished her husband would get well again, she told him that she'd leave him if he didn't seek medical attention. After therapy and with medication, he had been better, so she decided—for the sake of the children—that she'd give their marriage another chance.

As Jill drove her friend's car, she was angry with herself that she hadn't done more to prevent the boy's death. If she had been more persistent, maybe the boy would still be alive and Mrs. Binkley wouldn't have suffered such a dreadful loss. Jill clenched her teeth, changed lanes, and floored the gas pedal.

"Send someone to Mrs. Binkley and ask her where her husband could be!" Matthew shouted into his cell phone. "He isn't home, and we haven't found him yet. I don't expect him to return home, so, where the hell is he? Yes, I'll hold." Matthew ran a hand through his hair. He looked up to Nicolas. "The officer's on his way to her."

Nicolas noticed he had missed Jason's call, so he called him back. "All right, we're stuck. What have you got?"

"There was something odd about the bedroom of the Nyeburn house." Jason's voice sounded intriguingly upbeat. "Do you remember that she had the house remodeled after her husband's death? Well, she did much more. I took a locksmith to open it up and guess what I found? Yes, the bedroom's got a separate wall. You can't see it when you're standing in the room, but I compared the crime scene photographs from three years ago to the situation now. We found the door, and well, I'm standing in a special effects studio every theater would want. She's one of the killers, Nick, no doubt about it. Everything's here—wigs, make-up, clothes that look like three sizes bigger. I informed the surveillance team to arrest her, but she's gone. As if she knew we'd find out her secret."

"No. She got wind that Mrs. Binkley and her son were admitted to the hospital. We just heard the kid died."

"Oh my God! And now she's on a revenge trip. Any idea where the husband is?"

"None. We're waiting for Mrs. Binkley's statement to see if she can shed some light."

Matthew lifted a finger to get Nicolas's attention.

"Good work, Jason. CSU will have a blast." He ended the call. "What's up, Matt?"

"A cabin in the woods. Fifty miles west, at the Cumberland State Forest." He slipped into the passenger seat. "I'll give you directions."

Jill knew that this time it would be close to impossible to pretend she had been someplace else at the time of the murder. The specialists from the Crime Scene Unit would find the tire marks and compare them to her friend's car. Even if her girlfriend testified for her, Jill had no intention of involving her in a murder investigation. Binkley wouldn't die of an accident, either. She had no coherent plan, no clue what to expect, and there was no time to prepare anything.

She laughed a bitter laugh. *Maybe he shoots himself. There is no boundary for idiotic behavior.*

Looking back, it was a miracle how many *accidents* the homicide detectives and the ME had accepted and stopped investigating further. She claimed she was clever, but was it possible she was *that* clever? She wondered whether Detective Bartow, who had informed her about the investigations against her, had influenced his colleagues and claimed that the accidental deaths of molesters, rapists, and violent husbands were of no concern to the homicide division. If so, both murderers and investigators had played their part in cleaning the city of those despicable criminals.

Her smile hardened to a grimace as tears trickled down her cheeks. Jill couldn't count how many women and men she had advised and helped so that they could finally leave their abusive partners. She had saved lives—one way or the other. She was content in her skin. She had done the right thing. She had made the right decisions and swept the dirt that needed sweeping up from the road. She had acted on the weaker partner's behalf and only killed those who would never have stopped molesting. If Jill ever faced a jury in court, she would testify that the judiciary system favored the molester. Even if the wives and children survived their brutal treatment, they were scarred for life while the wrongdoer served his time and returned to freedom—sometimes to take revenge on the people he had mistreated before.

It was intolerable that the same person showed up in the victim's life again.

She left Route 60 at Cumberland. The tears dried. Her partner in crime was on her way. Binkley had an hour to live.

Matthew tried to call the Cumberland Sheriff's Department to ask for assistance, but since they were crossing an area with poor radio communications, he couldn't get a connection.

"Maybe it's for the best," he muttered after the third unsuccessful attempt. "I doubt that the sheriff would try to negotiate. These kinds of officers preferred a more direct approach." He played with the phone while Nicolas slung the car around the corners and accelerated along the straights, driving like a maniac.

The siren and flashing blue lights continued to clear the route for them, but still they had twenty miles to go.

"Did the shrink call you about the debrief?" Matthew asked after a while.

"His assistant called me. I've got an appointment for the day after tomorrow." Nicolas glanced to the right. "Why?"

"How do you cope with the situation?"

"The way we all do. Accept that you survived and move on."

Matthew made a sound in his throat.

"You think I'm lying?"

"Don't bite my head off, but I think it's not that easy. While the trial against my former wife was going on, my colleagues beat me up in my own house. They came at night, pulled me out of bed and into the hall, and gave me a thrashing. I remember one of them shouting to not hit my face." He huffed. "Of course, they wouldn't want anyone to notice what they did to me."

"I'm sorry, Matt. I didn't know."

Matt made a gesture as if he were over the memory. "What I'm saying is this—you have to face the truth. Katherine and her accomplice attacked you and Jacky's aunt in *your* house. You survived because you reacted quickly and because the aunt knows how to use a weapon. There was a lot of luck at play."

"I know."

"Back then, I had no chance, and it wasn't luck that saved me. If Fatsy and his flunkies had arrived with the intention to kill me, I'd be dead. It took me almost a year to accept that the invasion of my private domain didn't mean I'd never be safe again."

Nicolas pressed his lips tight and said nothing.

"Use the meetings with the shrink and—"

"Who said I wouldn't?"

Matthew lowered his chin, chuckling. "Because you're a badass agent. But even you are allowed to have feelings."

Nicolas left Route 60 toward the small road leading into the forest. "Showtime."

Chapter Seventeen

Jill Nyeburn knew the sort of men like Binkley too well, so she had perfected the role of the kind woman from the neighborhood, the one looking like a helpless victim. For Dobson, she had played the easily flattered realtor, a role that had the deputy mayor captivated within seconds. His bodyguard had been the real threat, but even that professional had been impressed and distracted.

Binkley stood in the doorway, anger and fear mixing in his look. He was sweating buckets of stinking liquid in the dry heat as he crushed the can in his hand. Beer foamed through the opening and dripped on to the wooden floor.

"Yes?"

Jill's heart skipped a beat. *The man is a monster!* From the nurses' description, she had expected a strong man, but her opponent was more than six feet tall with bicep muscles that threatened to rip apart his shirt sleeves. She swallowed her shock, knowing she had no choice but to continue. This deed had to be done.

"I'm really sorry to bother you, sir, but my car's making strange noises, and I hoped that someone could help me."

He looked left and right as if expecting a brigade of soldiers.

They're close, but not here yet.

"Sir, would you mind having a look?"

"What makes you think I'm a mechanic?" Binkley threw the can onto the porch, sneezed, and wiped his nose with the back of his hand. "I'm not. Walk, if you have to." He was about to step back and close the door when Jill's friend smashed his head with a baseball bat.

Jill let go of her breath as the man dropped to the floor, dazed and groaning. Behind him, Melissa Roberts stood, a grim smile on her face.

"I told you he's a giant," she said matter-of-factly. "You look kinda pale around the gills."

"Let's take him inside. We don't have much time."

Together they pulled Binkley through the room toward a wooden chair with armrests.

"Perfect." Melissa pulled the chair to the center of the room. With considerable effort, they hauled the senseless hulk into a sitting position, tying his wrists to the armrests and his ankles to the chair legs. They were sweating and cursing and had to pause to catch their breaths in the blistering and confining heat of the cabin.

"How did you get here?" Jill asked, wiping her face. She felt better now that the monster was under control.

"I told Tessa to cover for me. She understood without another word. If anyone asks, she'll find a suitable story and let me know. And you?"

"I won't be able to find any excuses this time. I came in Susan's car. There was no other way. The agents were watching and waiting across the street." Jill shook her head as she fought to control the emotion that threatened to overcome her. "Looks like this is the last time we work together."

"That's not fair." Melissa touched Jill's arm. Her look was full of compassion. "We can make this quick and run, if you want."

Jill shook her head as she thrust a potent smelling salt under the nose of the abuser to wake him up. "No. I won't run. I've never run in my whole life, and I know how to defend my hide."

Melissa's words were full of admiration. "Oh, yes, I know

that."

Binkley lurched forward as he opened his eyes, found out he was tied up, then he stared at Jill. "You fucking bitch!" He turned his head, spitting the words. "And another bitch. I'll give you a beating you won't forget!" He tore at the ropes, but couldn't wriggle free. "Fuck you!"

Jill took the baseball bat and swung wide to hit the man's right kneecap. Binkley's next curse was cut off, and he howled in pain.

"That was for your wife! You won't hurt anyone anymore. Not ever again!"

She took position on the other side of the chair, swung again, and in spite of Binkley's protest, smashed the left kneecap. His cry was louder than before. He cursed so hard that spittle flew from his lips.

"That's for your son! Your *dead son*!" Jill stepped back, gasping for air. She handed Melissa the bat. "Your turn."

Melissa raised the bat over her head.

"No!" Binkley looked up pleadingly, his eyes wide with terror and pain. His bold machismo was gone as he finally realized the dire condition he was in. He tore at the ropes again, but this time it was with desperation, not anger. "No! Don't! I'll do what you want, but don't hit me again!"

"Did your wife plead the same way? Did your children cry and hope you'd spare them?" Melissa gave him time to understand the words, then smashed his right hand. "Or maybe you're left-handed? I won't take any chances." She went around the chair.

"I'm right-handed!" Mr. Binkley screamed. "Right-handed! Please, stop hurting me!" He made a fist and tried again in vain to wriggle his arm loose.

Outside they heard the sound of a car, distant but obviously racing along the road. Binkley started to scream for help pathetically.

Melissa and Jill exchanged glances, and a deep understanding passed between them. "No cover-up this time."

Jill had never felt better, convinced from the bottom of her heart that her cause was just. "Do what you have to do."

Despite his trust in Nicolas's driving skills, Matthew was bathed in sweat upon arrival. He got out and heard a man screaming in agony. He pulled his gun and ran for the door.

Nicolas was at his heels. "We're too late." The man inside screamed again as the agents took position left and right of the door. "On three. One, two, three."

Matthew kicked against the door, but the thick wood didn't budge. Surprised and hurt, he limped backward and let Nicolas try—with the same result. Once more, there was the ominous sound of something hard hitting a soft object and a pitiful cry that turned to sobs and barely coherent begging to spare his life. Nicolas turned toward the closest window and smashed it with the butt of his gun. Quickly, he cleared the shards of glass from the frame and clambered through before Matthew could utter a word of caution. He followed through to stand beside Nicolas, directing his weapon at Jill Nyeburn and Melissa Roberts.

Matthew's breath caught in his throat.

Binkley sat tethered to a chair, tears rolling down his bearded cheeks. His hands and knees were dark red and swollen from the brutal beating. Breathing raggedly, Matthew saw that the man was still begging, be it very weakly, for his attackers to let him live and that he was sorry for what he had done to his family. Melissa Roberts stood on his right side, the bat clasped firmly in both hands, lifted up high for a further swing at his face.

"Stop! Drop the weapon!" Nicolas shouted, four steps away.

Matthew trained his weapon on the nurse. "Drop it, or I'll shoot!"

"And he lives?" Roberts glanced over her shoulder. "No way."

She swung the bat the same moment as Nicolas threw himself forward to knock her down, thus forcing Matthew to hold fire. The bat bashed the side of Binkley's head but not at full force. The nurse hit the ground with Nicolas on top of her. She screamed in frustration and tried to free her hands to club Nicolas's face. She dropped the heavy bat to fight with her fists instead. He held her fast with both arms and his weight until the struggle stopped and only her heavy breathing remained.

Matthew put away his gun and walked toward Nyeburn to handcuff her. "You're under arrest for the attempted murder of Mr. Robert Binkley and for several other murders within the last eighteen months. The DA will make a list." He turned toward the tethered man, checked his pulse, and was relieved that the victim was alive. Blood was dripping from many wounds and making a sticky puddle on the dirty floor. Looking at the injuries, Matthew wondered whether the man would ever walk again or hold anything in his hands.

Nicolas pulled Roberts up and pushed away the baseball bat just to be sure it was over. "You're under arrest for—"

She spat in his face. "You have no idea what he did! He killed *his own son*! He would've killed his wife and second son, too, if we hadn't taken action! Ask the other wives and partners! Without me, none of them would ever be happy or safe again!"

"You admit that you murdered several people?" Nicolas asked as he locked the handcuffs around her wrists.

"Don't say another word," Jill warned. "Wait for the trial."

"Yes, you'd better." Nicolas read her her rights. "There's a lot you have to explain, Miss Roberts."

Matthew called an ambulance. He kept an eye on Nyeburn,

who looked sad and disappointed rather than frightened that she would face a trial.

"We did nothing wrong," Roberts stated, nodding with conviction at her justification. "And we'll prove it."

No one was surprised that Senior Agent Sullivan didn't mention the agents' names when praising the *team* for its successful completion of the investigation. His statement consisted of announcing that the women were responsible for the deputy mayor's death and would—hopefully, following a trial—be sentenced with the full force of the law. Asked about Jill Nyeburn's spotless reputation and her service to the city, Sullivan stated that her actions didn't reflect on her behavior as a lawyer. Vigilante justice would never be tolerated. He ended his press conference with the well-known sentence that from now on, the citizens of Richmond could sleep without fear.

Matthew leaned back on his chair, sighing. "I doubt that the victims of domestic violence agree with him. Those in need will mourn Nyeburn's absence."

Nicolas handed him a cup of coffee, ignoring Jason's glare. "Turns out, Detective Bartow was eager to close the files once there was a chance it was an accident. The ME is an old friend and certainly on his side. The internal division couldn't prove that both men deliberately obstructed the investigations, but it was clear that they certainly took the easy way out, not going to great lengths to declare them as murder cases if they didn't have to. There's no decision yet, but their colleagues hope they'll get off with a slap on the wrist. Looks like no one wanted to see the abusers go free."

"Talking about monsters—how's Binkley? I heard he's alive?"

Nicolas made a face. "Alive, yes, but the women destroyed

his knees, his hands, and almost broke his breastbone. The final blow to his head caused a massive concussion. He might live but wish he was dead. If I have it right, there's no chance that he'll ever use his hands again."

Melissa Roberts admitted under interrogation that she had used a quiet moment in the ER to inject the paralyzing drug into Mr. Chávez's arm when he expected a tetanus shot. She had known the victim would drive his car and most likely die on the highway.

They packed up their files, cleared the borrowed desks at the homicide department in Richmond, and left without much of a farewell. Matthew had the impression that not everyone regarded them with scorn but that the detectives were happy that the agents would no longer be looking over their shoulders. Matthew longed to go home, cuddle with his dog, and catch some sleep.

"What's your plan for tonight?" he asked Nicolas as they got into the car.

"Oh, I don't know. Read the paper, watch TV. Maybe I'll go to bed early."

Both Jason and Matthew laughed heartily. "You and catching sleep? At home? We doubt it!"

Epilogue

Nicolas entered Lesley's *Cave of Love* and was surprised that the interior resembled a lawyer's office rather than a dungeon. There were elegant leather chairs, glass tables with business magazines, and tasteful paintings on the cream-colored walls. The lady at the counter wore a sophisticated yet sexy dress, and her smile was inviting as he approached the light brown marble desk.

"I'm Nicolas Hayes, looking for Miss Hollander."

"Oh, Lady Hell." The secretary's smile brightened. "Please, use the door to the left. There's a reception hall with a waiting area. Someone will be with you shortly."

"I'm not a customer, Miss. I'm—"

"Please, take the door to the left." Her smile said that many men tried to deny they were here to see a dominatrix.

Nicolas sighed and went through the door. The hall at the end of the corridor was more like he had expected. The lights were softer, the furniture black, the pictures on the wall showed women in leather bras and skirts making kissing lips while holding whips, paddles, and shackles in their hands. The men at their feet didn't look equally happy—tied and muzzled. The magazines on the low tables had similar very distinctive covers.

He looked up to find small black cameras inserted in the ceiling, masquerading as fire detectors, but he knew the difference. He wondered if Lesley told the customers they were being filmed. Two men were waiting, one of them dressed in casual jeans and shirt, the other one in suit and tie. Both appeared to be frequent customers, judging by their relaxed behavior. They scrutinized him inconspicuously, and he didn't like the fact that they thought he was a paying customer.

The rear door opened, and a dominatrix stepped into the light. She could've been a cover model—full bosom, female hips, long legs, all dressed in dark red leather and high heels. Her face was unrecognizable under a thick layer of make-up, so he couldn't tell if she was twenty or thirty years old. Her short black hair was sleeked back, stressing her beautiful cheekbones. Making mewling sounds in her throat, she gave Nicolas the eye, and he held his breath when she came straight up to him.

"You're new."

"I'm waiting for someone," Nicolas replied quietly and made to step out of reach.

She followed and rubbed her leg against his crotch. "Aren't we all?" She ran a gloved hand across his shoulder so he caught a wisp of her perfume. "With me, you don't have to wait anymore."

"Hands off him, Alissa," a stern voice commanded from the rear door. "He's spoken for."

Nicolas took another step to the side while the dominatrix turned with a disappointed sigh to walk back to where she had come from. The two men on the couches glared at Nicolas. The one in the suit checked his jewels and let go of his breath.

Lesley strutted through the room. Nicolas wondered how she could safely move in the too-tight leather skirt matched with her precipitously high heels that made her legs seemingly endless. The leather bra lifted her bosom, and since she wore not much else, Nicolas's attention was drawn to the jewel flashing in the piercing in her midriff. His mouth was dry, and his heart was beating in his throat.

Her smile seemed to encompass the seduction techniques that every woman had ever exploited since Eve sinned and was thrown out of paradise. She stopped in front of him, purring exquisitely. "Lost?"

"Not really." Nicolas found it hard to breathe, and his voice sounded strangely squeaky.

She linked arms with him, blew kisses to the waiting men, and led him through the rear door toward another corridor. "They already have hard-ons just seeing me," she told him confidentially. "What about you?"

Nicolas would have died before admitting that so much sexiness made him horny. Lesley made eye contact and cocked an eyebrow.

"I thought so."

There were four doors on each side of the corridor, each carrying a small plate with a word on it. Nicolas squinted to read them.

"Themes," Lesley explained. "In every dungeon, you have different playrooms according to the players' preferences."

Despite himself, Nicolas was impressed by the ingenious arrangements that prompted his imagination to add what he couldn't see. Lesley had turned the former industry hall into a parlor of lust with a heavy touch of class. Halfway down the corridor, a naked man knelt on the floor, close to the wall. Besides shackles that kept him from getting up, he wore a head harness—a tight arrangement of leather straps with an attached ball gag and eye patches. He made a sound in his throat and moved his butt left and right. Nicolas couldn't help but gape at seeing a tail wag in the man's ass.

"Raiden's my pet." Lesley patted the man's head. He had long and wavy brown hair, a full but cropped beard, and tattoos along his upper arms and massive chest. "He has to wait a little longer, don't you, boy? Close your mouth, Nicolas, I'll take you to your mistress before you come in your pants."

"I wouldn't—"

Lesley laughed out loud. "This is the last place, Nick, where you have to deny an erection. It's a requirement, and I'm flattered that my interior inspires you, too." She stopped and turned to him, one hand shooting out to grab around his genitals. "Don't forget—I know how well you are equipped." She opened the door to his right. "Go on in and have fun."

Nicolas went through the door and stopped, rooted to the spot. He couldn't decide whether he stopped breathing because Jacklyn looked fantastic in her new dungeon outfit or if the collection of medieval torture instruments scared him so much. The rack and the Saint Andrew's cross were touched by torchlight, adding to the menacing mood. Nicolas couldn't stop thinking that Jacklyn had previously maltreated a paying customer.

She made a satisfied sound. "There you are. I thought you wouldn't come."

Nicolas knew he should claim that he had come solely with the intention to take her home and wasn't the least interested in what he saw in the interior of this place, but the words stuck in his throat. "Well, I'm here," he mumbled breathlessly.

Jacklyn, the experienced mistress, instantly saw through his façade. "Since you're here—would you mind staying for another hour? I could show you some new . . . things."

He kissed her sensuously and whispered, "If you don't do something with my beast right now, Lesley will be right and I will drill a hole clear through my pants."

Jacklyn giggled and opened his belt and his pants. "Then I'd better hurry up and punish that naughty beast for its eagerness, hmm?"

The End

You may also enjoy the following from eXtasy Books Inc:

Blind Trust
Ann Raina

Excerpt

Katherine smashed her bag on the table, took off her coat, and glared at the joyous group of four men handing out beer bottles and chips and giving high-fives to each other as if celebrating the super bowl win. She counted to five before she opened her mouth.

"Tell me, all of you, are you out of your fucking minds?" The men fell silent. "Is that what you call professional? You busted this! You almost got caught!" She looked at Herman—Manny to his friends—her eldest brother, who was the only one able to stand her glare. "Tell me, Manny, how's it possible that officer was so close on your heels you could smell his cologne?"

Herman, tall and broadly built, flashed a cocky smile and opened his arms wide. He could've embraced his younger brothers and his sister in one swoop. "He wore aftershave? Man, I didn't notice that!" The other men laughed. Herman quickly lifted a hand to stop Kate's reply. "Hey, calm down, okay? We got away. Plans B and C worked smoothly. No one got hurt—"

"None of us," Benjamin cut in, lifting a bottle of beer and receiving nods and cheers from his brothers.

"Okay, none of us." Herman exchanged a high-five with Benjamin. "We saved most of the money and escaped smooth as a baby's butt. That's all that counts."

"Don't say . . ." Katherine looked from Herman to Benjamin and his twin, Theodor, then to their friend, Tom, who had driven the van. Their expressions were of mild amusement and—to her chagrin—contentment. "That's how you see it? It's enough for you that you had such a narrow escape?"

She took the small glass Benjamin handed her and looked around. The scent of malt whiskey reminded her of the evening before when they had sat together to review the plan one last time. She had anticipated the robbery would run as smoothly as the previous ones. Katherine had thought they all knew their places and actions by heart.

She took a deep breath before she continued. "And that the van didn't burn? That's just bad karma, or what? Come on, don't gimme that shit!" She gulped down the whiskey and slammed the glass on the table, then pointed at Herman. "You screwed up! What about the cameras at the metro station? Are you sure you didn't get caught? Seen? You know nothing."

"Fuck, Kate, stop bickering! I just can't take it anymore." Theodor poured himself a drink while he shook his head. "You're right. The van didn't blow up, and one of us might or might not be on tape. So what?" He shrugged. "We've changed disguises every time. Who'll know it's us?"

Katherine loved her brothers dearly, but at that moment, she wanted to knock their heads on the table. She only restrained herself because they were stronger, and she'd have embarrassed herself trying to wrestle one of them. Instead, she turned her glare on Theodor. "Who'll know? The fucking FBI will know. The two who chased you through the station were with the FBI, not metro police. That means they have stacked up personnel and will be much more alert to every unusual move around the banks in DC. We've got to leave this turf, or we'll get caught."

"Well, we'll get caught. That's right. Not you." Herman's deep voice carried, though he spoke quietly. "You'll sit somewhere safe in a car and judge our work."

Before Katherine replied, Herman lifted his hand to stop her.

"Right, you do the planning. We got that. And you worry. Fine. But, hey, did you notice that our asses are at stake every time we go out there?" He looked around for the other men's approval. "So, stop throwing shade at us, will ya? Give us some credit. We do what we can. And we did get away, okay? Acknowledge that at least." Smiling like a winner, he toasted her with a bottle of beer.

"I've planned these robberies meticulously."

She watched Tom take off his overcoat to reveal muscled arms. If you didn't look closely, you could mistake him for the fourth brother of the group—the introverted thinker in contrast to the boasting others. Looking at him, mellowed her anger. He met her gaze, and his apparent desire sped up her heartbeat. She wanted to embrace him and call it a day.

She collected her thoughts and continued in the same stern voice. "I work hard to make sure you all get out. Don't gimme that blah-blah about credit because it's your ass that'd be taken to jail. If you had followed my plan every step, no one would've been in danger." Katherine accepted a second glass of whiskey and knocked it back quickly.

"Who could've known the FBI would show up?" Herman put down the already empty bottle with a frown and stretched for another one. "We thought the police were occupied with guarding the demonstrations. You can't put the blame on us. We made the best of it."

Katherine fumbled for a hair tie to bind back her curly hair. "Why didn't the van blow up? Was something wrong with the fuse? Ben, didn't you check it?"

"Why not watch the news?" Benjamin hit the button of the

remote. "I bet it's the top story of the night."

Katherine felt the alcohol kick in and dissolve the tension she'd endured since the FBI car had sped up behind the van. For fifteen painful minutes, she'd been afraid that her brothers and Tom would get caught. Though she'd been relieved seeing them unharmed, their sloppiness bothered her.

She shrugged, discarded her cardigan, and slumped on the couch. Theodor glanced at her with his dark blue eyes. Like his twin, Benjamin, he had an angelic face, a fair complexion, and blond hair. Without effort, he could charm the ladies and get any woman he wanted, no matter what the time or place. He smiled at her, then turned toward the kitchen to take care of dinner. She heard him open the fridge as her stomach grumbled.

Herman pulled up a chair and sat with his bulky forearms propped on the backrest. It galled her to find him at ease, even smiling, but that was his way of dealing with stress. He joked and moved on as if danger didn't mean anything to him. Katherine was torn between scolding and applauding his attitude. She'd always envied his easy-going manner.

The anchorman of the local news station had a serious expression. "According to police sources, the bank robbery was executed with brutal force. The wounded guard is still in critical condition. The bank's tellers and customers are being treated for shock and minor injuries. The robbers looted about fifteen thousand dollars—"

"Yeah, and we almost got it all!" Theodor clapped his hands.

"—and got away by dumping their van at the Federal Triangle to slip through police forces securing the station. One officer was injured during the chase, and the police assume the three robbers escaped on one of the trains during the turmoil. So far, the perpetrators haven't been identified. The FBI has taken over the investigation and is examining video surveillance footage. If you have any information about the robbers, contact your local police department or the FBI. There is a reward for clues leading to their arrest."

Benjamin turned to Katherine. "See? They don't know shit."

Katherine lowered her chin and snorted. "Since when do the police give all their information to the media? The FBI will strip down the van and the weapons for evidence. Is there anything you haven't told me so far?" Once more, she glared at the men. "Like leaving chewing gum for their DNA experts? Or someone working without gloves? No? Okay, so you may have survived this one." She got up again to pace back and forth through the room, gesturing with both hands. "Still, I don't understand why the van didn't blow up. What the fuck happened?" She stopped and turned her attention back to her brothers. "Ben? What happened?"

"I don't know." Ben dropped his gaze and then—as if gathering strength—looked back at the TV program. "Must've been something wrong with the fuse," he growled.

Katherine was silent for a moment and pursed her lips. "Fact is, the plan for our next coup is gone, ruined, smashed to smithereens. Washington Trust and Loan will live without being looted. I'll need time to come up with another target."

"Fine." Theodor bobbed his head and put down a bowl with fried rice. "As always, we'll stay out of the way, play it cool, and stand at attention whenever you call."

"Very funny." Herman slapped his younger brother's head. "Why not ask what she's got in her mind? Maybe we can help with the preparations." He smiled amiably at her. "What do you want us to do?"

"Stay low-key and don't bully the neighbors."

Herman smirked. "I love you so much, sis."

About the Author

Ann Raina lives and works in Germany with cats and a horse (which has its own home). Riding and writing are her favorite hobbies without putting one above the other. Her latest series, starting with Twisted Mind, deals with FBI Agent Nicolas Hayes, his cases of capital crimes, and his demanding and commanding lover, Jacklyn Hollander. In all her books she combines romance, suspense, and humorous elements, for no thrilling story can stand without a comic relief.

www.ingramcontent.com/pod-product-compliance
Lightning Source LLC
LaVergne TN
LVHW020540100826
845148LV00010B/1544

* 9 7 8 1 4 8 7 4 2 9 4 1 6 *